STE
THE W(

MW00639547

STELLA Dorothea Gibbons was born in 1902 in London. She was educated first at home, then the North London Collegiate School for Girls, and finally at University College, London, where she did a two-year course on journalism.

Her first job, in 1923, was as cable decoder for British United Press. For the next decade she worked as a London journalist for various publications, including the *Evening Standard* and *The Lady*.

Her first published book was a volume of poems in 1930. This was followed by the classic comic novel *Cold Comfort Farm* (1932) which remains her best-known work. In 1933 she met and married Allan Webb, an actor and singer, the marriage lasting until the latter's death in 1959.

From 1934 until 1970, Stella Gibbons published more than twenty further novels, in addition to short stories and poetry, and there were two further posthumously-published full-length works of fiction. She was a fellow of the Royal Society of Literature, and was awarded a *Femina Vie-Heureuse* prize in 1933 for *Cold Comfort Farm*.

Stella Gibbons died on 19 December 1989 at home in London.

FICTION BY STELLA GIBBONS

Novels

Cold Comfort Farm (1932)
Bassett (1934)
Enbury Heath (1935)
Miss Linsey and Pa (1936)
Nightingale Wood (1938)
My American (1939)
The Rich House (1941)
Ticky (1943)
Westwood (1946)
The Matchmaker (1949)
Conference at Cold Comfort Farm (1949)
The Swiss Summer (1951)*
Fort of the Bear (1953)
The Shadow of a Sorcerer (1955)
Here Be Dragons (1956)
White Sand and Grey Sand (1958)
A Pink Front Door (1959)*
The Weather at Tregulla (1962)*
The Wolves Were in the Sledge (1964)
The Charmers (1965)
Starlight (1967)
The Snow-Woman (1969)*
The Woods in Winter (1970)*
The Yellow Houses (written c.1973, published 2016)
Pure Juliet (written c.1980, published 2016)

* published by Furrowed Middlebrow and Dean Street Press

Story Collections

Roaring Tower and Other Stories (1937)
Christmas at Cold Comfort Farm (1940)
Beside the Pearly Water (1954)

Children's Fiction

The Untidy Gnome (1935)

STELLA GIBBONS

THE WOODS IN WINTER

With an introduction by
Elizabeth Crawford

DEAN STREET PRESS

A Furrowed Middlebrow Book

FM63

Published by Dean Street Press 2021

First published in 1970 by Hodder & Stoughton

Cover by DSP
Shows detail from an illustration by Leslie Wood. The publisher
thanks the artist's estate and the archives of Manchester Metropolitan
University

ISBN 978 1 913527 81 5

www.deanstreetpress.co.uk

To
John Oliver
and
John Rose

Long live the wild and
the wilderness yet!

Gerard Manley Hopkins.

INTRODUCTION

The Woods in Winter (1970) was the last of the novels that Stella Gibbons published in her lifetime. Its opening words, 'Some forty years ago...in North London...', take us back to the early days of her career as an author and to the place where it all began, locating some of the scenes in areas of Hampstead and Kentish Town that she had known so well, the one loved, the other hated. She had enjoyed a long career; shortly before the publication of *The Woods in Winter* a production based on her first novel, *Cold Comfort Farm* (1932), was enjoying a repeat showing on television. However, early success had been both a blessing and a burden. 'That Book', as she came to call it, had been a great popular success, had received rave reviews on both sides of the Atlantic, and in 1933 had won the *Prix Étranger* of the *Prix Femina-Vie Heureuse*, much to the disgust of Virginia Woolf, a previous winner. An excoriating parody of the 'Loam and Lovechild School of Fiction', as represented in the works of authors such as Thomas Hardy, Mary Webb, Sheila Kaye-Smith, and even D.H. Lawrence, *Cold Comfort Farm* was also for Stella Gibbons an exorcism of her early family life. There really had been 'something nasty in the woodshed'.

Stella Dorothea Gibbons was born at 21 Malden Crescent, Kentish Town, London, on 5 January 1902, the eldest child and only daughter of [Charles James Preston] Telford Gibbons (1869-1926) and his wife, Maude (1877-1926). Her mother was gentle and much-loved but her father, a doctor, although admired by his patients, was feared at home. His ill-temper, drunkenness, affairs with family maids and governesses, violence, and, above all, the histrionics in which, while upsetting others, Stella thought he derived real pleasure, were the dominating factors of her childhood and youth. She was educated at home until the age of thirteen and was subsequently a pupil at North London Collegiate School. The change came after her governess attempted suicide when Telford Gibbons lost interest in their affair. Apparently, it was Stella who had discovered the unconscious woman.

Knowing it was essential to earn her own living, in September 1921 Stella enrolled on a two-year University of London course, studying for a Diploma in Journalism, and in 1924 eventually found work with a news service, the British United Press. She was still living at home when in 1926 her mother died suddenly. Stella promptly moved out into a rented room in Hampstead, no longer feeling obliged to stay in the house she hated. Incidentally, the house in which we first encounter the central character in *The Woods in Winter*, Ivy Gover, is located very close to the Gibbons' family home in Malden Crescent, allowing the author the opportunity of evoking foggy, bedraggled Kentish Town as she had known it.

Then, barely five months after her mother's death, her father, too, died, leaving his small estate to Stella's younger brother, who squandered it within a year. As a responsible elder sister, Stella found a new home to share with her brothers in the Vale of Health, a cluster of old houses close to Hampstead Heath. In *The Woods in Winter* this little house, 'Vale Cottage', is re-imagined as the home of Miss Helen Green, who employed Ivy as a char-woman and is identified by Stella's biographer as 'perhaps Stella's fullest portrait of her younger self'. These Hampstead years were to provide a rich source of material. Not only the topography of the area but friends and acquaintances are woven into future novels. One young man in particular, Walter Beck, a naturalised German to whom she was for a time engaged, appears in The Woods in Winter as Helen Green's elusive Jocelyn Burke, who was 'quite rich as well as being beautiful'.

In 1926 Stella's life was fraught not only with the death of her parents and the assumption of responsibility for her brothers, but also with her dismissal from the BUP after a grievous error when converting the franc into sterling, a miscalculation then sent round the world. However, she soon found new employment on the London *Evening Standard*, first as secretary to the editor and then as a writer of 'women's interest' articles for the paper. By 1928 she had her own by-line and, because the *Evening Standard* was championing the revival of interest in the work of Mary Webb, was deputed to précis her novel *The Golden Arrow* and, as a consequence, read other similarly lush rural romances submitted to the paper. This at a time when her own romance was ending unhappily. In 1930 she was once more sacked, passing from the *Evening Standard* to a new position as editorial assistant on *The Lady*. Here her duties involved book reviewing and it was the experience of skimming through quantities of second-rate novels that, combined with her Mary Webb experience, led to the creation of *Cold Comfort Farm*, published by Longmans in 1932.

In 1929 Stella had met Allan Webb, an Oxford graduate a few years her junior, now a student at the Webber-Douglas School of Singing. They were soon secretly engaged, but it was only in 1933 that they married, royalties from *Cold Comfort Farm* affording them some financial security. Two years later their only child, a daughter, was born and was, in turn, eventually to give Stella two grandsons, on whom she doted. In 1936 the family moved to 19 Oakeshott Avenue, Highgate, within the gated Holly Lodge estate, where Stella was to live for the rest of her life.

For the next forty years, in war and peace and despite the death of her husband in 1959, Stella Gibbons continued to publish a stream of novels, as well as several volumes of poetry and short stories. Her final offering, *The Woods in Winter*, reveals Ivy Gover as one of Nature's 'wise women', moving to a derelict cottage in rural Buckinghamshire and proceeding to tame man and beast. Other characters, more interested in Progress than Nature, are subjected to the author's somewhat merciless gaze. The novel ends with a coda set in the 1970s, bringing the reader back to the world in which the author was living, where the horror of Progress was mitigated by the actions of some members of the new generation, who were willing to protect the Land. It is quite clear throughout the novel with whom Stella's sympathies lie.

After *The Woods in Winter* Stella wrote two more novels, but declined to submit them to her publisher. As Reggie Oliver wrote in *Out of the Woodshed* (1998), 'She no longer felt able to deal with the anguish and anxiety of exposing her work to a publisher's editor, or to the critics.' She need not have feared; both novels have subsequently been published.

Despite a marriage proposal from her literary agent, Stella never remarried. Although avoiding literary and artistic society, for some years she did hold a monthly 'salon', attracting a variety of guests, young and old, eminent, unknown and, sometimes, odd. She died on 19 December 1989, quietly at home, and is buried across the road in Highgate Cemetery, alongside her husband.

Elizabeth Crawford

Some forty years ago, there used to be in North London a place called St. Phillip's Square. Its three-storeyed, narrow houses, built of grey or yellowish bricks, looked mean and cold, in spite of a parapet, unexpectedly crenellated, which had been added to each one, presumably as an adornment; and only a few dahlias and chrysanthemums, blooming in its long straight front gardens, offered any strong colours.

It was not a true square, but a rectangle, open at one end to a main road, along which trams and buses ran up to Hampstead Heath; a drab yet swarming place, where some of the front doors stood open all day. Its windows were curtained in dirty cotton or imitation lace.

But two of them, giving light to the top-floor front of a house at the short end of the Square which faced the main road, had curtains of white muslin starched so stiffly that they looked fierce, and behind their rigid folds, on the evening of a glaring October day, someone was sitting and looking out.

Eyes, so dark as truly to deserve being called black, stared over the Square, where children were shrieking on the hop-scotch lines scrawled across the pavement. They noted Davis's eldest, hurrying round to the newsagent-tobacconist's shop for Davis's *Star*, and one of those Corners, the roughest inhabitants of the Square—though, even so, less rough than the inhabitants of the Mews just around the corner—slopping along in bedroom slippers with a jug to the *Mother Shipton*. The Square simmered in the early autumn plague of heat, sending up its shrieks and shouts and heavy footsteps to a pair of small ears that carried two beads of heavy gold, chased with a design that looked ancient, on delicate lobes.

The view was dim because of the frosty intervention of the curtains, and the noises muted because the windows were shut, but the hoarse barking of a dog, uttered at intervals of a few seconds, pierced through the general clamour to those ears as if it were the only sound in a midnight quiet.

Ivy Gover suddenly stood up, walked quickly round the room, snatched up a rag, and vigorously rubbed it over the surface of a strange old sturdy table, with a seamed surface gleaming from years of such rubbings; then as abruptly returned to her seat. The barking went on.

She got up once more and returned to her polishing; now with a furious, short motion, then with long sweeps of her arm; her brown brow frowned, and her lips were compressed.

The floor boards were stained with permanganate of potash crystals, and their only covering was the remains of a large Turkey rug, which now consisted mostly of greyish threads but showed a few gleams here and there of orange and indigo. The greater part of the room was filled by a double bed, whose brass framework pitched back the glare of the evening sun in dazzling rods and bars of light. Then the eye sank into the soft snow of a marcella quilt. Beside these plain glories, a picture hanging above the bed looked a nothing; it wasn't needed, though the dark face of the young male spirit was tender, and the female spirit whom he had come down to welcome in the blue gulf of sky had an enviable double-veiling of her plump back in some five yards of pure white chiffon and great quantities of brown hair.

The name of this picture was *Reunited*. Ivy had been moved to buy it in a second-hand shop, frame and all, for half-a-crown after her last husband had been killed three years ago. It was only after she had brought it home, and was studying it with an eye in which the satisfaction of the bargain was strangely mingled with resentful grief, that a slight irritation had come upon her.

It took the form of a scarcely shaped question: "What about George, and that Eddie?" Yes, there had been three of them; three husbands; that Eddie (and a poor skinny bit of a thing *he* had been, though meaning well, she supposed) and George, who had worked on the building, when he could get a job, and had liked his drop; and the last, Stan, who had been drowned when the *Connaught* struck a mine left over from the war while patrolling in the China Sea . . . Royal Navy, he'd been.

So Ivy had gone out charing again as she had done since she was eleven, and on the proceeds, with the help of pension money, she lived.

But she had ceased to look at *Reunited*, especially as she was not certain how to say its name. "Re-you . . ." was as far as she could get with it, and that, when she did think of it, was how she thought of it; "Re-you . . ." and accompanied by a vague sense of irritation.

The bed, the ghostly rug, a stout armchair covered in scratched leather, and some photographs (including one of the skinny but well-meaning Eddie, looking apprehensive) together with some old cups and saucers with sprays of blue grass on them, a brown lustre teapot and an old deal chest of drawers, were Ivy's home. For saucepans and frying-pans she used biscuit tins, to the scandal of such decent matrons as ever penetrated beyond her usually firmly shut door, though she did own one saucepan, which had a prehistoric air, so dinted, heavy and smoky was it.

The hoarse bark broke in on the absent satisfaction induced by her hearty polishing. That was two hours he'd been at it. Them—must be out.

Ivy did not use such words casually. When she allowed a word with foul associations to come out between her small firm lips she meant every vowel and consonant, and she used such a word now, meaning it more than usual.

But there was something else to which she could turn.

Having dipped a hand into one of her tin boxes, she went over to the windows and slid one of them up; as the curtain was attached, it went up with it. The smell of dirty dust and sun-baked slates and dustbins came up to her as she leant out, and the thick, sickly air smoothed her face. She put both hands on to the sill, which showed signs of having been recently cleaned from bird-droppings, and, leaning out, looked upward.

There came a dry, silky whistling sound, and down out of the glare sailed a pigeon, and alighted on her shoulder and stood there, serpentining its shining neck and uttering its rich note of seeming love. The cold eye looked out at nothing.

"There . . . beauty," said Ivy, and slowly put up one hand and stroked the feathers of its back with fingers light as one of themselves, "'ungry, are you?"

She brought out her right hand, and held it level with the sill, the palm filled with hard yellow grains. "'Ere, supper, Cooey," she coaxed, and the bird walked down from her shoulder, gripping the dark stuff of her blouse in its claws, until it reached her arm, which it sidled along until it could dip into her palm. She waited for the moment when she would feel the touch of the beak on her skin.

It came; peck, peck, peck; too sharp to be quite agreeable to most people, and precisely the feeling to be expected from a beak belonging to the owner of that eye. The pigeon gulped down the last grain, then turned and sidled back along her arm, across her breast and on to her shoulder. The warm, stiff wing brushed her cheek as the bird fluttered clumsily off and away.

The sun had set behind the squat black tower of the nearby pencil factory. Shadow filled the Square, making a child's white pinafore, a woman's white apron, glow bluish-white, and giving a deeper colour to red dahlias and yellow chrysanthemums.

Ivy lingered at the window, her face set in lines of pain against the barking. Absently, feeling in biscuit tins while she kept her eyes on the factory towering above the roofs against the golden sky, she fished out a crust and a lump of cheese and ate them; sitting back, now, in the comfortable armchair.

In the warmth and the growing stillness, as the children were dragged inside and people sat down to eat, she dozed; a rare thing, with her, but the barking had pressed upon her, and drawn from her. When she awoke an hour later it was dusk, and the shape of the window-frame was faintly thrown upon the floor by a full moon.

Glancing at her loudly ticking clock on the marble mantelpiece, she sprang up, darted to the window, and leant out.

Yes, there he came, round the corner, walking slowly after the heat and trudging of his day, with the now almost empty sack slung over his shoulder, and the red and blue of his uniform showing clear even in the dim light from the Square's few lamps.

Ivy waited until he had walked the length of the Square, pausing only twice to deliver letters and give the familiar knock, and saw him turn to go along the short row of houses at the end. Ah! There might be something for her.

She moved across the room, drawing a key from her overall pocket as she went; opened her door and went through, locked it with one smooth turn of the key, and was down the stairs and in the hall just as the knock sounded through the quiet house.

Neither loneliness nor a desire to communicate with the relatives of her three dead husbands prompted this descent, which had the appearance of a manoeuvre made expert by repetition. Ivy preferred solitude, and felt neither regard nor any sense of duty towards Eddie, George, and Stan's numerous relations, with their Christmas cards and their postcards of bunches of roses on her birthday—especially towards Win Smithers; she was the worst of the lot.

But if there was a letter for Ivy, she meant to have it, and most people were nosy devils; Mrs. Pierce on the first floor, for instance.

Something white landed on the filthy coir mat and Ivy pounced.

"Mrs. Stanley Gover, 28 St. Phillip's Square, Kentish Town, N.W."

"Lucky I come down," muttered Ivy. And typewritered too. *And* sent on from Alperton Place. Mrs. Curtis, that must have been, not a bad old stick. She began to re-mount the stairs.

A door opened below as she reached her own landing, and a voice shouted:

"I saw yer, 'couraging them filthy birds—and their dirt. They're Walker's, they are, and they're valuable, 'ave to 'ave special food. I shouldn't wonder if you wasn't arter pinching one."

"Go on—you're dreaming," Ivy shrieked back, without turning her head or pausing, and went into her room and locked the door.

2

BUT it was full of long words.

It would not be true to say that she could not make head nor tail of it. She gathered that it was from some bloke in a place called Nethersham—and Ivy knew that name, of course—and there was also the name of Tom Coatley, who was her great-uncle. When she had scanned the typed lines on the thick white paper two or three times, she began to feel excited.

If they meant what she thought they meant—

But hold steady, Ive (that was what Stan used to say) hold steady. You got to be on the watch; it might be a take-in.

Wanted her to call, seemingly, to give her the key.

Well, it *seemed* straight enough. But you just never knew.

Ivy looked up sharply at the serene moon, as if daring it to produce a take-in. Ought to ask someone, really. But no, they'd all be after Number One, if she knew anything about her relations by marriage, and Nobby Clark, Stan's friend, was all right, but ignorant; not ignorant in a nasty way, but no book-learning. She needed someone with a bit of book-learning . . . like Miss Green, the one she worked for.

That was it. Miss Green. It was a Saturday; Miss Green would be home, perhaps; she didn't always go away over the week-end, and a breath of air would be all right, over the Heath; get away from that barking. Ivy felt in her purse and found twopence for the bus-fare. It was only just after nine o'clock.

From a large cardboard box she took out her winter hat (she possessed two, one for the summer) and as she set it firmly down over her brows she heard the dog start again; a harsh, tormented noise. She locked her door, and ran down the stairs.

Helen Green was at home. The young man she was in love with did go away at week-ends, and sometimes she went with him, but on this Saturday they were in the middle of one of their partings for ever, which took place every three months or so, and he had gone alone.

As Ivy approached Miss Green's cottage, which was in the Vale of Health on Hampstead Heath and was very vaguely reputed once to have been occupied by Leigh Hunt, Helen was sitting at the open window of her bedroom, and looking out.

But on a prospect very different from St. Phillip's Square: a quiet little street, made up of grey pavement and a long brown wood fence, above which looked the innocent head of a may tree whose berries were just beginning to redden, all lit faintly by the gold of the ascending moon. A bird was singing, far off in the dark woods of the Heath—perhaps even a nightingale—anyway, it was a heartbreaking sound, and Helen thought that she was exceedingly unhappy.

She rented the putative Leigh Hunt cottage from the mother of one of her friends; and as living there was almost as quiet as living in the country, she was fortunate—though of course she did not feel it. She felt little, except the emotions aroused by love and poetry; and there can be no doubt that everyone in the world outside her private dreams was unusually forbearing with Miss Helen Green, or she would never have succeeded in holding down a job, much less earning enough to live on.

Yet she did both, and she also contrived to employ Ivy Gover to clean her cottage for ten shillings a week.

And surely there was Ivy, coming down the little street, in her navy coat and skirt and her black felt hat with the red ribbon. They had only parted at twelve o'clock that morning, so what could Ivy want? Helen hoped, in a detached way, that nothing was wrong.

She was usually so interested in observing human beings, in a dreamy yet concentrated way, that it seldom occurred to her to wonder if they were unhappy or worried; she only studied them, taking them into her mind, and then enjoyably imagining what they were. When people were beautiful, she just watched them, without thinking about them at all, as if they were giraffe or deer.

However, this enviable state of mind was at last beginning to alter, and it was Love which had begun the change.

And she did like Ivy, whose cleaning had a fierceness that gave to it a heartening gleam and polish, and who got on with the job without talking, or demanding that Helen should come and see how nice it looked. She relished, particularly, Ivy's silences on Saturday mornings, when Helen wanted to moon over a poem she was writing, or to sit gaping at the door, which opened directly on to the little brown and grey street; or to go wandering over the Heath, looking at the trees and falling into small holes, without remembering that Ivy was in the cottage at all. Also, she liked Ivy because she suspected, from various slight indications, that Ivy liked the country.

When Helen saw that Ivy was almost at the door, she leant out of the window and silently waved, then ran downstairs.

Unrestrained by any middle-class theories about staring, Ivy had been looking in over the small white curtain veiling the window set in the cottage's queer little front door; when Helen opened it, the moon-light and a soft, exquisite smell from trees and grass stood silently there.

"Hullo, Ivy." Helen sounded neither cordial nor surprised. "I didn't expect to see you until Monday." (Ivy chose her own hours to come to the cottage, and had her own key and was sometimes still there about six o'clock, when Helen got home.) "I hope things are all right?"

She meant *I hope nothing's wrong*. A year ago, she would have put the question in that form, but during the past twelve months she had parted finally from Mr. Jocelyn Burke three times. They sometimes joked about it, but the recurring event was teaching her things.

"Can't say," Ivy answered, looking dead straight at her employer, as always when she addressed anyone, "I got a letter. Brought it along. Thought I'd ask you about it. Miss."

"Do come in," Helen said, and Ivy stepped off the white stone step and on to the parquet, "and do sit down." Ivy sat on a chair whose every curve was as well known to her, from past rubbings, as the inside of her winter and summer hats.

"It's typewritered," she pointed out, as she took the letter from her jacket pocket and held it out, "Miss."

When Ivy said "Miss" or "Sir" to anyone, she added it to the end of her sentence, thus making it sound like an appendage; an afterthought and a concession.

Helen studied the letter. The cottage's one living-room was a dark little place, because it was panelled in wood painted shiny brown and the floor was dark, too. There were a few flowers about, but they were deep red chrysanthemums and gave no effect of light. Helen bent her head, with its short, straight fair hair, over the sheet, and thought, while she read.

She was almost certain that Ivy could not read as an adult does; not, that is, fully to master the sense of a paragraph, and Helen's growing new attitude towards the feelings of other people made her want to avoid hurting? insulting? annoying? Ivy. Oh, how difficult it was, this remembering to treat human beings as if they were living, hurtable creatures!

She tried to get around her difficulties by murmuring the letter aloud.

" . . . Gardener, Elliot and Son, 24 High Street, Nethersham, Buckinghamshire . . . beg to inform you . . ."

"I don't want nothing to do with beggars. Miss. Got no use for that sort. Bone-idle, mostly."

"It doesn't mean that kind of begging, Ivy. It's just an old-fashioned way . . ." (here Helen was pulled up by remembering that, to Ivy, 'old-fashioned' would mean something quite different from what it would mean to herself) " . . . just a way of being polite."

Ivy's face said nothing and neither did her lips. But her eyes under the hat sent out an impatience to hear.

" . . . The late George Coatley, your great-uncle . . . deceased October the twenty-fourth . . . The cottage known as Catts Corner . . . vacant possession . . . leasehold . . . would be glad if you could call upon us at your convenience . . . They will then be pleased to hand over to you the key. And they sign themselves your obedient servants."

Helen looked up, tucking a plume of hair behind one ear with a slowly-moving finger.

"Reckon it's a take-in?" Ivy demanded.

"Oh no, I'm sure it can't be." But then Helen paused again, unable to follow up her statement because she did not want to imply that Ivy was such an unimportant object, such a mote amidst millions of other motes, that no one would bother to take her in.

But to Ivy, of course, Ivy was not a mote. Unless she had been very lucky in her loving, the most important thing in the world to Ivy was Ivy. And about Ivy's loves or loving, Helen knew nothing.

"These people," she went on at last, gently waving the letter, "are solicitors. They . . . arrange things when people die . . . and . . . and . . . that sort of thing. Your great-uncle would have paid them something to make his will for him—"

"D'you reckon I'll 'ave to pay them something for this 'ere cottage?"

"I'm *certain* you won't. That I *am* sure of. But of course there may be a little to pay them for managing it all—unless your uncle did that before he died."

The two ignoramuses confronted one another, with considering expressions.

"Just a little, perhaps . . ." Helen's voice trailed away.

"*I'm* not paying *them* nothing." Ivy stood up, and reached out for the letter. "It was my uncle, and now it's my cottage, seemingly. *I'll* manage it, if there's anything to manage." She rammed the letter into her pocket. "What's 'deceased' mean, then? Miss."

"Dead, Ivy."

"Then why can't they say so?" Ivy was at the door. "Sure you don't reckon it's a take-in?" She stood there, a black little woman, straight as a pin, with eyes glittering beneath the brim of her uncompromising hat.

"I'm *sure* it isn't!" Helen almost cried; she felt that the positive aspects of the event were more than due for their innings, "Think, Ivy—it's a cottage of your very own, in the country!"

Suddenly, there swept along the landscape ruled by her mind's eye the majestic vision of the Nethersham beeches; towers and castles of rustling green; benign father-gods of the woods, filled with their gently-stirring life in the blue air of summer or roaring slowly in winter's gales. "Just think, Ivy. It's beautiful country there. I . . . know it quite well." Her light green eyes looked limpidly through Ivy's face, as Jocelyn Burke joined the vision of the trees.

Ivy was not interested in what Miss Green knew.

"It was all right I come, then," she said. "I'll send 'em a p.c. Good night. Miss."

"Good night. And congratulations, Ivy. It's lovely for you." Ivy merely nodded as she turned away, and Helen shut the door.

3

THE autumn was short, that year. The heat wave suddenly ended, and frosts brought fog. In London, a week later, it was the thick dark yellow of a sunflower's heart, but in Nethersham it was white and chilly, rolling down from the low hills, crowned with beeches, that stood above and around the village.

Mr. Gardener, senior partner in the firm of Gardener, Elliot and Son, Solicitors, had already glanced out of the windows at four o'clock, when a cup of tea and a biscuit were always brought in to him, and decided that he would leave early. Houses on the other side of the long, curving Nethersham High Street were mere shapes, just showing through the white fog, which was thickest over the stream and its bordering willows that ran down one side of the road. Yes, I'd better go before it gets dark, he decided. His chauffeur was off duty today because an old war-wound had flared up, as it did occasionally, and Mr. Gardener, who was over sixty though active, disliked driving himself at night.

As he was rising from his desk at half-past four, his senior clerk entered with the announcement:

"There's a . . . lady to see you, sir, Mrs. Gover."

Greddle had been with the firm for forty-five years. Mr. Gardener did not hesitate to exclaim in a tone mingling annoyance with incredulity:

"In this weather!"

Greddle looked correct. If he already had his views on Mrs. Gover, formed by her manner and the two remarks which she had addressed to him, he did not allow views of any kind to show in his expression.

"Well—show her in, show her in," said Mr. Gardener, and sat down again.

Woman lived in London. She would never find her way back to the station through this . . . there would be fuss, complaints, even requests for help . . .

"Oh—Greddle—will you telephone Mrs. Gardener as soon as I have left, and let her know I am on my way, please?" he added.

"Yes, sir." Greddle disappeared and returned, followed by a shape, looking no more than dark and squarish as it followed him up the dark stairs.

"Mrs. Gover, sir." The shape came into the room.

Woman looks like a gipsy, thought Mr. Gardener. Tidy enough, but if there isn't gipsy blood there I'll eat my hat . . . never saw it in old Coatley, though. Must be on the mother's side.

"Good afternoon, Mrs. Gover. Sit down, won't you, please . . . unpleasant weather, isn't it? I hope you didn't have much difficulty in finding your way from the station?"

"Good afternoon. Sir. No," said Ivy. She put a large old rusty-black umbrella and a worn black handbag, capacious and bulging, carefully before her on Mr. Gardener's desk, then seated herself, folding both hands on her lap and looking straight out at him from under the brim of the winter hat.

"I'm glad to hear that. Perhaps you . . . er . . . know the village? Your great-uncle lived at Catts End for many years; I remember him when I was quite a small boy."

"Yes."

Mr. Gardener was not sure if this meant yes, she knew Nethersham, or whether she was commenting on his reminiscence. He was not finding her easy to talk to. Still, taciturnity was better than the rush of twaddle he had anticipated.

"Er . . . in your letter, Mrs. Gover—"

"Postcard." Ivy gave a sudden jerk with one black gloved hand to her hat, bringing it further over her eyes.

"Yes, of course—in—on your postcard you didn't mention any particular day or time for coming to see me, and I was . . . er . . . awaiting further details from you—I was, as a matter of fact, about to leave the office when you arrived. So—"

"I said, when convenient. Fit in with my work," said Ivy.

Convenient. So *that* was the word. He and Greddle had puzzled over it more than once.

"Quite . . . well, I am sure you will understand that I should like to be as brief as possible, in the circumstances. My chauffeur is laid up today, poor chap, he has a war-wound that is troublesome sometimes, and I shall have to drive myself home—through all this. You see, had you suggested a definite date and a time, I should of course have set aside—"

"All I come for is the key," Ivy held out a small paw, black and steady as if carved from jet.

"Certainly, I have it here." Mr. Gardener slid open a drawer. "But there are one or two other details which must be mentioned."

Ivy took her bag off the desk, opened it, and carefully put away the key.

"The cottage, you see, is not freehold," began Mr. Gardener.

"Does that mean it ain't really mine? Sir?" Ivy's eyes seemed to flash suddenly, under the brim of the hat.

Mr. Gardener shook his head; benignly, he hoped.

"No, no, of course it's yours, Mrs. Gover. I shall give you a copy of your uncle's will and you will see that it belongs to you absolutely, for your lifetime. But as to your children . . ."

"I never had no children," said Ivy. And Mr. Gardener was trying to decide whether a word of commiseration was expected, when she added, "Thank goodness, *I* say. Always been lucky."

Mr. Gardener checked some straying thoughts. "Ah . . . you are widowed, then, Mrs. Gover?"

"Three times." Ivy nodded. "Go on about the cottage being what you said."

"Leasehold, yes. Your landlord is Lord Gowerville, who owns it, and the land it is built on, and all the woods round about, for that matter. Of course you will communicate with him, if it should ever be necessary, through the agent, Mr. Stone."

Ivy nodded. He could not see her expression clearly under the hat, because of the fog and the gathering dusk.

"Your great-uncle was quite a character, you know," he went on.

"We . . . all of us here in Nethersham . . . were thankful that his death was so sudden. At his age, a long illness—"

"What he die of, then?" Ivy demanded, "I bin wondering. On and off."

"Oh, old age—just old age. Ninety-three, you know. He was digging in his garden one evening, and he fell on to the earth he'd just turned over and didn't get up again. Death must have been instantaneous, the doctor said. His heart simply stopped. Unfortunately, he wasn't found until the next morning; Sam Lambert, who works at Benneys farm, found him, on his way to work."

Lord Gowerville, Sam Lambert, Mr. Stone—the place was all over strange men, thought Ivy. Well, that was better than strange women. And she had the key. Just let any of them try to get into her cottage.

"And now I know you will excuse me, Mrs. Gover." Mr. Gardener rose from his desk. He knew that, as she was a client though a humble one, he should make some enquiry as to her plans for returning to London. He could not bring himself to do it. He hoped that she would not ask about buses; Greddle had informed him, nearly two hours ago, that the bus had stopped running. "I must make my way homeward," he said.

Ivy, too, had risen. "That your car outside, sir?" she enquired, referring to a Renault whose characteristic blunt nose was parked beside the kerb.

Mr. Gardener was so surprised that his mouth remained open for two seconds before he said, "Yes." It was long enough for him to have a wild idea of saying no. But he got no chance to say anything. Ivy pounced.

"My cottage is on your way 'ome," she said, "so you could give me a lif'. I'd like to 'ave a look at it."

"But you can't have a look at it—" exclaimed Mr. Gardener, almost adding *my good woman*. "It's nearly dark, and very foggy, and freezing. It's down a narrow lane, two miles from the Little Warby road, and it was raining yesterday—the mud down there will be shocking, if it isn't frozen hard. And how will you get back to the station? I really think . . ."

"I'll manage, sir," and Ivy snapped her lips together as she looked at him steadily. She had sized up Mr. Gardener from her first glimpse of him: she had also remembered where the Gardener family had always lived; out Little Warby way.

"Well . . ." he said, in a helpless kind of way. Ivy moved towards the door.

Mr. Gardener did not lack an occasional detached sense of the humour in situations which, had he been as dignified as he looked, would not have seemed to him to possess any. His lips twitched: Mrs. Gover was bustling him out of his own office.

But when, after looking in on Mr. Elliot to say 'good night', and just glancing in at the four clerks at work on the ground floor and then stepping out into the icy fog—which did, however, appear to be thinning—he found that he could not persuade the Renault to start, his momentary amusement vanished.

"Get in, please, Mrs. Gover, won't you," he said, as he stooped for the third time over the starting handle. But Mrs. Gover was already in, and beside the driver, too. Really . . . Mr. Gardener put his annoyance into his fourth attack on the handle, and at once a reassuring chugging noise broke out inside the car. It was so quiet that before he tackled the handle, he heard the Nether rippling under the little bridges made from a single stone, which, at intervals, led across to the houses on its further side.

In silence, they drove off into the dimness, the headlights showing up moving coils and wraiths of mist. Jove! it was cold; it was undoubtedly freezing. What with the composed silence of the figure seated upright beside him nursing bag and umbrella, and an icy current of air playing across his left cheek that would inevitably give him neuralgia, Mr. Gardener's spirits became low indeed. His former relief at Mrs. Gover's lack of chatter was replaced by an illogical wish to hear the woman make some cosy remark.

Whew! A lorry bound for the North was suddenly almost on them, looming high-laden out of the swirling mist with headlights glaring. He had of course both seen the lights and heard the engine as it approached and had thought himself prepared, but it had been a near thing—this mist was terribly confusing—he braked and swerved only just in time.

In spite of the freezing air, he wanted to mop his forehead, and this was the moment chosen by his passenger to make the notably uncosy observation—

"That's a good job, that is. Driving them things. No one nosying about. All on your own. Wouldn't mind it myself."

"For a young man, no doubt," retorted Mr. Gardener, allowing some acerbity to colour his voice. What kind of a woman was this, who "wouldn't mind" an all-night drive of five hundred miles in freezing fog? If the late George Coatley had been a character, his great-niece seemed likely to step into his shoes.

They drove on at a pace reduced, since the encounter with the lorry, to some fifteen miles an hour, in the rapidly thinning fog. They passed no other cars, only a ghostly figure on a bicycle, who called out 'Good night, sir,' as it vanished into the mist.

"Sam Lambert," explained Mr. Gardener, "he . . . er . . . found your great-uncle, you will remember."

"Ar . . ." said Ivy, on an indefinable note, which was certainly not one of gratitude. Now why should she sound like that? pondered Mr. Gardener, who could not know that her uncle's being a corpse when found by Sam Lambert invested the latter, for her, with an aura of nosying-about.

The mist suddenly thinned away to the lightest of veils, the hedges on either side looked out dark and thick, and there, above hills crowned by lofty trees that showed solid against the sky, was the waning Hunter's Moon.

"Almost gone . . ." Mr. Gardener said heartily; another twenty minutes, and thank goodness he would be home, "and here's your turning, Mrs. Gover." He slowed the car down, and braked, keeping the engine going. "But are you sure you want to go down there tonight? It's freezing hard. Let me . . ." he made a real effort, and his voice sounded kind, ". . . won't you let me drive you on to the station? It will . . . be a pleasure."

She was, after all, a client. And her great-uncle had made the effort, quite a considerable one at ninety-three, to walk along the lane, and catch the bus into Nethersham, and climb the three-hundred-year-old stairs into the offices of Gardener, Elliot and Son, to have his will properly drawn up, signed, and witnessed.

When the bill came in, he had got Sam Lambert to go into Great Abbey with a few bits of china and a funny little old table made with two round tiers that he had owned, and sell them to raise the money to pay it. Not one penny had been found in the cottage by the willing neighbours from Little Warby, who had put things straight there after the funeral. They reckoned he had about run out when he died; the landlord at The Swan did not seem to tire of telling how George Coatley had stood treat all round, the night before he went. Seemed as if he knew . . . A fine old man. Mr. Gardener felt that he owed the niece something.

But the niece, competently clutching umbrella and bag, was climbing out of the car.

"I really think, Mrs. Gover . . ." said Mr. Gardener.

At which she turned on him, so quickly that he actually started, demanding in the controlled voice used to a child just before one's patience snaps—

"Now what in the name of goodness joo think is going to 'appen to me, sir?"

"Why—er—nothing, I suppose," Mr. Gardener answered, more feebly than he liked, "except that it really is exceptionally cold, Mrs. Gover—and suppose you were to—er—fall, and sprain your ankle—"

"Then I'd 'ave to stay where I was until someone come along an' found me, wouldn't I?" Ivy snapped. "P'raps it ud be *Sam Lambert* . . . 'e could carry me to the 'orspital."

She turned, and walked unhesitatingly across the thickly rimed road towards the rutted lane leading down between taller, less carefully kept hedges. Mr. Gardener, not without indignation, called pointedly, "Good night, Mrs. Gover," and at that she turned.

"Good night, sir," she called back. "Now don't you go a-worrying about me, I knows it round 'ere like me own 'and. I was born not two miles from 'ere."

"Oh, oh, well of course, if you know your way . . . Good night."

Tiresome woman, why couldn't she have said so before? The car began to move; she passed out of his view, but as she did so he caught out of the corner of his eye a last, backward wave, careless and perfunctory; she had not even troubled to glance round.

*

The mist was drifting rapidly away, and the moon was riding in a clear sky. Down the lane marched Ivy, along the top of iron-hard furrows, between the narrow pools of glistening ice. She looked about her, now; at the leaves withering on the hedges, at wreaths of bryony, colourless in the moonlight, at the twigs making a black pattern along the top of the hedges against the sky. These hedges were so tall that they shut off everything from view except the lane, but a mile or two away were still the hills, and crowning them the woods; dark woods, with the glittering stars above them. The air smelled of dead leaves and cold earth. There was not a sound. Then a fox uttered its wild abrupt cry, far off.

"Two miles, my foot," Ivy muttered, after half an hour's quick, light walking, "it's nearer three. All the better. 'Ullo—'ere we are."

She stopped, settled her hat, and stood staring.

"Just the same," she said at last, in a lower tone.

The lane had taken a sharp curve, and ended. It opened out on to a ploughed field, where the ridges sparkled with frost, and on the edge of this the cottage stood; a small place built of whitewashed bricks, with a thatched roof, and shadowy weeds crowding up against its walls. There were four little windows, two above and two below, staring out of its whiteness at the moon. In the pallid tint of the thatch, high up by the chimney, was a dark, roundish hole.

"'Ave *that* seen to," Ivy muttered, as she stood studying her property.

As she spoke, a bell began to sound from somewhere near at hand: one . . . two . . . three . . . six; a sweet sound, with an ancient quality. Ivy frowned; that would be St. Peter's; just round the corner at Little Warby, that was. A nuisance. Ivy neither went to church (except to be married, of course) nor supported or approved of those who did.

Her stare went over the faintly glittering ridges and beyond, up a noble slope of grass, colourless in the moonlight. Up and up it swept, broadening out at last into a wood of beech trees; giants with vast, thick, silvery branches still laden with their leaves, and sweeping round in a half-circle that must have covered a good three miles. The faint light of the moon deepened their silveriness. Absolutely still they stood, in the freezing air, and between their titanic boles Ivy's eyes, keen as those of some predatory bird, could trace the way into solemn glades filled with shadow. The fox barked again, nearer this time, and, frowning, she turned away from the marvellous sight.

The dog—was the dog barking, at home, in St. Phillip's Square?

Had it been barking hoarsely, desperately, since she had left Marylebone early that afternoon?

"I don't care about *nothin'*..." she muttered, as she turned off down the lane and began her walk to the station, *"that"* (meaning the cottage) "that can wait. But I got to do something about that dog. I *got* to."

4

THE course of true love never did run smooth and throughout the circles moved in by Miss Helen Green it ran bumpily indeed.

There was plenty of love, true and otherwise, in those circles, which consisted of young painters, poets, journalists, sculptors and actors, and a few young newly-married creatures who provided a room—and something to eat—where they could all gather.

Love had a bad effect on the careers of those few among them who had to earn their living by doing something inartistic, such as working in a bank or an office, where it frequently caused them to neglect their tasks. The artistic ones got their work done in spite of love, and it did not hamper the actors at all.

Some of the girls in the set did not work, either artistically or inartistically. The Cartarets, Pearl and Coral, for instance; Daddy was in business and they lived in a handsome house in Belsize Park and kept three maids. The Cartarets worked at nothing but golf and trying to make themselves look even prettier than they were, which was very pretty: Helen had privately named them Snow White and Rose Red. Coral the elder, was also keen on knitting, which she did beautifully, producing jumper after jumper in softest wool the colour of porridge. Pearl did not even knit, and her drive was weak compared with the alarming force and judgement of her sister's.

Later that autumn, about a fortnight after Ivy Gover had been to inspect her inheritance, Helen was replacing the receiver of the telephone in the cottage, and looking grim—an expression to which her straight features and deeply set light-green eyes and small mouth were rather well suited.

Young men! Really!

When she had heard that Pearl Cartaret was engaged for the second time, Helen had merely remembered, without bitterness, that she herself was not the kind of girl who became engaged. It cannot be said that she felt pleased for Pearl; why feel pleased for someone to whom a pleasant but inevitable event had happened? When the first engagement had been broken off, it is true that Helen had felt for Pearl, assuming that Pearl's feelings would resemble her own, had *she* been in the inconceivable state of being engaged to Mr. Burke and the engagement had then become what Coral called Off.

But what Helen did not remember was that on the first evening—it was in May, two years ago—that he had shown signs of becoming rather grave in his manner towards her and just slightly uneasy—like a horse eyeing the snaffle—she had walked home trader the chestnut and flowering almond trees with one thought ruling the confusion in her head—*If I'm married to anyone I shall never be alone.*

And now Coral had interrupted the turning of the heel of a peculiarly complicated sock to ring up and say wasn't it ghastly and she thought Helen ought to know that the second engagement was Off too. She had said that she was in the very middle of the heel. But she had simply had to ring up.

"How *awful*," breathed Helen, inwardly recording 'one lost soul more,' "is she in a state?"

"Oh, well, I wouldn't say in a state. She's a bit upset, naturally. They'd already bought a lot of things, and decided the date, you see, and they'd half-got a flat, and some presents have come in," said Coral robustly.

"How awkward," observed Miss Green, on the demure note which occasionally caused her more conventional friends to glance at her quickly. To nethermost blazing hell with the 'things' and the flat and the presents, she thought, when she's lost *him*. "I don't mean to be inquisitive, but who . . . ?"

"Oh, he did. That's what's so disgraceful. Mummy and Daddy are simply furious. Mummy wants Pearl to bring an action."

"A—what do you mean? For *breach*?" Helen managed to bring but the sentence without letting her disgust and horror into her tone.

"Yes—it would serve him right. Pearl would have been very well off, you see."

"I do see." It was the demure note again. "But she won't, will she?"

A picture of Pearl's small fair face and shingled hair the colour of new chicken presented itself. Helen preferred Pearl to Coral; though she often used Coral's society in order to take into herself great refreshing draughts of stodge.

"She says she won't. But Mummy's keeping on at her. Pearl's still a bit soft about him, I'm afraid."

"When did all this happen?" Helen demanded.

"Oh, yesterday. He wrote to her (funked phoning, I suppose). Just said he'd decided they weren't suited. I ask you!"

"Well, if it only happened yesterday I suppose you'd expect her to be."

"Be what? (I *must* do a bit of that heel; Daddy's taking us to the pictures after dinner.)"

"A bit soft about him."

"Well, *I* shouldn't be. I'd feel so *furious*, so *insulted*. Wouldn't you?"

"I don't know . . ." Helen murmured. Coral would never understand, happily for Coral, that a girl could feel furious and insulted *and* still be a bit soft about someone.

There was a pause. Coral's thoughts returned to the sock heel, but mingled with her calculations were thoughts about Helen Green's dimness (well, writing poetry, I ask you), and her cheap and ungracefully worn clothes. Coral jerked her Kasha dress down over her hips, and a gold bangle slid down one plump arm. How could Helen, poor and peculiar and dowdy, be expected to know about engagements or how nice people lived? She never seemed to be going about with anyone, and no wonder. Who would look at her, in those clothes?

In fact, Mr. Burke was quite rich, as well as being beautiful. Why he had looked at Miss Helen Green, who shall say?

"Well," Coral said on a final note, "I thought I'd let you know. I *must* get back to that heel."

Helen nearly retorted "For God's sake, do," but controlled the impulse, and asked Coral to give Pearl her love.

"Just my love. Don't say anything about my being sorry, or anything like that."

"Rightee-o—oh, I nearly forgot to tell you! Daddy says he'll start Pearl and me up in a tea-shop! In Nethersham. Near our country place, you know . . . isn't it a yell? Imagine us *keeping a shop*! All Mummy's friends'll think it's simply crazy."

"How thrilling," droned Helen, "that's near where Ivy's cottage is."

"Oh, that peculiar female who works for you? Has *she* got a cottage? Really, the way these people go on nowadays . . . I simply must fly, Helen. Cheerio." She firmly hung up the receiver, as if to discourage Helen from another half-hour of gossip, and Helen made an absent kind of farewell grimace.

Ivy was moving in tomorrow morning, she remembered, as she went across to her fireside. Her expression was still decidedly grim. She sat down.

Almost at once, the telephone bell rang again.

"It's me—Ivy," said the telephone, very greatly to Helen's surprise, "could you do me the favour to 'ave a dog? Miss. For one night, it'll be."

"A dog?"

"I'm just going to take him orf. Can't stand it no longer—bark bark bark . . . I'd be obliged."

Helen had never before heard Ivy use any word that implied a request. 'Oblige', 'favour' and 'kindness' were not heard from her lips, and 'please' and 'thank you' infrequently. Helen was interested. *Take him off?* What was Ivy up to?

"What kind of a dog, Ivy?"

"Dunno—never seen 'im. Can you 'ave 'im. Miss?"

"Is he—er—well-trained? I mean, he isn't savage or—anything?"

Bark bark bark suggested a dog that might not be trained at all. If he were only snappy it would be more than Helen felt capable of dealing with just now. She had owned a dear mongrel who had died because she had neglected it in order to give her full attention to Mr. Burke, who, unhappily quite certainly, did not want her full attention. Perhaps the hesitation to shelter this dog arose from some remorse.

"I got to get on. Miss," Ivy said urgently. "The fog's lifting, and that won't 'elp. 'Ow about it?"

Ivy is going to steal that dog, Helen decided. If I have it here, I may have the police as well. What a bore (it was her strongest term of disapprobation). Oh well. It's only for one night.

"All right, Ivy, I'll have him. When will you—"

"We'll be along in about 'alf an hour." Helen expected to hear more but all she heard was a bang as the receiver was put down.

She resumed her seat by the fire. Ivy was excited; Helen had heard it in the urgency of her voice, felt it in that slam. I hope, thought Helen, who was no night-owl, that I'm not going to be up until three in the morning. But I probably shall be.

The Mews, just around the corner from St. Phillip's Square, was the roughest place in the neighbourhood. On the frequent occasions when the police were summoned by some breathless and dishevelled non-participant to go down there and break up a fight, they went in pairs, as they did to the more famous and even rougher Litcham Street, in the back regions higher up towards Hampstead.

The narrow entrance was dark, and overhung by an old brick archway, and one pale yellow lamp, an ancient one set into the wall, cast its feeble light a little way into the gloom. At this time of night, those dwellers in the Mews who had any money were drinking themselves silly in the *Mother Shipton*, and those who had not were well, they'll be indoors, thought Ivy, loitering past the entrance in the choking yellow fog, and they'll be the trouble. If there is any.

An unpleasing and melancholy, yet somehow majestic, clanging sound now approached, and in a moment a tram crept state-lily past, with its golden lights glimmering through the drifting wraiths. The fog muffled all noises; the few passing footsteps from unseen feet, occasional ghostly voices, a boy's jeering laugh or a girl's shrill one.

Ivy knew where them Slessors, who kept the dog, lived; she had made her casual observations during the past week. Second house on the left down the Mews. Not really a house, a kind of loft and some small rooms, over a stable. And they kept the dog in the stable. Gawd, demanded Ivy silently, with sternness, make 'em 'ave that door open . . . not that they're the lock-up kind . . . if anyone makes trouble you see to it it's an old 'un, Gawd—I can just give an old 'un a good push in the belly. Now, for a moment, there was utter silence; fog, and the fog's reek, and silence.

She pulled her collar higher round her throat, jerked her hat down, and, noiseless as a cat, darted in under the pallid glow of the lamp—and vanished into the gloom.

The dog had been silent for the last half-hour. Wore out, thought Ivy, moving lightly over greasy cobblestones. Asleep, p'raps. A few dim lights shone in upper windows; suddenly a woman's voice burst out into shrieking and crying, and a man shouted. Now don't you start nothing outside, for Gawd's sake—Ivy's lips were moving, in her passionate yet cold excitement—just you keep on shouting and take their minds off of me . . .

No lights in Number Two; the wide wooden door faced her, black and saying *No*. But—she glided forward and saw a darker streak against the blackness; oh Gawd, thank You thank You, it was ajar. The dog suddenly began to bark—the desperate sound, coming out of the absolute blackness behind the door, hurt Ivy as it had never done before, throughout the three months that she had endured it.

Recklessly she swung the door right back, letting in the faint light from the archway's lamp. A disgusting smell came to her, and she looked down; the stone floor was smeared and clotted with ordure. Some sort of white bowl glimmered at the far end of the place, and above it, green and glaring and wild, she saw two small lights; lights with a red gleam in their emerald, above a long pale blur. The unbearable sound went on.

She felt in her pocket and took out a small electric torch and pressed its button down, directing the beam first on to the floor. Filth, filth everywhere, and the barking filling up the darkness of the place with desperation and harsh echoes. Grey straw. The beam of light moved cautiously, tenderly forward, into the focus of rasping, torn, choking sound. Upwards, carefully, so as not to frighten him. The grey straw was scattered all around, as if, in his fury and pain, he had made a whirlwind.

But he was not ill, he could not be ill, or he would be curled up in his dirty straw and silent, with dull eyes; he would not be stretched to the full length of a piece of rope, with eyes glittering and golden neck extended so that it gave him the look of some strange animal that was not a dog. He was well, he was plainly very strong, and he was young.

The sound he was making seemed full of blood. Ivy went squelching forward. Not for a second did she take her eyes from his insane emerald ones, but went straight up to him, with nothing in her but passionate pity and love, and put her hand gently on to the narrow, burning head.

"There, beauty. There." She kept her hand still, and felt his blood throbbing under it.

The barking ceased.

The dog stood absolutely motionless. Then it growled. Ivy did not move, but very slowly her hand began to move down the head, in a caress.

The growling ceased.

Then she heard a soft, broken, hissing sound, as the long nose moved cautiously along her skirt, her stockings, her shoes, while he smelt her. She knelt, not troubling to lift the hem of her skirt, and let him smell her all over, and thrust his dry, hot muzzle against her face. She could feel his head trembling, and she moved her hand down until she was stroking his neck, in long, powerful sweeps.

"There, there, beauty. Ivy'll take you. Ivy'll take you away. Now, now. There, beauty. Come with Ivy."

Keeping her hand on his neck and gently pulling him with her, she moved down to the end of the rope where it was fastened to a staple in the wall, and taking a sharp penknife from her pocket, she severed it and let it drop to the floor. Now she was planning and thinking again; now she was wondering if he would make one bound for liberty when they got out of the place, and be off.

Well, better get run over than tied up here.

But he stayed near her; he stayed close by her skirt, almost pressing against her side while she pushed open the door and they got out into the Mews once more. The fog was thicker; the light from the lamp above the archway was scarcely visible.

A woman was crying in one of the upper rooms, but quietly, not screaming any more. Ivy heard the sounds now; while she had been in the stable she had forgotten them. She kept her hand lightly on the dog's head . . .

. . . 'Ullo. 'ere's trouble. She paused, pressing her fingers a shade harder into his scalp.

There, at the limit of visibility, which was now some four feet, stood, undoubtedly, someone. Not a post, not a bit of wall, not a half-open door. Someone. Sex and age unguessable. When it spoke, as it did after what was a long and apparently indignant stare, the voice was weak and piping.

"'Ere, what joo up to?" it said.

"Taking the dog. Should think you could see," retorted Ivy, now going on towards the archway, and speaking over her shoulder. No need to worry about pipy-voice.

"What right you got? That's Slessors' dawg, that is, you know what 'e is. 'E'll just about kill you, 'e will. An 'oo are yer, anyways? Takin' dawgs orf."

"I'm—" (Ivy exerted herself, calling upon her memory), "I'm a repersentive of the Royal Society of Animals, that's 'oo I am, so you can shut yer bleedin' mouth."

"Cor!" said the voice, awed. Then it went on, "An' quite right, too. I bin thinkin' for a long time it's a disgrace. Keepin' the por thing there. 'E's a beauty, ain't 'e? . . . Just shows, you never know 'oo's got a eye on yer."

"'E's a beauty, all right." Ivy was at the archway now. The wan light of the lamp gleamed on the dingy gold pelt pressed against her skirt.

"'Ere, good dawg, nice dawg," said the voice, showing a tendency to shuffle towards them with an outstretched hand. The movement was checked by a truly appalling growl, and a movement of the dog's head.

"'E's got a nasty temper, though," said the voice, retreating.

"So'd you 'ave, if you'd been chained up in your own dirt for two months. And 'e don't like anyone but me. So 'oppit," said Ivy, and passed on with the dog out into the freedom of the fog and the night.

5

IT WAS about half an hour later that Helen jumped from her chair at the noise of a triumphant tattoo on the knocker. She hurried to the door; Ivy's usual knock was a business-like dab.

She opened it hospitably wide, dismissing a thought about shadowing policemen, and saw them there, together; Ivy's eyes glittering under the brim of her hat and one hand resting on the beautiful, strange head of a superb young collie. On seeing Helen he uttered a murderous growl. Thanks, Helen thought.

"'Ere we are," Ivy announced, proving how out of her usual self she was, for as a rule she never made unnecessary remarks. "Excuse if there's a smell—I did give me shoes a good wipe on the grass but it's on me skirt as well—them Slessors ought to be . . . but I won't speak of it."

"Do come in . . . The Slessors are the people you . . . who had him, are they?" They came in, with the dog keeping close to Ivy's side, and Helen shut the door. Then she knelt, and confronted the dog, who stared straight back at her, rigid and in menacing

silence. Then his lip slowly curled back over his teeth and that
sound came up from inside him again.

"Do you think he'll bite?" asked Helen, looking up at Ivy.

"'E will if you let 'im," Ivy said—not helpfully, her hostess
thought. She addressed the dog, "We don't want none o' that, now.
I knows 'ow you feel, but we don't want it. See?" She moved her
hand lightly along his head, and Helen, still kneeling, went on:

"So thin—and his poor coat. What frightful creatures those
Slessors must be."

"Ah, you may well say so. Sods, excuse me."

Helen got up, and the dog growled again. "Come to the fire,"
she invited, "you must be frozen."

The dog's unkempt nails skittered on the parquet. Ivy sat
down in Helen's chair.

"You sh'd 'ave seen 'im run up the Malden Road!" she burst
out, "went off like a mad thing and I thinks '*e's* gone', but back
'e come, going like a Derby winner—didn't you, beauty?" She
stroked his back, where he sat upright, close to her. "Jumped up
at me and nearly 'ad me over. All the way up 'ere, 'e done that."

"I *do* hope he'll be all right. I think he's beautiful." Helen's
eyes were shining. "What's his name—do you know?"

"Nebukedzer," Ivy answered unhesitatingly. "Least, that's
what I'm calling him. Don't know what them bleeders called 'im.
If 'e was pinched—and I'm dead certain 'e was, 'e must 'ave 'ad a
name. But who's to know? Nebukedzer'll do, and Neb for short."

"It suits him," murmured Helen, who collected words. This
name could only be a form of Nebuchadnezzar, and where had
Ivy found it? Perhaps at school she had chanted,

> "Nebuchadnezzar the King of the Jews
> Sold his wife for a pair of shoes . . ."

"Considering the awful time he's had," Helen said next, "he
doesn't look too bad."

"Ah, you may well say an awful time," Ivy muttered. "'Is soul
'as been among lions, 'asn't it, beauty."

Helen kept still; this really was a collector's bargain, and she didn't want to scare Ivy off. Her small ears suggested two idle shells, and her expression was placid.

". . . and so 'as my soul been among lions, listenin' to 'im barkin'," Ivy went on.

"That's a . . . true way of putting it," said Helen, not too emphatically, "I never heard that before."

"In the Sarms, that comes. Me great-uncle used to read the Bible to me when I was a nipper. Kep' on for hours. I didn't half used to wriggle about neither. Then 'e'd cop me one and go on, read-read-read, drive you mad."

That explained Nebukedzer, too.

"Could you drink a glass of beer, Ivy?" Helen knew that Ivy did not like tea. She drank it, because it was cheap and tastier than water, but she did not like it.

"You try me," Ivy retorted, with the first full flash of teeth that Helen had ever seen from her. They were a startling beauty, in that brown, unfriendly face.

Helen kept beer in the house for one of her young men friends. She now opened a bottle, and poured a glass for Ivy.

"You not 'aving any?" Ivy asked; she had drawn up her skirt to the fire, showing laddered pink silk stockings and a blue petticoat of a material called Locknit.

"I don't like it. I'll have water." Helen spoke from the kitchen, no bigger than a large cupboard, to the sound of the running tap. "Now, Ivy," as she returned, sipping from a cup, and looking at Ivy over the top, "the question is—will he stay with me all night? Suppose he wants you, and tried to get out? Shall I shut him in the bathroom, in case?"

"Let 'im go, then." Ivy did not hesitate, wiping froth off her lips with the back of her hand. "'E can't land up with anyone worse than them bleeders, can you, Nebby?" turning to him. He looked at her. Nothing of him moved; his tail hung down like an uncurled feather. But his eyes shone.

"You'd really let him go, sooner than make him stay here?"

"I muss say it ud about kill me to lose 'im now I've got 'im," Ivy burst out, passionately, "my soul *would* be among lions then, and no error . . . but if 'e wants to go, 'e must."

Oh dear, thought Helen, what a pair . . . *he* looks *capable du tout*, as well, and she glanced over Nebukedzer's filthy matted coat and drooping tail, beneath which shone, unmistakably, a fine breeding: I can just see him going off to the guillotine in a cart with that tail straight up in the air.

"He'll probably be all right," she said soothingly, "but Ivy, have you got anything you can leave here? Then he can lie down on it, and the scent will make him think you're near . . . people do that with dogs."

"'Ere . . ." Ivy began tearing off her jacket.

"You can't go home like that—it's too cold—I've got a spare coat—half a minute . . ."

Ivy grunted impatiently, but Helen had opened the door shutting in the little staircase leading up to the two bedrooms, and was halfway up it.

"Here . . ." she said, coming down with an exiguous elderly tweed coat over one arm. "You can bring it back tomorrow morning."

"Might 'ang on to it," Ivy said, and actually uttered a loud, short laugh, "smells posh." She slipped her arms in the sleeves.

"Yes, that's *Ambre Antique*," Helen rattled on before she could collect herself, "Old Amber—I'm glad you . . ."

But Ivy was kneeling down in front of Nebukedzer, who was whining, silently caressing his bent head.

Miss Green, moved out of reserve by the circumstances, had actually been about to confess that the scent had been bought with money which she had been paid for a poem.

Good thing I didn't, she decided, now, she'd have thought I was bats.

"I'll be back ter-morrer, Nebby. You be a good dawg. Stay 'ere. 'Ere's Ivy's coat . . . thass right, smell it, good boy." She thrust it gently against his dejected head, and he sniffed the cheap, worn serge.

"Perhaps if you put it down by the fire, he'd go to sleep beside it," Helen suggested, and that was what Ivy did, coaxing the dog towards it, inch by inch, though he resisted, clinging to her side, whining.

Helen glanced at the clock; they looked like being at the task until the small hours.

"It's no use, Ivy, you'll just have to *go*. I'll hold him, and you run." She took a firm grip of Nebukedzer's neck-fur and he turned on her, snarling.

Ivy stood up, looking desperate, then knelt again, and whispered, with an earnest look, into the pricked ear. It was a long whisper. Helen was interested, but she also swallowed a yawn.

"There." Ivy got up. "Now don't you forget, Nebby . . . stay 'ere, and be a good dawg. Ivy'll come. Promise faithful. Ivy'll come and fetch you in the morning."

She turned to Helen. "Eight, we'll be 'ere. Goodnight. Miss." She did not look back at the dog.

Helen nodded, and Ivy darted to the door, flung it open and herself outside, and slammed it.

Then Helen was almost jerked off her feet by Neb's frantic leap across the room. She had no chance at all of gripping his neck. He flung himself against the door, howling wretchedly and making long deep scratches with his nails down the paint which Helen's landlady had recently had put over the ancient wood.

Helen observed him while she rubbed her jerked arm and gathered together such forces as she possessed for the struggle to come.

"You," she remarked to him, "remind me of someone else I know—so good-looking, and never a minute's peace."

The sunlight of ten minutes to seven, pretending that it was ten minutes to eight, shone cheerfully in at the cottage window. It should have revealed Helen, sitting at her breakfast table, eating bacon and eggs and reading Gibbon. It revealed her deep in sleep upon her big sofa, and Neb also deep in sleep, as far as he could possibly get from her, at the opposite end. Helen was, so to speak, draped across one of the sofa's arms, with her head thrown back, and her legs dangling down on to the floor, in order to get as far as possible from Neb.

They had crawled on to the sofa at the hour of three in the morning accurately prophesied by Helen, after Neb had bitten her wrist and she, trembling but calm, had hit him quite hard four times. On his back. With a length of thickish string, and exclaiming "There!" at the end of the ritual. He had yelped with rage and tried to bite her again but she had rushed away and shut herself into the kitchen, whence she had emerged, half an hour later, with three Oval Rich Tea biscuits and a basin of water.

Neb was lying desolately close to the door, and looked at her with dull, wretched eyes. Offered the biscuits, he sniffed them and deigned to take half of one into his mouth and to drink most of the water. Helen was rather tearful by now, the ceremony with the bit of thickish string having required an expenditure of nervous energy, and while coaxing him to eat, she told him about Emily Brontë's epic beating of Keeper. ". . . and nothing," Miss Green had assured Nebukedzer, "simply *nothing* stands between you and a beating like that, except the fact that *I* am no Emily Brontë."

She then slid down on to the floor beside him and cried for some time, telling him incoherently that it might be better if she sometimes beat Jocelyn, while Neb, catching the infection of unhappiness, howled subduedly but dismally for Ivy.

At last in desperation, as he would neither stop howling nor go to sleep on Ivy's jacket, Helen cautiously unlocked the door (having fastened the fatal length of string about Neb's neck) and off they went for a ramble through the black, still, foggy Vale of Health at half-past two in the morning, returning in half an hour both feeling not disagreeably exhausted, and ready to retire together (Ivy's jacket having been placed under Neb by Helen), at a formal distance from one another upon the sofa.

Cold winter sunlight shone on the dirty golden dog and the big, fair-haired girl. Asleep, Helen looked quite fourteen years old, and this was understandable, as in many, many respects fourteen was her age.

"Well, I never," remarked Ivy, peering through the glass upper part of the door, while Nobby Clark sat patiently in the cabin of his van, "never went to bed, seemingly. Must 'ave 'ad quite a night of it," and she chuckled harshly.

Though Nobby was under Ivy's spell as thoroughly as any wood-cutter ever fell beneath that of some waterfall-witch, his sympathies were with the young lady that Ive had bamboozled into having a mad dog all night. Well, if not downright, near-mad. But he only said, "Best get a move on, Ive.'"

Best, too, not to think about the football match he could have been watching this afternoon, or the job taking a wardrobe from a house in Lissenden Gardens to one in Belsize Park. Ive had a way of making you do things. His van was full of her furniture, and a proper disgrace most of it was.

Ivy did not answer, but rapped sharply once on the cottage's knocker. Instantly, it seemed, Nebukedzer was off the sofa and over the room and on his hind legs at the window, thrusting the curtain aside so that it draped itself across his nose, and uttering hysterical yelps of rapture. Helen stirred; large but beautiful stockinged feet, arms in their striped green and white jumper, fair head, all came into slow motion.

She went over to the door, and opened it, and Nebukedzer shot out and on to Ivy. Helen smiled to see the two, wrapping the handkerchief tighter round her throbbing wrist.

At the appearance of the young lady, Nobby touched his cap, from a dim conviction that *someone* ought to act polite. It certainly wasn't any use expecting Ive to.

Downright ignorant, Ive could act, and usually did. If only . . . if only . . . those teeth, and that way she had. Fair got you. And her nearer fifty than forty! Must be; Stan would have been fifty-three this year. But she got you, somehow, just got you, all the same. *And* a good cook—when she liked. But telling a man to keep an eye on some bleeding pigeon, when he'd just asked her to marry him . . . that he was not going to stand for.

It had all been done right; no funny business; and her with Stan's pension and now this cottage: sell it and put the money in the P.O., all working out right—and then a bleeding pigeon. And now the dog. Not but what it wasn't a nice dog, but excitable . . . might go mad any minute, and anyway he wasn't asking Ive again, so *let* it go mad: only not, he hoped, in his van.

He turned away from the farewells being hurried through at the cottage door.

"Good-bye, Ivy. I hope Nebby settles down, but I'm sure he will, all he seems to want is you," Helen was saying.

"And all I want is 'im, so we're a pair," Ivy answered, with a most unusual expansiveness. "We'll be off, then. Miss." She kept her hand on Neb's head as she spoke, and gave a dismissing nod.

"Wouldn't your friend like a cup of tea?" Helen asked, being aware, through experience rather than deduction, that friends looking like the chap in the van would always like a cup of tea.

"'E don't want no tea," said Ivy firmly, "we got to get on. Come on, Nebby. So long, then," and she led him, frisking and squirming, to the van.

Still keeping his head turned away, Nobby had unfastened the door so that she could get in, and in she got, helping Neb to scramble up beside her. He settled himself heavily on her feet.

"Got to 'ave 'im just there, I s'pose," said Nobby, compelled to break what he regarded as his perfectly legitimate reproving silence, "'is tail 'ull get all caught up in the gears."

"It won't if you drive sensible," Ivy snapped. "There, boy, now you'll 'ave a nice ride. Thass right, you 'ave a look round," for Neb had suddenly sighed, sat up, and was looking out with bright eyes through the cabin window at the winter morning.

"Ought to 'ave let 'im 'ave a run," Nobby suggested, while he was turning the van to take the road leading up and out of the Vale of Health, "don't want no accident."

"You can stop up the 'ill—if you're worried. Proper old aunty, you are."

Nobby said no more. What was the use?

They drove off, and Helen turned back to her cottage.

All I want is him.

The words sang on in her mind, and it was tempting to think that they were true of herself and Jocelyn. There was abandon in them, and grief, and whole-hoggedness, and the luxury of being a whole-hogger. But even as syringa is sweet in the nostrils, and can suddenly turn over-sweet, suddenly Miss Green . . . not Helen . . . began to feel that the words were not true.

She did not only want Jocelyn; she wanted to write poetry, and to walk, and to pick wild flowers, to see her friends, and to laugh. She had once said something of the kind to Jocelyn, and he had appeared (the thought was not comforting) to be slightly relieved.

The room was exceedingly untidy. There were crumbled biscuits, and the ominous shortish bit of string, on the floor, and over all hung a strong smell of unwashed, neglected dog.

Now I'll have a nice time tidying-up, thought Helen, and she began.

The bite in her wrist continued to throb, and occasionally she examined it, marvelling over the complete absorption in Neb which had prevented Ivy from noticing a handkerchief wrapped round the wrist of someone who had been looking after a savage dog all night. She did not condemn Ivy, she only marvelled. Her detached interest in Ivy's state of mind replaced any resentment.

She disinfected the bite. It continued to throb, and halfway through the morning it occurred to her that it might be as well to submit the perfect blue marks of Neb's teeth to the eye of her doctor.

6

NOBBY's silence continued. Through Hampstead, through Hendon, Watford, Pinner and Rickmansworth, out into true country, it stayed unbroken, while Neb sat on Ivy's feet, looking out at the sights, and Ivy occasionally stroked his head. Both of them gave the impression of two people having a nice ride.

Nobby had begun by enjoying his silence, with a stem, self-justifying relish, but as the time went on he began to feel plain miserable. You couldn't get the better, seemingly, of Ive. He'd lay ten to one she hadn't even noticed he wasn't speaking to her.

One of the qualities in her that fascinated him was "the way she wasn't everlasting jawing".

It wasn't like most women; yet it wasn't sulks, neither; and then when she laughed, sudden-like, and showed them teeth— which he would also bet was her own—well, he had begun to fancy her before old Stan was killed, and that was the truth. Next to

Ivy Kathy and Cis, even Eileen, seemed like a kid's jelly-sweets; no taste to them.

Yet she could be that unkind. Bleeding pigeons. No, best keep off.

"You was asking me," observed Ivy suddenly as the van drove past the few small general shops and red-brick cottages of the suburbs of St. Albans, "about marryin' you."

"Just remembered, 'ave you? Thanks and all that," was what Nobby meant to say, and what he did say, turning eagerly to her, was, "Well, what's the answer, eh, Ive? I got a bit saved up, I told you, and now you got this 'ouse—"

"Cottage, and the roof's half off."

"—Cottage, then, we'd 'ave a place of our own, and I got the van. We could—"

"The answer's no. Thank you for askin' me. But I could 'ave married again times over, since Stan—*if* I'd felt like it." She moved her fingers gently along the top of Neb's head, kneading the dirty golden fur, "Get you barfed, first thing when we get 'ome, won't we, beauty?"

"'Oo was that, then? Arst you?" demanded Nobby, so jealous that he hardly realised he had been refused. (But he had known that he was, of course; you don't, even if you are Ive Gover, go on about some bleeding pigeon if you've just decided you'll have a chap.) "Recent, I mean."

"Oh—some feller up the Malden Road. Keeps a terbacconist's. Used to go in there for me fags regular on me way 'ome from work, and one evenin' 'e says, ''ow about you and me getting married?'"

"You thought 'e was jokin', and I'll bet 'e was," poor Nobby said.

"No I didn't. Kind of 'ung over the counter and caught 'old of me. Knocked off a lot of books on the floor. Wasn't 'alf in a state," Ivy ended. "Look, Neb, there's dawg biscuits. In that winder."

"'Oo else?" Nobby insisted, "recent, I mean," and swung the van round a curve in the lonely lane. A low branch, laden with russet leaves, scraped against the roof.

"I s'pose I might say it ain't your business," Ivy's tone was tranquil. "But me and Stan's known you a goodish time . . . Old Clarkson, it was. Lives over the shop. 'Er father."

"'Im! 'E must be eighty!" exclaimed Nobby, scandalised.

"Seventy-three," Ivy corrected.

"Well, 'e *looks* eighty."

"That don't matter to me. I'm not 'aving 'im any more than what I'm not 'aving you nor the chap in the terbacconist's. 'E can look a 'undred, for all I care."

Nobby was feeling slightly better. He was not the only victim of Ivy's peculiar fascinations, and the others—and how many more might there not have been, between her first and her last marriages?—had been declined, apparently, as casually as himself. He was not alone in feeling the fetchingness of those eyes that were as near black as he ever saw, and the teeth, and the 'ways' that were unlike the ways of other women.

And he was not going round crying Onions for Sale over Ive Gover, not him. Well out of it, if you asked him. A cottage with the roof half off, and a dog that might go mad any time (not but what it hadn't behaved all right up to now, but then Ive had control over it, you could see)—no, there wouldn't have been much of a life. And he suddenly realised it was getting on twelve, and that a bite to eat would be all right.

The Swan, at Little Warby, stood on the verge of a quiet, meandering, leafy lane, with still fields stretching behind it away to low blue hills. As Nobby stopped the van and as the engine's racket ceased, one big leaf floated down from a chestnut tree overshadowing the little white weatherboarded place. A faded sign showing a swan whose snowy feathers were now cream colour, hung above the door.

The entrance to the saloon bar opened to his hand; it led into a low-ceilinged, small room offering the smell of old beer, and a rough table with benches. Two farm-workers were already at the bar with their pints. The landlord was leaning across it, smoking a pipe.

"Morning," Ivy and Nobby said together, as they came in, seemingly, so small was the room, to fill it completely, and followed, close at Ivy's skirt, by Neb. "Morning," everybody nodded.

Neb stopped, and growled.

"Here, here," said the landlord easily, not taking his arms off the counter, "what's upsetting your lordship?"

"Just bought 'im. Been with a rough lot what kept 'im on the chain," Ivy explained, and sat down at the table. "'E'll be all right. Neb, lie down. Down, boy," and he flopped on to the stone floor at her feet.

"You Mr. Tuckett's son?" she next demanded of the landlord, to Nobby's surprise: she had given no indication of knowing this little place.

"That's right. But he's gone. Went fifteen—must be nearer sixteen—years ago," the landlord answered.

"I'm sorry to hear that. Me great-uncle used to bring me 'ere for a swig of ginger pop when I was a nipper, and *that* must be—no, I'm not telling 'ow long ago that is," and out came Ivy's smile, effecting the usual transformation upon herself and those who saw it, "Outside I'd 'ave to sit, course, while 'e 'ad 'is pint inside."

The landlord slowly studied Ivy. Nearer fifty than forty. Respectable. Didn't look like London somehow, in spite of wearing gloves.

"Coatley was the name. George Coatley. I used to live round Nethersham way. Me father worked up at Weaver's Farm," Ivy added.

The landlord's expression changed completely. "O' *course* I remember George Coatley—remember! He hasn't been gone three months. Had a great big beaver—" the landlord expressively moved a hand up and down between his chest and his chin—"snow white, it was. White as snow. Used to come in here regular. Walked over from Catts End."

"Lived there . . . yes, that's where my cottage is. He's left it to me."

The landlord stared. "Left it to you? You and your husband'll be settling down there then?"

Nobby, who had joined the pair at the bar, looked around him rather huntedly. A half-day spent in Ivy's company had given him the feeling that he preferred it in short, exciting flashes. She was too much. She led you into embarrassing situations. For example, had he been mistaken for Kathy's or Cis's husband—and especially Eileen's—there would have been laughter all round, and perhaps they might have coloured up a bit—Cis certainly would.

Not Ive. She answered immovably, "'E isn't my husband. I'm a widder. He's a good friend of my husband's. No. I'll be living there alone."

Nobby's embarrassment gradually subsided. What he wanted now was his dinner.

They arranged to pay one and sixpence each for the steak and kidney pie, potatoes, sprouts, stewed apples and custard that the landlord said his family were having themselves; and Ivy asked, in her usual calm tones, where the Ladies was, and went off composedly to find it. A nicely-ironed, if coarse, cloth was laid on the table, and they enjoyed their meal and Neb had his bowl of something, and a bone.

The landlord shook hands with Ivy on their leaving, and called her "Mrs. Gover". Perhaps the relish with which she had drained two pints of stout convinced him that she, like her uncle, was going to be a regular customer.

Nobby's first glimpse of Catts End convinced him of the desirability of getting back to London as soon as possible. That roof, with rotted black straw streaming out of it which birds must have pulled off for nesting, and that grass half-way up the front-door ... for the first time, Nobby felt downright *thankful* that she had refused him. He sighed quietly to himself. No thanks.

All you could say was, the windows wasn't broken.

Although it was still early, an expectancy had drawn down over the day like a veil. Soft colourless clouds packed the sky, and the distant hill, crowned by its grey and russet beeches, looked dark and clear. The withered grass did not stir; only a robin, drawn at once to the place by the presence of man, first flew on to a branch of an elder bush growing in the cottage garden, and then began, almost below its breath, to whistle its song. But there was nothing to expect but dusk and rain.

"Gawd!" Nobby burst out, "if I 'ad to live 'ere I'd go off me nut."

"Just as well you 'aven't, then." Ivy was standing, with Neb close at her side, sniffing the air with lifted head, and surveying her cottage by daylight.

"Cor—rain, now," was Nobby's next disgusted remark, while he was unlocking the back of the van. Ivy was putting the key into the front door.

"Pardon?" She did not look round.

"I said it's *rainin'*," shouting, "Yer *stuff*'ll get wet."

"Then it'll get wet, won't it?" Ivy marched into her drawing-room, dining-room, scullery and kitchen, and stood, studying it.

Of course, it looked different without Uncle's bit of carpet, and the plants he used to have on the window-sill. Where had that bit of carpet gone? And the little round table? Wore out, most like. But the old black wood dresser was still there, and three of the remembered red and blue cups were hanging on it.

There were three of the old chairs left, and Uncle's Windsor; that was where he used to sit while he read to her out of the Bible. She remembered particularly him calling it the Windsor.

Neb had followed her in, and was sniffing at the chair-legs and round the wall, deepened to dark cream by smoke and age but unmarked by any sign of damp.

"'Ome, Nebby," she said, on a low note, moving her hand towards him. He stopped his inspection, and turned, and looked up at her, "this is your 'ome, now. You can go for a run, any time, as far as you like, but you always come back 'ere. 'Ome. Understand?"

"Ive!" An exasperated roar from outside, "you might come and give us a 'and . . ."

"I'm seein' upstairs," Ivy roared back, not with a loudness given by any irritation but with a sudden astonishing projection of her voice; and up the narrow, ladder-like stairs she went. Neb followed.

The two little rooms were empty but for an old iron bedstead big enough for two, with its mattress neatly rolled and tied up with rope; and a marble-topped washstand, on which stood a large white china water-jug patterned with salmon-pink flowers, and a chamber-pot to match on the floor.

"Done it all up tidy, I will say," Ivy muttered. "But 'oo come round 'ere doin' it, I wonder? *Sam Lambert*, was it, or *Lord Gowerville* or *that Mr. Stone*? Nosying about."

The names were perfectly and accurately pronounced in a biting tone, while her eyes were moving over the splashes of white on the bare boards in the smaller room, and the dull beam from the grey sky that came down through the large hole in the roof. Down with it, too, came a fine drizzle (she held her face up and felt it); and here there was a damp mark, a big one, on the sloping ceiling. The little window panes were dim with old dust from the fields.

She went downstairs again. Fire, that's the next thing. I can smell mice. That'll be all right; mice.

Nobby was setting down another rolled-up mattress on the floor. He remarked that the place smelled of mice; didn't half was how he put it.

"That won't kill me. Wood's the next thing. Got all the stuff in? We'll 'ave a fire. 'Ere." Ivy took the familiar pale green and brown packet of Woodbines from her jacket pocket, and held it out to him. Gloomily, he accepted one, and they both lit their own.

"Got it all in?" she repeated.

"All but your chest o' drawers, Ive. That's a bit awkward—with me shoulder."

It was awkward because the muscles had never fully strengthened again after the thrust he had taken at Loos. The Jerry had gone for his belly, as per instructions, but Nobby had struck up the bayonet, quick as lightning, with his own weapon, and luckily someone had at that precise moment stabbed his attacker in the right place. Not, however, before some other Jerry's bayonet had gone through Nobby's shoulder.

"Wot you got in the war? All right—I'm comin'," and Ivy came out into the drifting drizzle, followed by Neb.

If that wasn't Ive all over! Made you feel you could do 'er in, and then acting friendly-like.

But though there was a good scent of damp woods and fresh earth in the air, and the rain was floating, so light was it, rather than falling down, and though they had a good laugh over Ivy's hat being knocked sideways against some bush all over shiny black berries near the front door while they were carrying in the chest of drawers, Nobby's thoughts continued to play around fish and chips and the Late Night Final *Star*, in London.

"Ive!" he burst out suddenly, when the chest of drawers had been with difficulty carried up the stairs, "you surely ain't going to sleep 'ere alone tonight? It ain't my business . . . but I know Stan wouldn't a' liked it—you bein' here on your own."

"Well if you think Stan wouldn't like it, you stay 'ere with me. There's two rooms." She glanced at him mockingly under her hat brim, her teeth gleaming pearly in the dusk.

"I didn't mean nothing wrong, Ive; you know that."

"You! You'd never mean anything wrong." Ivy's tone was neutral; all the same, Nobby did not like this sentence. "S'pose I ought to say thanks. (Thanks.) But come to that Stan was used to me being on my own—sometimes I wouldn't 'ear from 'im not for three munfs. For all 'e knew, I might a' been under a bus. You give me a 'and getting in some wood, and then we'll 'ave a cup of tea and you must be off. I got Neb, ain't I, beauty?"

The plumy dirty tail thumped uncertainly on the stone floor.

"First time 'e's done that," Ivy said with satisfaction. "Now for that wood. Reckon we'll 'ave to go acrost the field and up to that there kind of a forest." Her tone was full of relish.

"Wot—in all the rain, Ive? That there field's been ploughed, recent, I noticed. We'd get stuck." Nobby's tone, by contrast, was quite subdued by horror. "*I* ain't goin' and that's straight."

"Well—p'raps there's some in the hedge."

There was; the hedge had not been cut owing to the persistent drunkenness, and consequent final dismissal, of Lord Gowerville's hedger and ditcher; and they found plenty of snapped-off thorn, dead hazel, and even a treasure of small sawn-up logs of holly, either prepared and stowed away for his own use by the hedger, or even, so weathered and overgrown were they, by George Coatley.

Two armfuls for the taking, and the logs. As they trudged away from the hedge in the rainy dusk, Nobby was reflecting that there was not a ha'penny to pay for the load. And the price of coal in London! Brightly gold as the vision of fish and chips gleamed, he admitted that there might be something to be said for living in the country.

7

Ivy had lit candles, and stuck them in two old beer bottles on the table. The grate was huge and blackened, below a high mantel-shelf dark as itself, and wind had started to moan miserably in the cavernous chimney.

Nobby experienced a return of former feelings. Them candles gave you the creeps. Couldn't hardly make out a thing, and not a sound in the place; not a sound outside, come to that, except some bird screaming its head off over in the woods. If it was a bird.

He glanced for comfort towards his van, just visible across the road. It announced reassuringly—you could just make it out—that J. Clark was willing to undertake light removals. J. Clark was wishing heartily that he could remove himself.

Ivy's alarm clock, standing commandingly on the mantelshelf, and looking out with the eye of regularity and order across the discomfort, announced that it was a quarter to four, and at that moment Nobby heard another sound beside its confident ticking—the engine of an approaching car. He dropped his armful of wood on to the brick hearth.

"'Ere's someone coming!" he cried.

Ivy was busy with paper bags and tins at the dresser. "Visitors already, seemingly," she retorted, not pleased, and Neb sprang up and bounded across to the door, making his snake's neck and uttering his frightening bark.

"Here, missus—call him off, will you?" a voice shouted. "Want any bread today?"

Nobby eagerly opened the door, and there in the wan light stood no Wandering Jew, no creepy figure from the dark woods, but a boy in his early twenties, with a cheerful rosy face, and a basket over his arm filled with golden-brown loaves.

"You're the baker, are yer?" Ivy asked, as if he were someone else, disguised. "Neb, you lie down, see."

"Wattle and Son, Nethersham. Used to come out regular Wednesdays and Saturdays to the old chap. Him being *that* old, and it being three miles. On me way to The Hall and saw your light."

"That's a wonder," Nobby put in, wishing to detain this fellow-male until, if possible, their two vans (for he could see by the cheerfully bright headlights that the baker had come in one not unlike his own) could set off together in jolly fellowship.

Let her get on with her candles and her hole in the roof and her mad dog.

"I'll 'ave a 'ome-baked," Ivy said briefly; she was now screwing up newspaper into rolls, "you still do 'ome baked?"

"Course we do—how'd you know that, missus? Since my grandad's time, we've done our home-baked."

"George Coatley was me great-uncle and I was born round 'ere—and this place is mine now and I'm goin' to live here." Ivy began to shy the rolls of paper unerringly into the grate. "You bring me a home-baked twice a week same as what you done my uncle, see?"

"Right you are, missus, and pleased to welcome a new customer."

He edged into the room, keeping one eye on Neb, and rested the edge of his large pale-yellow withy basket on the table, while he took out a comely loaf and put it on the gleaming seamed surface.

Ivy had tossed some wood on to the paper, and lit it, and it was beginning to flame up. It did make a difference, thought Nobby, though the place was still cold enough to freeze you. The walls looked a kind of red, now, with the flamelight, and you could see better . . . I *hate* candles, I downright *hate* 'em, Nobby decided, with passion.

If it had been Cis or Mary, or even Eileen, kneeling there by the hearth and tending the fire, she would have said that she had only moved in an hour ago, and something about the place being still in a muddle. Mary or Cis, even Eileen, would have asked the baker to stay for a cup of tea.

Not Ive, though. Trust her.

All she said was "Thanks. Good-evenin'," and before Nobby could thrust in some remark to detain him, the baker had snatched up his basket, nodded and smiled, and gone whistling away. Nobby went to the door, and dismally savoured, to the last crumb, the sight of the van being started up and its lights vanishing down the road beside the field that presumably led to this here Hall. Nice road to lead to a Hall, he must say, it looked as if it dropped off over the edge, somewhere further on.

He turned back into the room. And there was Ive's little blue kettle settled on the blazing logs, and a cloth had been whirled on to the table—clean, he must admit—and a bit of marge (in the paper . . . even Eileen . . .) and a great knife beside it what looked more like it was for doing you in than cutting bread. Two chairs had been drawn up.

A fire certainly did make a difference. Nobby sighed, and sat down in the Windsor. Ivy darted about, in silence.

Presently there crept out on the air a soft singing noise, a wandering sound that in no way suggested the crying of the wind, but belonged to the hearth and shut the crying of the wind away. Nobby looked up at the faint sound.

"Where'd you get the water, Ive? There ain't no tap as I can see . . . 'ow you're goin' to manage in this place *I do not know*, gel. If it was Cis Roberts, now—"

"Well, it ain't Cis Roberts, and there's a well. Outside at the back. I remember. But I brought a drop in one of me bottles. 'Ere—" she deftly whipped the kettle off the fire, with a hand wrapped in her skirt. "Boils before you can turn round—always 'as. Cut the bread, will yer."

While he used the fearsome knife on the new loaf, she worked off the lid of a tin of golden syrup, where a rather horrifying picture showed a dead lion with a swarm of bees hovering above it.

"'Out of the strong comes forth sweetness," muttered Ivy, spooning treacle on to thick slices spread with margarine.

"Pardon?"

"Says so on the tin. Thass out of the Bible, too."

Nobby gave it up. He supposed she knew what she was talking about, but all he wanted was his tea.

"Give you the creeps, them windows," he observed, when they had been seated at the table, and eating and drinking in silence for some moments, "you want some smart curtains up there, Ive." The small panes were pitch-black in contrast to the golden candlelight and rosy firelight in the room; black as Egypt, thought Nobby, and outside there might have been nothing—or anything.

"P'raps I will—and again p'raps I won't, we'll 'ave to see, shan't we, Neb?" She put a hand down to caress his head where he sat, more as a house-bred dog would have, now, beside her chair.

Sitting there in her hat eating bread and treacle and the water out of a well (upset you, most like) and a half-mad dog for company—Nobby felt a strengthening wish to order her about. It wasn't *right*, the way she went on.

"You'll 'ave everybody lookin' in, Ive," he warned.

"There ain't no one 'ere to look in, 'cept the rabbits, and I don't mind them."

"Rabbits! Them windows is a good five feet orf the ground!"

"The rabbits round 'ere is extra tall," and then she fair burst out laughing, looking at him over her cup with her eyes black as the windows and shining; downright shaking, she was—and what was so funny? Nobby took a deep pull at his tea, and in the silence there came a rap on the front door.

"Now you keep still," Ivy ordered Neb, leisurely getting up, "and we'll see oo *that* is—nosying round when we was all comfortable."

She flung open the door in her usual royal style, and there stood a tall fair man with a long face above a parson's collar, under an umbrella.

"Mrs. Gover? Good evening. I'm your Vicar, Mr. Henderson—I saw your light and guessed you had moved in, and I came to say 'welcome' to Catts End . . . Your great-uncle, Mr. Coatley, was one of my parishioners, of course."

"Good evening. Sir," Ivy stated, after a pause filled with the low, rumbling, unceasing growling of Neb. "You live round 'ere, then?"

"Yes," Mr. Henderson replied after a pause, "I expect you will remember, Mrs. Gover, that the church is at Little Warby, and the Vicarage is just by it. You *were* born here," he smiled at her as he shut up the umbrella, "weren't you?"

Three bloomin' cheers, thought Nobby, who had got up from the table and was standing almost at attention. 'Ere's someone who's got Ive's number at last.

"'E told you that, I s'pose. Sir. Mr. Gardener," Ive said, making no movement towards inviting her visitor in.

"You've got it looking very cosy," was all the Vicar said, after a calm glance round.

Kath, Cis, even Eileen would have offered the gentleman a cup of tea first thing—and him a clergyman, too. Ivy said not one word in reply to the pleasant comment.

"'Ow about a cup of tea, sir?" Nobby said suddenly, in his deepest voice. The one he had used for making the new recruits jump to it in '16.

"We ain't got no more milk," Ivy snapped instantly, even as there was a distinct—"Thank you—that's very kind—but no thank you . . ." A pause, "I shall see you both at church on Sunday, no doubt."

"'E ain't my 'usband. And I shan't be going to church. There'll be too much to do. Sir."

Ivy spoke clearly, with a jerk of her head, and Quentin Henderson looked at her with hidden amusement. A character, Mrs. Gover.

"Mrs. Gover's a widder. I'm a friend of 'er late 'usband's, sir. Won't you come in out of the rain? It's a nasty night."

Nobby did not care how Ive glared at him; the gentleman was a clergyman and should be treated proper. As Mr. Henderson came in, observing clearly that Evensong was at six and he must only stay a moment, it occurred to Nobby that it might do Ive a bit of *good* to belt her one now and then, let alone the relief to a man's feelings.

He drew up the Windsor, first dusting it with a bit of something he snatched up, and Mr. Henderson sat down. Neb stood with outstretched neck and glittering eyes, silently baring his teeth, and Mr. Henderson glanced at him.

"Good boy?" he said, without nervousness, "I like dogs."

"Ive!" commanded Nobby. "If you can't make Neb be'ave hisself, put 'im outside."

For a moment, he really thought that it was Mr. Henderson who was going to be put outside. Ivy's eyes under the hat were as fiery as Neb's; Nobby could have sworn they had the same dark emerald glare.

Then she said quietly, "Lie down, Neb. 'E's been chained up for months," she explained, turning to Mr. Henderson, "and e's still very wild. 'E only got away yesterday. I reckon 'e was stolen."

"Poor fellow, that explains it. People can be much worse than the brutes."

"And that's true. Sir," Ivy said loudly. "But 'e got away, 'Thou 'ast delivered David thy servant from the peril of the sword'!"

"That sounds like your uncle, Mrs. Gover. He was a great reader of the Psalms and Bible. Not a churchgoer, but he did know his Bible and Prayer Book."

"It was me uncle taught me. Well—I say taught me. Used to keep on read-read-read while me auntie was dishing up. Always seemed to take a turn for it while she was dishing up."

"Yes, that's how I remember him best. Sitting in this chair," he tapped the arm of the Windsor, under which Neb was now lying, "with the Bible or the Prayer Book on his knee. A fine old man, I miss him."

"I couldn't stick 'im," Ivy said simply, and Mr. Henderson started. His fine lips just moved at their corners.

"Always 'ave 'ated read-read-read, I 'ave, nor anything to do with it. Can't stand a book near me. Like some silly fools is with spiders. Used to make me sit still and listen and then, if I moved, 'e'd cop me one."

"But not a very hard one, I'm sure," Mr. Henderson was smiling broadly now.

Ivy said sternly, "It seemed 'ard to me, I wasn't above four years old."

"And 'e come along to give me a 'and with the moving," she added suddenly, nodding towards Nobby.

"Couldn't very well leave 'er to manage all by 'erself," said Nobby—and Ivy's instant glare revealed that she had of course taken it the wrong—or rather, the right—way.

"'E 'ad this van," she said, letting the remark fall into a cold silence, and after a pause Mr. Henderson resolutely got up, and said that Evensong was in half an hour, and he must be going.

Only poor Angela Mordaunt would be there, with her soft wisps of greying hair, and her pretty, anxious eyes. Church-going had dropped off since the war; the fact had to be faced.

Nobby accompanied him to the door, holding it open so that candle and fire light shone out into the darkness and the spinning rain; the wind had risen.

"Very obstinate, Mrs. Gover is," Nobby confided in a near whisper, while the umbrella was being put up; Ivy, after a curt "Good night. Sir," was clashing cups about. "Livin' here alone. Not the right thing for a woman 'er age—any age, come to that. Wouldn't you say so, sir?"

"She'll be perfectly *safe*, of course." Mr. Henderson paused in the doorway. "She has the dog, if a tramp were to come past, by some hundred to one chance. But won't she be nervous?"

"Nervous? Ive?" Nobby gave a despairing kind of laugh. "So'd a rattlesnake be—not that I mean calling names, sir, but she's *that* independent, Ive, you get browned off, sometimes."

"I'll try to keep an eye on her—if she'll let me," and Mr. Henderson twinkled, "Good night, Mrs. Gover," he called, swinging away into the darkness.

"A nice gentleman," observed Nobby, shutting the door.

If it had been any of the others, even Eileen, they would have said sharply, "What was you saying to him? Come on, now—something about me—I heard you."

But not a word. The alarm clock said half-past five.

Neb had come out from under the Windsor and was lying on the hearth again, and Ivy was kneeling beside him, stroking his neck with long firm strokes of one small hand, her head bowed under the hat, her profile dark against the flames.

"Well . . . think I'll be off," said Nobby at last, as neither of them were taking the slightest notice of him. "It's pitch dark and raining cats and dogs and it's hours and hours back to Kentish Town."

"All right, then. P'raps you'd better. Thanks for giving me a 'and. Send us a card some time. I'd better know 'ow you're getting on—I s'pose."

"*Thenks.*" Nobby jerked himself into his old mackintosh, slapping his pocket for tobacco, matches and latchkey. "You're very kind, I'm sure." He dragged a button through its hole, glaring at her.

"And at Christmas I'll send *you* one," Ivy promised. Was there a sly gleam of pearl under the hat brim? He was just not going to look. "Wiv a rabbit on it 'stead of a robin."

"That mattress ought to be aired," he said sharply as he jerked open the door.

"Oh go on, aunty. Go on, for Gawd's sake. 'Oppit. Thanks, all the same."

Neb rolled over on one side and gazed at him indolently. It was the last straw, and without another glance, Nobby slammed the door on the pair of them. Having turned the van with much difficulty in the churning mud, he drove away.

Send her a card, he thought. I don't think.

Ivy sprang up. Up the stairs she raced, light as a leaf, with Neb after her, and in a minute down tumbled her mattress, almost into the fire, while Neb barked and pounced around it. She spread it out before the flames, dragging it, straightening it with determined kicks from her sturdy small boot.

"Airin'! It don't need no airin', do it, beauty? But we'll 'ave it nice and warm, and sleep down 'ere, what say? In front of the fire?"

Neb sent out a long, rolling bark, crouching before her.

"Up—up, beauty," she coaxed, "up to Ivy," and patted her chest. Up he reared, and she grasped both paws, enjoying the feel of the hair and pads against her hands.

She began to dance; round and round the table and between the mattress, pulling him after her in awkward mimicry while their shadows reared and dwindled, reared and dwindled, against the fire-painted walls.

Green and blue flames from the logs on the fire were their torch-light, and Neb's wild barking was their music. The cottage rang, glowing like some fiery cave.

Sam Lambert, bicycling home from Benny's farm with a gas cape over his shoulders against the rain, saw the flickering light and heard the distant sound of barking, and wondered what was going on. But he did not go up to the windows and peer in; he was more than ready for his supper, at the end of his day as a tractor-driver, and Ma, even if she was everlasting keeping after him, always had a good supper waiting.

Better than some wives, happen. But Ma needn't think things would go on for ever. She was nearing sixty-nine. She'd die, some time. Not that she looked like dying; it was a joke with them up at *The Swan*. He rode on, and glow and sounds fell behind into the darkness.

Calmly and irresistibly, the singing and light flowing out from the cottage with *something else*, began to pull. They pulled with heat, and luring sounds sweet and harsh, and the other force that has no name. In the woods, away across the dark field and up the hill; and in hollows in the hedges, and in crevices which had remained dry under the grass swept sideways by winter winds, this pulling was felt; and strange, microscopically small eyes opened, as soft or horny lids stirred, and faint shivers ran along spines covered in chitin or fur. The wind swept greatly over the great trees, rocking slowly in the blackness.

8

"OH, DADDY will get Dickie Stone to look round for us—he's got a job down there," said Coral Carteret.

She and Helen Green were walking on Hampstead Heath. Coral had telephoned earlier that Saturday afternoon, saying that everyone was out and someone had let her down for golf, and could Helen come round? Helen had suggested the walk, adding, as inducement, that it was a nice day. In fact, it was one of those afternoons in early winter that suggest, in colour and light, that we are being given a preview of Paradise, but naturally one did not say that kind of thing to Coral, who must, Helen knew, be hard up indeed for society if she had had to telephone herself.

Coral frequently announced that she loathed and detested being alone, and as it undeniably was a nice afternoon, she agreed to go for a walk. Even Helen's company was better than solitude.

There had been a little difficulty about their choice of a way, Coral wishing to go where there were people to look at and Helen preferring to ramble through the most solitary glades the Heath offered. By deftly steering the conversation on to knitting, Helen had got her sly way, because Coral had become so absorbed in the account of a jumper she was working on that she did not notice where they were going.

They were walking down a dry, bare hill, with a small copse of yellowing beeches to their left and a few hawthorns, still clothed in bronze leaves and red berries, on their right. The air was cold and very still, the sun declining in purple smoke and pink clouds. Far off between motionless trees, the pond in the Vale of Health gleamed calm and still.

"Who is Dickie Stone?" Helen didn't add, as some girl worthier of acquaintance might have done, "Do I know him?"

In fact, she had once seen him from afar at one of the sisters' parties, to which she had kindly been invited *(wore a frock made out of some kind of old Arab shawl, my dear, most peculiar).*

She recalled stubbiness of form, a small fair moustache, keen eyes, and a noticeably loud and harsh voice, combined oddly with a jocular manner.

"Oh, we've known him for simply ages. His people used to live near us. He's agent to old Lord Gowerville now. Just outside Nethersham, you know. Dickie knows everything that's going on down there; he'll be just the person to find us something."

Helen had slipped in the question, "How is the shop going along?" with an expertise acquired in the management of many conversations, not only with Coral; for the subject of sewing the seams of the jumper together was moving, regrettably but peacefully, towards its end.

"I was thinking that you wouldn't want all the fag of finding a place and deciding about the rent and everything yourselves," she added.

"Oh lord, no." Coral clutched her coat more closely about her, looking unseeingly across the glowing trees and pale water. "Besides, Daddy wouldn't trust us to!" She laughed.

"And how is Pearl feeling? Is she looking forward to it?" In the forsaken Pearl's place, Helen would not be looking forward to anything. But other people were different.

Coral made a face. "Oh I suppose so. She doesn't say much. She's still feeling a bit soft about that awful young man, I'm afraid."

"And of course you want to be right in Nethersham?"

"Oh yes. It's mad, of course, starting in the *winter*, but crowds of people go out for drives, and there are quite a lot of our own kind of people living round about there and coming in to shop. They'll all want tea and cakes. I'm having lessons in *book-keeping*—isn't it a scream?"

Miss Green, studying the landscape with the afterglow reflecting itself pinkly on her calm face, agreed that it was, indeed, a scream. "Will you live at your cottage?"

"That's the idea . . . except at week-ends, of course . . . Daddy can't spare us at week-ends!"

Helen reflected upon this news with satisfaction. Now she and Jocelyn would not have to steer clear of Nethersham on their Sunday drives.

"Will Pearl make the cakes?"

"Yes: we'll have other help, of course, but Pearl adores cooking; she's always been in and out of the kitchen, ever since she was a tiny. Mummy used to get quite cross with her. Cooks do hate it, you know."

"I suppose they do; yes."

Helen reflected upon Mrs. Jordan, big and ash-blonde, jolly and spiteful, who had been their cook-general for a year. Mrs. Jordan, who detested Helen, had once told her that she was "ate up with *sarcasm* and glorying in wickedness", and even at eleven years old, Helen had mulled the phrase over and relished it.

"Ivy's cottage is at Catts End, about five miles from Nethersham," she remarked in a moment, coming in just as Coral was about to say that there didn't seem much to see round here.

"Oh yes, you *said* something about her having a cottage, on the 'phone the other night. I never heard of anything so extraordinary. How on earth did she wangle it?"

"An uncle left it to her. In his will."

"Good heavens—whatever next?" Coral demanded of the setting sun, "his *will*? No wonder these people are so bolshy . . .

The trouble Mummy had with our last parlourmaid you wouldn't believe . . ."

Helen was wondering what Coral would have thought of the Green servants, a procession curiously linked, in one way or another, by Love: Nelly, white-faced and blue-eyed, who had wept for love of Helen's tall handsome father; sixteen-year-old Katie with the large brown eyes, painfully but silently suspected by Helen of being in love with the schoolboy living next door secretly loved by herself (Helen had been in love with someone or something since she was five years old), and Mrs. Jordan, and tall, unkind Cissy.

To say nothing of a procession of seduced governesses . . .

And then, as if these vague thoughts—hardly thoughts at all; these warm emanations, so to speak, from the mighty form of Love—had drifted out into the icy November air and into the neatly shingled head of Coral Carteret, the latter exploded the following bomb.

In her loudest, most cheerful voice; turning those sharp brown eyes full of healthful sparkle straight upon Helen; Helen, dismally aware that, in the vulgar phrase, "*she* didn't miss much," and instantly terrified and armed against attack.

"By the way, I saw you with Jocelyn Burke the other night. Coming out of the Queen's Hall. We were in Daddy's car, on our way back from a cocktail party at some friends in Knightsbridge. I remember I thought it funny, at the time, because no one else was coming out . . . The programme can't have been over so early. I didn't know you knew Jocelyn that well."

"I don't know him *well*," said Helen with an awful calm, which she felt must be visible all around her, as a kind of glassy, Coral-proof fence, "I happened to be at the concert, and he was there, and we saw each other, and in the interval he said he'd got musical indigestion from two Beethovens and a Brahms straight off, and wasn't going to stay for the Mendelssohn and the Grieg, so would I go to Appenrodts' for some coffee and sandwiches."

As she rapidly lied, she was thinking of the expression that would appear upon Coral's face if she, Helen, were suddenly to announce just how well she did know Mr. Burke. The glassy barrier nearly shivered in a loud hysterical laugh.

"He's rich," was all Coral said, in a respectful, but also a relieved, tone.

All was well. Young Mr. Burke, so eligible, so eminently marriage-able, had not been hooked by peculiar, poor Helen Green. He was still there, floating lightly in the pre-matrimonial currents which at any moment might drift him across Coral's own path. She did not particularly want him, but really, with all that money, and so good-looking, it would be highly *unsuitable* for Mr. Burke to drift up to Helen Green. Not the thing at all.

"Is he? Oh yes—I suppose he is."

"I just thought it was funny," Coral ended.

Helen felt what has been called 'a great surge of relief', though she wished that Coral had not made this last addition.

"Do come in and have tea with me," the insincere girl now said expansively, made cordial by relief, "look, we're quite near the cottage."

"Well, thanks, I will. I always like seeing your funny little place. Though I don't know how you stand it being so dark, and as for living there alone! I should die."

"Oh, I survive," Helen said, and led the way down into the Vale of Health, that little cluster of old houses lying below the highest point of Hampstead Heath, in a valley beside a pond. Tradition, which usually says something pleasantly romantic, in this case murmurs that the name dates from the time of the Great Plague, when (presumably rich) people came up from London into the purer air of Hampstead to escape the pestilence.

Past the fairground they went, where the yellow swings and gay roundabouts were wrapped up and stilled until Easter; up one of the Vale's two brief, narrow streets; with an ugly little red brick house at the top where D.H. Lawrence once lived for a short while and where no one seemed to have succeeded in living for long after him; it was usually 'To Let'. A turn to the right, past some other little houses of the purest self-conscious prettiness, and there was the creamy plaster face of Helen's cottage, and its blue half-door with the window sparsely curtained in net which,

Coral's jetty eyes at once observed, needed washing. Helen's heart swelled with love for the place as she took out her key.

"Opening right on the street. I shouldn't sleep a wink," Coral shivered, as they went in.

"Oh, I sleep lots of winks . . . do sit down, Coral."

Coral sat, and began to stare about her.

The fire was not quite out, and the two threepenny bunches of violets in a clear glass pot on the round table had been bought that morning. The dim little room smelt of them, and of woodsmoke. Helen turned on a lamp under a creamy shade, and all her familiar soft shadows appeared.

"I'll just make the fire up." She disappeared.

"Do you keep the coal *indoors*? Doesn't it make an awful mess?" Coral, who was watching, observed in a minute.

"Not particularly." Helen re-appeared, laden.

"There's a postcard for you." Coral's tone implied that any event was a treat in a life as dull as Helen's.

"Is there? Thanks . . ." She dusted off her hands and picked it up. "It's from Ivy. 'Hope you are well. Neb don't fight with the . . . rates'? What can she mean—oh—*rats*. (Neb's her dog.) I wish she'd send my coat back."

"Has she got your coat?" (If Ivy had Helen's coat, how was Helen 'managing'? For it was unlikely, surely, that she owned two?)

"I lent her an old one . . ." Helen skipped the details; she was filling the kettle and putting it on the gas cooker in her dark little cupboard of a kitchen, "Do you take sugar?" *(Oh, so it was an old one, was it?)*

"Yes please."

Coral's face became calm—or perhaps stony would more accurately describe her expression—as always when fattening foods were mentioned.

It was fashionable to be thin; of course, one followed the fashion; but she was not thin, and was not going to try to be. Helen was not thin either, but her frame was large, and her fat (Coral thought of it as 'her fat') seemed somehow to be distributed over it more . . . well, anyway, Helen was not thin either. Now Pearl; Pearl was really *slim*. This did not make Coral any fonder of her sister.

"You ought to dig her up about it," she went on, meaning the coat, "that class will always pinch something if it gets half a chance."

"I will, sometime."

Helen made a face at the ceiling as, safe behind the kitchen door, she poured boiling water on the tea. Why had she wasted an hour of a precious Saturday afternoon having Coral Carteret in the cottage?

However, Coral was running true to form. That was always worth seeing.

She brought the tray into the sitting-room just as Coral said helpfully, "There's someone at the door."

So there was; a van parked outside, and a large male visible through the glass panes. There came a knock; but he was not looking in. Nice manners; better than those of some of the people Helen knew.

She went to the door and opened it, while Coral avidly yet haughtily looked on. This was a common man, in a greasy cap and a rough jacket.

"Afternoon, miss," said the man, touching the cap.

"Good afternoon . . . You're Ivy's friend, aren't you? You drove her down to Catts End."

"That's right, miss." A shade, if anything as slight as a shade could be described as marking that large, sensible face, seemed to pass across it, and Helen (more used now, to noticing shades) gathered that the friendship was either badly dented or had ceased. He held up a familiar object, which had been draped over his arm: "Does this 'ere happen to be your coat, miss?"

"Yes, that's mine." She took it. Its former scent of *Ambre Antique* had been replaced by that of fried fish. "Thank you very much . . . did Ivy give it to you for me? How is she?"

"So far as I knows, *Mrs. Gover* is very well," was the awful answer. "No, she did *not* give it to me. Your coat, miss, was lying in the back of my van all last week. She must a chucked it there. Meaning to give it back, no doubt, but forgot. The dog being there, and her not innerested in nothing but the dog. So, noticing it after I left a load up Harringay way this artemoon, I thought, that's the young lady's coat, that is, I'd best take it back. She may be wanting it. I did give it a bit of a dust, but . . ."

They surveyed the coat, together and in silence.

His use of 'but' was understandable. One and sixpence for cleaning, thought Helen, and *at once*.

"It was Mrs. Gover, miss, chucking it down like that," he said suddenly. "Course, if I'd noticed it . . . But there's a lot of old stuff I keeps in there, and it was lying about a 'ole week."

"Well, it was very kind of you to bring it back, and thank you very much," Helen said soothingly, and she smiled, which always made her look kind, and jollier, and altogether different from the severe sort of chilly Valkyrie she set herself up to be.

Nobby smiled too. A big, pretty young lady; he liked her. Behind her, however, he caught sight of quite another sort of face. Cor! Keep off the grass, thought Nobby, and would have liked to wink at Ivy's young lady, only of course he didn't. He understood, though, why this time he wasn't offered a cup of tea.

"Well I'd best be getting along, miss. So I'll say good-afternoon."

"Yes. And thank you very much, again. Good-bye."

She shut the door on him.

"Good gracious, what a dreadful smell of fried fish," cried Coral. "Is that the coat you were talking about? Whatever have they been doing with it?"

"I can't imagine," said Helen with decision, carrying it through the kitchen into her minute and now twilit bathroom, and dropping it into the bath. She was not going to endure fifteen minutes discussing a fried fishy coat with C. Carteret.

"But you ought to make her pay for having it cleaned! I would. I'd sit down tonight, and write to her. It's disgraceful. Why, there's quite a lot of wear left in that coat." (For *you*, at any rate, was Coral's unspoken ending.)

Helen poured herself out some tea; she felt in need of refreshment.

"But *fried fish*!" Coral went on implacably. "I suppose he *lives* on it. They usually *do*—and kippers. Disgusting!"

"Perhaps he was in the Navy and got used to fish. I mean, Ivy's husband used to be," answered Helen, rather wildly. Mr. Burke had mentioned that he might possibly telephone around five, to make plans for an evening excursion. It simply must-not-happen while Coral was there; Helen had been mad to invite her in.

"Is that man 'walking out' with your char? How killing." Coral sipped tea; entertained, for the moment; not in a hurry.

"Ah, that I don't know . . . Coral, you won't mind if I go up and change, will you? I've got to go out."

As Helen spoke, she realised that she couldn't go up and change, because Coral would then answer the telephone (making up the fire, carrying a tray, opening the door to a greasy man, no: answering the telephone, yes; because then she might find out who Helen *knew*, awful people as a rule, no doubt, but you could never be completely sure).

And Helen also thought: got to go out. Got to, indeed (and not the best grammar). Like someone under a spell, like someone following the twitch of an enchanter's wand.

Helen, do not be an ass. You are not in the least under a spell, unfortunately. You know exactly what he is; he told you; and you will not face it. You haven't 'got to' at all. You will be lucky if he telephones.

All the same, she decided that she had better be dressed and ready.

"Of course not, my dear. I must fly, too." Coral drained her cup; Helen had offered no other refreshment, she noted.

Coral rearranged the bit of lynx round her neck. Ten minutes' walk up the hill, fifteen minutes' walk down, and she would be home. Someone would be in, by now, and she or Pearl could 'phone somebody or other and go out.

"Where are you off to? Somewhere nice?" she asked.

"A party in St. John's Wood. Friends of Celia's," Helen lied.

"Oh." Coral did not like Helen's closest friend. So long as it was not somewhere really nice . . .

They parted amiably, Coral marching off with the lynx muffling her nose against the freezing air, and Helen darting back into the cottage and snatching off the receiver, in triumph, just as the telephone bell rang.

9

THE fact, verifiable and solid, that Mrs. Gover was George Coatley's great-niece, and had been born in a cottage now finally tumbled down and gone somewhere between the two Warbys, established her in Nethersham and the surrounding beechy, rolling district as someone to be said 'good-morning' to.

Mr. Gardener had mentioned to his head clerk, that Ivy was George Coatley's great-niece, which fact Greddle had received with correct interest, having recognised it from his first sight of her. He did not, of course, discuss the firm's clients, outside the circle of his own fireside, but it had soon got round; young Wattle the baker, having set the news cheerfully rolling at every house, including The Hall itself *and* The Beeches, at which he had called later on that first Saturday afternoon.

His mother, who had always admired George Coatley's garden when the family walked past it on their way to church on Sundays, wondered if Mrs. Gover would Keep It Up? and, on hearing that the said Mrs. Gover put candles in bottles, instead of having a decent lamp, and wore her hat in the house like ladies did, and had a fierce dog, shook her head.

She then recalled that Mrs. Gover's grandfather on her mother's side had been a gipsy, so what else could you expect? Her mother had been a regular slut, too; no wonder Alfred Slater drank. Their cottage had been a pigsty and Ivy was out charing, up at The Beeches, soon's she left school at eleven. That was before Miss Angela was born; poor Miss Angela, didn't seem much chance of her getting married now, did there? Well, there were two million in the same boat, the papers said; all those girls whose young men had been killed in the war. That old Kaiser; he had something to answer for, he had. Miss Angela's young man, too. She'd never got over it, poor thing.

Mrs. Wattle ended her remarks, which took place over the tea-table one evening when Ivy had been living at Catts Cottage for a month, by recalling that "Ivy's hair was as black as that teapot," stretching across to tap the fat, lustrous object, "used to plait it and tie it up with a bit of string. A shilling a week, she got. Their cook told me. Impudent, she was, too, in a funny kind o' way. I can see her now."

A few miles away, on that evening, Ivy was walking fast along the road to Little Warby in the starlight, with Neb bounding at her side.

The air stung with frost, and every star in the universe seemed to be out, up there; chips of crystal, minute silver blurs, steady throbbers of fire. Not a leaf shivered on the hedges, now, and far off on the hilltops the beech trees gleamed solemn and silvery and still. The eerie light was so brilliant that Ivy and Neb cast faint shadows on the road.

Ivy had added a long purple woollen scarf to her coat and skirt against the cold, and Neb, to his incredulous disgust and even with an attempt to bite which had been ignored save for a murmur, had at last been bathed: he now looked feathery, which added a frightening touch of frivolity to his aura of fierceness. It was noticeable that people, when commenting on Neb, usually began to say, "That's a nice—" and then changed it to a 'fine', or a 'beautiful' dog.

By a short cut across a field, where turnips used to grow but which had recently been put down for grazing, it was two miles from Catts End to The Swan. Ivy strode over the bleached grass where frost glistened heavy and white along the blades, walking with lifted head and eyes moving from the distant hedges to the withered, ghostly flowers underfoot.

Halfway across, she saw from the corner of her eye a shadow slip out through a dark gap in a hedge on the left, noticeable because, in this well-fostered country, gaps in the hedges were not common.

The shadow came gliding towards her, low to the ground and no colour in the starlight; no more than a darker shade in the pale surrounding grass that moved, and it had a bushy tail.

"Neb," said Ivy, low, and with unmoving head, "now that's a beauty, like you. A beauty, boy."

Neb drew close to her skirt, all his newly-clean fur quivering, and his eyes alight with their emerald flare. He whined quietly, on a pleading note.

"A beauty, like you, boy," said Ivy again. "S'sh. No."

The shadow was almost level with them now, trailing them, but keeping well to the rear of Ivy's skirt, white at the hem with frost brushed off the bents. Her stout small boots crunched softly on the stiffened blades, and that was the only sound in the darkly-brilliant, ringing silence.

Turning her head, so smoothly that the movement seemed reptilian rather than human, she looked full down at the fox, and it lifted up its belly from the grass, under the power from her eyes, and crept up to her side—nearer and nearer, until it was trotting beside her like a dog; three creatures now, two half-tamed and one wild, moving together over the grey grass in the bright grey starlight.

"Come on, boy," Ivy said, low and coaxing, "come on, Neb; play with him—beauties together; play, beauty," keeping her eyes on the fox, "play with my Neb."

But they kept her between them. She could smell the fox's rankness, and see how the fur stood up along its neck, and she smiled; a full, tender smile, like that of a mother watching her children. Neb whined rebelliously now and again; the fox was silent, only its teeth gleamed sometimes, as its black upper lip drew back, down near the icy grass.

The three turned on to a path leading into a coppice of hazel and oak saplings, at the far end of which, perhaps half a mile away, lights shone. This was Little Warby, consisting of a few scattered cottages, The Swan, a small general shop which was also a post office, and St. Peter's Church and vicarage, which stood in as nearly inaccessible a situation, down a lost lane and through a small but thick and ancient wood, as its founders in 1598 had been able to decide upon.

They had had the convenience of the Gowervilles at The Hall in mind; a faint, very old track swung round and out of the valley in which The Hall stood, and round to the lonely road whence the lost lane opened. A horse could get to the church in twenty minutes; never mind Hodge; let him flounder through mud and briars, and if he didn't get there at all, the priest would soon be down on him to find out why.

The path led out on to a road, and there was a stile to cross, for the coppice was enclosed; this marked one of the boundaries of Lord Gowerville's land. As the three approached, Ivy marching along the narrow way and her companions passing soundlessly over the fallen leaves at either side, the door of a cottage standing on the far edge of the trees opened, letting warm light fall on to a small garden made neat for the winter, and a man came out. Neb uttered a loud angry bark, and the man started, turning towards them.

Ivy, with a quick lissom movement, stooped silently to the fox and it had gone. A shade joined the other shadows among the hazel saplings and the brambles: Ivy was innocently employed in getting over the stile, Neb still passionately barking, with extended neck.

"'Ere—whose dog be that?" the man standing by the cottage door called loudly.

"Mrs. Gover's, from up Catts Cottage, Catts End, and I'm 'er," Ivy called in jeering answer, "you afraid, mister?"

"I bean't afraid o' dogs, not usually, but he be a new 'un—I've heard o' he, though. Young Charley Wattle said as he be a bad-tempered beast."

"He won't bite you while I'm with 'im, so keep your hair on," said Ivy. "Neb, you mind your manners, now."

She looked full at the man, who was tall and well-set-up. Been in the Army, prob'ly, thought Ivy, who noticed when men were well-set-up.

"What's your name?" she demanded, "told you mine, now it's your turn."

"Sam Lambert. That's me. The one as did find your great-uncle when he wor gone west," and he grinned, though it was more a grin of embarrassment than one of heartlessness or grisly humour. They were standing in the glow of light from the cottage, Ivy and Neb (who had stopped barking at her reminder) at the gate, and Sam Lambert in the middle of his well-weeded path of crushed ashes. Suddenly—though with no effect of haste, a voice came out from inside the cottage.

"Who's that you're a-talking to, Sam? Lily Perkins, is it?" It was what Ivy thought of as a soapy voice; the voice of a nosyer-about. His wife or his mother? Sounded oldish.

"No, ma, it bean't Lily . . . I be just off," and, winking at Ivy, Sam went on down to the gate.

Ivy's lips were compressed. She felt that he had intruded upon her family affairs by coming on her uncle's corpse. But a sense of justice, painfully, and even irritably, learned from the example set by Stan Gover (a fair-minded man) during their years together, now told her that she should express gratitude.

"S'pose I really ought to say thanks," she retorted, but did not say it; only turned off in the direction of *The Swan*, whose low, weather-boarded buildings and dim red-curtained windows glimmered further down the road.

Sam easily caught up with her, on long legs, and was just behind her as she turned the handle of The Swan's door.

"What say?" She turned, at the sound of a sentence, deep and quiet, with amusement in it.

"I says—where be t'other dog, missus?" He was grinning again; his smiles occurred too frequently for Ivy, no smiler herself.

"What other dog? There's only me and Neb."

"Ah—I saw 'im. I bean't blind, missus. It isn't everyone as could walk 'crost a field with a dog-fox . . . and I knows *your* sort, missus, I do."

She turned her back on him, and, opening the door, swung it wide.

"Evenun', Mr. Tuckett," she said clearly, into the silent room, "Mrs. Gover from Catts End. You remember—a month ago I come in. Evenin' all."

After a stunned pause, a series of mutters and nods ran round the row of brown, creased, heavy faces, and Will Werry (luckless, as usual) was the one who had to move up and let Ivy sit down next to him with her pint of stout.

The conversation her entrance had interrupted had not been the kind that a woman's presence would make embarrassing; but the fact that she was a woman now tied tongues never eloquent. Women did not come into *The Swan* to drink of an evening, not even with their husbands. It was just not done. A woman might very occasionally be brought in for a drink by a man driving a car, in this remote region where the communication by rail was not good, but those were ladies: another race.

However, as Ivy did not instantly break into a stream of chatter nor try to fascinate William Werry by giggling, the regulars became less disturbed, and talk was gradually resumed. A detailed discussion of the events leading up to, and following, the disappearance of a screw from a root-chopper, related by Jim Barber, ended in the loss of a shoe by the horse he had ridden into Nethersham to buy another screw.

"Which shoe was that, then?" hoarsely asked old James, known by no other name, and usually silent. He was shepherd on a lonely farm high up on the spur of the Chilterns above Nethersham, and came in only rarely.

"Right forefoot. I swore, I can tell you. But we was only a hundred yards or so from smith's. I got her there, no trouble, and he fixed her up."

Ivy sat in silence, sucking down stout occasionally, and keeping her eyes fixed upon Neb, at her feet.

He was still angry and baffled because of that shameful walk beside the fox, which, though looking like himself, had had the wrong smell and had joined itself on to them uninvited by friendly smellings. Checked instinct ran through his veins uncomfortably, coursing with his blood. Without looking up at Ivy, he suddenly growled.

"That's for me," she muttered, "I know. You be quiet, there's my beauty, now."

"He looks better than what he did a month ago, Mrs. Gover," said the landlord civilly. "You have much trouble with his temper?"

Every eye was instantly fixed upon Neb, who growled again, lifting his head.

"Not myself, I don't," was Ivy's composed answer, "but he don't get on with no one 'cept me."

A pause, while Neb, who had grown during his month with Ivy, was doubtfully surveyed.

"How old be he?" asked the shepherd suddenly. "I'd say a year—but how old *be* he, missus?"

"I don't know, to a month or so. Haven't 'ad 'im all that long. Some people as I knew up in London 'ad 'im chained up, never let 'im orf, and I gave 'em fifteen shillins for 'im."

"I'd say a year," repeated the shepherd, and began to rise, with an impression of creaks though none actually were heard, from his place on the bench, "let's have a look at yer teeth," to Neb.

Neb remained perfectly still but his eyes began to light up. Ivy put in, hastily, "Never did like 'earing a dog bark bark bark. Gets you down. Three months it went on. Upset 'im a bit, I s'pose." Shepherd, slowly advancing across the floor towards Neb, gradually came to a pause.

"Now if I was to look at him close, and handle him, that dog 'ud bite me," he announced slowly. "That dog would."

"Go along, and you been with dogs all your life," said the landlord. "That's because why. I knows when a dog will bite. I reckon you're right, missus," turning to Ivy, "he's only all right with you."

That's what I said, isn't it, and I s'pose I ought to know, thought Ivy. But she drowned the retort in a swallow of stout. Three husbands had taught her that though you might be right, saying so to men only made matters worse.

It was good stout. She was relishing it. She decided that she would come along here sometimes of an evening. On top of a good brand of stout, you never knew what you might hear that would come in useful.

But a feeling of disapproval, slight but distinct, had fallen upon the group and, after one of their pauses, someone observed in a measured, gruff, and faintly dismal tone that could have served for *The Swan's* collective voice:

"Last time I was up your way, missus, I see a great hole in your roof and they messy birds was in and out."

"There is a 'ole," Ivy conceded, and said no more.

"Your uncle," the voice went on (it came from the back of the room, where a bench was situated farthest from the glowing coal fire) "he was going on ninety-four when he was took, he was always arstin' the Lord to do summat about that there 'ole."

"He allus was the religious sort," Ivy snapped.

Praying about a hole in the roof! Yet she was not surprised. Anyone who read read read all the time in the Bible would do just that kind of thing.

But a subdued laugh went round.

"Lord Gowerville, Johnny meant," the landlord explained, "very sharp, the new agent is. Mr. Stone. You don't get nothing done except the place falls in on you. Thinks a lot o' hisself, too, Mr. Stone does. You been to see he yet, missus?"

"No, I haven't. I'll get around to it," Ivy promised, with her face in the stout mug. Silly fools. Anyone could take a thing the wrong way.

"That's right," Shepherd said, in the kindest tone heard in *The Swan* that evening, "you write a letter to he. Or go up The Hall and see 'im. There be a little office kind of place there, and there he be, and sees people."

"I'll see . . ." Ivy said again; then, excited by the sudden idea that this Lord Gowerville might pay for having her roof mended, and feeling a girl's desire to show off, she added casually,

"Come to that, I might mend it meself."

The silence following this announcement was so charged with outrage, disapproval and collective shock that she actually glanced quickly round the room. What faces! Like Satan's on washing-day. She stared at Sam Lambert through the dim lamp-light and the smoke from pipes and cigarettes, and her irritation concentrated itself upon him. Grinning again; he didn't seem to know what a straight face was.

"You'll 'ave Tom Wattis arter you," someone said feebly at last, "women don't do thatchin' work."

"I don't see why not." Ivy was not going to be put down, unless, of course, it suited her to be, "'Tisn't all that difficult, putting bits of straw along a roof."

"'Tis a skilled trade, thatching, and they holds theirselves very close 'cause there bain't much thatching work about anyways," said someone else.

"'Sides, you might fall off, missus, and where'd you be then? A broken leg, or a broken back, p'raps. And people's all for slates nowadays, they wears better," the voice ended, on a note of calm dejection. "Even the Lord," it added after a pause so long that Ivy, but no one else, had concluded that it had said all it had to say that evening.

"You take my advice, Mrs. Gover," said Sam Lambert suddenly, his quicker, decisive tones sounding younger and more alive in contrast to those of the other men, "you put your money by until you've got enough to pay Tom Wattis yourself. You won't get nothing out o' Mr. Stone. He'll only tell you *you're* the one as has to pay for repairs to that cottage. Your uncle never would believe it. Time and time again, he arst the last agent, the one before Mr. Stone. Never would believe what was written down by the law. Don't you waste your time up there. That's my advice."

"But this here Lord Gowerville, he lives in a place half the size o' Buckingham Palace, I remembers it," Ivy protested. "Mean to tell me he can't afford to 'ave a bit of thatch repaired?"

"Ah, the times has changed for the gentry, since the war," the landlord pronounced. "Selling land all over England, they are. Hard up. Wages is up, and land values is down. The Lord he's hard put to it, it's well known. Not a lick o' paint inside or a bit o' repointing outside there these last ten years. They say there's even broken windows in that wing he's had to shut up . . . I like a nice bit o' thatch, myself," he ended irrelevantly.

"They birds is a pest, course. Pullin' the straw about. But they's always a pest, anywheres," Will Werry put in.

"Seems, if I'm to 'ave Tom Wattis arter me, and fall off and break me back, I'd better leave the job alone," Ivy said, and smiled for the first time since her entrance, with the usual effect. She was rewarded by slow smiles all round. It had been a joke. Not the sort of joke a woman should make, of course, but nevertheless a joke.

She drained the dregs of her stout, and got up, and Neb sprang up too, quivering to be off.

"Thanks fer telling me," she nodded to Shepherd, who silently lifted a big hand deformed by rheumatism in acknowledgement. "I'll be off, then. Night, all," and amid a chorus of good-nights that sounded relieved, but slightly more cordial, than the good-evenings that had greeted her arrival, she opened the door and went out.

"Black hair. I like black hair," Sam Lambert said, in a moment. There was a loud general laugh.

"'Ere, what'll Lily Perkins say?"

"You'll 'ave your ma arter you, you will, Sam Lambert."

"Wonder if it's dyed?" Sam went on, unperturbed.

"Go on, she's respectable, Sam, you can see that," the landlord said with a touch of reproof, "must be nearer fifty than forty, too; must be, if she was out charing at The Beeches 'fore Miss Angela was born, like Mrs. Wattle says. That must be over thirty years ago, and Mrs. Gover lef' school when she was eleven—yes, a good sight nearer fifty than forty."

"I like black 'air," Sam repeated. "Another pint, Bob, please . . . always have liked black 'air."

He was thinking that Mrs. Gover, as well as having black hair, was probably 'a wise woman'; a witch.

10

Now it was December. The last leaves had gone and the beeches stood naked and strong, and breathing out calm, or rocking slowly in the tearing winds that whirled their copper carpet in showers. With her winter hat rammed well over her brow, and followed by Neb leaping and pouncing after the flying leaves, Ivy walked in the woods, with step light as the racing clouds above; unnoticeable, dark and small in the bronze and russet glades, below the giant branches.

She met no one during the week; sometimes on Saturday afternoons or on a Sunday she passed a young man and a girl. With cheeks smoothed and rosed by the wind they would pass her, talking; if they noticed her they smiled and said, "Good afternoon." One Sunday she met Miss Green, walking with a young gentleman: Ivy saw a glint of gilt hair beneath a soft fawn cap, and cool blue-grey eyes. Miss Green looked much as usual.

"Hullo, Ivy!" she said, sounding more pleased than Ivy felt, "I wondered if we should ever meet you. This is Mrs. Gover; she used to work for me," she added to the young gentleman, who lifted his cap. "She lives near here—are you far from home, Ivy?"

"Down the 'ill and round the corner. Miss. 'Ow d'you think Nebbie's lookin' now?"

"Beautiful. He matches the leaves." Neb was rushing round in crazy circles some way off, sending up tawny clouds all around him. "And you're liking it, living down here, are you?"

"Suits me fine. Miss."

Helen studied her, with one quick stare that took in an increased thinness, a brighter eye, a still browner face, and some kind of a change in the line of the mouth—a softening? a lessening in its grimness? And one loose lock of wiry black hair—Ivy used not to show loose locks of hair. And she no longer wore her gold bead earrings.

"Well, it's nice to have seen you," Helen said, beginning to move away because she knew that he was impatient, "perhaps we'll meet again, one day. We often come here. Good-bye."

"Good-bye. Miss.'"

The young gentleman lifted his cap once more, and they walked on, through the softly-roaring wind and the glades scented with autumn.

"I 'ope we don't. We don't want no one, do we, Neb?" Ivy muttered, as they grew small amongst distant trees.

"She looks like a gipsy . . . she always did, a bit, but now it's much more noticeable. I didn't ask her if she could give us some tea because I thought you wouldn't like it," Helen said, in a moment.

"I don't expect I should . . . there's that place in Great Warby we went to before, we'll try there. That was a very well-bred dog, by the way. Did she steal him?"

"I've always thought so; yes."

On country walks you could nearly always find a dim little baker's shop in a quiet village, with a hand-drawn notice saying TEAS stuck up somewhere outside, and be served with strong tea in thick white cups in some stuffy, cosy back room that was plainly used as a parlour, looking out over a garden in all the romantic desolation, at this time of year, of delicate bare twigs and a few pale chilly roses.

Last roses.

Ivy had noticed Helen's quick stare. She was not annoyed by it; she was only rather irritated at meeting anyone she knew so near her new home. Nosying about? No: that inconvenient sense of justice she had caught from Stan told her that Miss Green, unlike most people, was not a nosyer-about. Bet she thought I look like a gippo, thought Ivy. Oh well, who cares? "Come on, Nebbie!" and away they raced through the racing leaves.

She had been in the cottage for over two months, and had still done nothing about the hole in the thatch. The short days passed quickly. Sometimes the red berries and few remaining brown leaves glowed in a bright cold sun and the beech trunks looked blackish-silver; sometimes sheets of rain veiled everything in mist. Most often there was stillness, and motionless, dun, soft cloud.

Ivy rose early, but not to sweep or polish; it was to share whatever she ate for breakfast—a bit of bread, a lump of stale home-made dough-cake—with the birds.

Dun and blue, brown and russet, sometimes black and white, or dark, sea-tinted starling, they screamed and squabbled before her open door; so bold on her second morning there that they flew down on to her outstretched arms and clung to her shoulders at her call.

She knew, well enough, that she was 'letting herself go'. In thirty years of married life, moving about the Home Counties with husbands who had all three been attracted to her because she was no homebody, she had met with, and seen, women who had let themselves go: stopped eating regular meals, stopped cleaning their home, occasionally stopped cleaning themselves. Sometimes it was laziness, usually it was a bad husband or too many children.

In Ivy's case it was because, for the first time in her life, she was living as she had always unknowingly wanted to live: in freedom and solitude, with an animal for close companion. Her new life had acted upon her like a strong and delicious drug.

She lived on scraps. When the longing for a kipper, her favourite dish, became too strong for her she walked into Nethersham and bought a pair for ninepence and also six pennyworth of beef bones that she boiled up with potatoes in one of her tins, making a thick soup. It was true; her clothes did seem to be falling off her.

On the very wet days she sat at home, spending hours playing with the mice, who soon came out to enjoy the big wood fire she kept up night and day on her brick hearth. She baked rough, coarse bread in the oven at the side—she soon gave up having the home-baked from Wattles; it was a tie; any regular habit was a tie—sharing her bread with the mice while it was still crumbling and hot. Neb liked to go out for half a day's ranging in all weathers; she could bring him home, when she thought it was time he came, but she was generous with his play-hours.

She would sit still as a stone for some time, then sigh faintly—a natural drawing-in of the breath, not the sigh of pensiveness—and in ten or twenty minutes there would come the bark outside, and she would open the door and in he would tumble, smelling of the icy fog, or cold with brushing through frosty grass or with his coat dripping with rain, and shake himself, and show his teeth at the rollicking mice; then lie down in front of the fire to sleep.

She did think to send a card to Nobby Clark; a brown picture-postcard of Nethersham High Street, showing one of the three little stone bridges that crossed the Nether and a view of the willow-shaded walk and houses on its far bank. "Hows' Yourself—from Ive," it had written on it; and when Nobby got it he snorted and muttered "Can't even spell".

For Nobby, though Ivy might think of him as without book-learning, wrote a clear hand and was one of those who, when they do have to spell, can. Besides—*yourself*. What kind of a scholar couldn't spell that? Anyone could spell *yourself*, even Eileen.

Another man had Ivy in mind that December; Sam Lambert, bicycling past on his way to Binney's Farm, saw no more than he had expected when, one fine morning, he passed her standing on her door-step almost hidden in birds; birds on her head, birds on her outstretched arms, all kinds of birds hopping and pecking around her feet.

What else would you expect of a woman who could walk across a field with a dog on one side of her and a dog-fox on the other? And if he kept these extraordinary sights to himself, and did not attempt to entertain the regulars at *The Swan* with them, it was because he had a dim feeling that a woman like that, who could walk with a fox, and have birds perching on her as if she were a tree, that woman, if you did anything to annoy her, could 'do things to you'.

So he called out "Good morning" or "Good night, missus" every time he bicycled past, and sometimes she answered and sometimes she didn't.

She was not always outside in the mornings, when he passed, gliding swiftly through the dim grey light and the marvellously pure air. More than once his countryman's eyes, unerringly taking in details on which his brain made shrewd comments, detected her climbing the great slope leading up to the beechwood, a black mark on the sweep of grass, with an amber dot racing ahead of her.

Why had Sam, the travelled soldier with ten or so French and Belgian girls to his credit—if credit it can be called—returned apparently without ambitions or regrets to Little Warby?

He liked the country, and his tyrannical old mother was quite easily deceived; also, she was an unusually good cook.

Ivy was not by nature a slut. One evening, towards the end of December, she slapped her teacup—full not of tea but of hot water because she simply had not bothered to buy a new packet—down on the table and said aloud, "Ive, my girl, this won't do."

The next morning, she sat in the same position, in the warm room freshly swept and even dusted, as if a start had been made against 'letting herself go' any further. The front door stood open to the frosty sunlight; it was nearly eight o'clock, and her sturdy boots were gleaming and she wore a new pair of bright pink artificial silk stockings. Blue-tits, finches, wrens and robins hopped in front of her, helping themselves to crumbs from her plate. Dozens of bright beads glancing out from softly-tinted tiny heads! Minute chirrupings and miniature battles, sudden alightings and sheerings away! Neb looked sleepily at the birds; they weighed less than the mice, when they perched on one's back, and at least they did not nibble one's fur.

Ivy remembered the way to The Hall. She remembered it well, but she had avoided it during her rambles. She did not want to see The Hall again. She had angry feelings, dim and silent and resentful, about it; memories of her father coming very slowly up the stairs, in the cold blue moonlight, pausing to rest, and breathing cruelly hard, and wiping blood from a wounded shoulder, while her mother cried, and she herself lay shivering and watching, under the thin ragged blankets.

The Keepers. That was the word that brought up the anger. She had never really understood it all; the next day, as there sometimes was, there had been pheasant for dinner, and she could remember as if it were yesterday the taste, and the good, full feeling afterwards. Her father had hidden the flesh wound under his thick old corduroy jacket. And there had been other times, when he was nearly caught . . . . Poaching. That was it. Dad had nearly been caught poaching again. Alf Gover's a poacher . . .

The Lord had all that land and that great house and couldn't spare a pheasant for people's dinner when they were that hungry . . .

The way went straight up the hill and into the beech forest, and then it turned right round, along a broad grassy ride bordered by oak and birch saplings and tangled blackberry bushes, for more than two miles. Gradually, the walker came among beech trees again, and then out on to a wide plateau overlooking a valley, shut in on all sides by hills that were crowned by the great silvery creatures.

That morning, the air was clear as glass. She stood there, looking down, and the angry feelings that had kept her company during the walk seemed to float away and to vanish into the still, icy light.

There it was, The Hall. Silent, with every crenellation and every ogive window and the long, long walls that swept about it and shut it into a great square, dressed in greenish moss. It seemed as if asleep, in the silvery air, with one fantastic chimney giving out a curl of blue smoke. The tall iron gates had a coat of arms, with a dragon on them, and they were shut fast, but there was a little door in the wall, with a bell-push at one side; she could see it plain as plain.

As she stood, looking down upon it, a bell began to strike clearly and softly from somewhere in the great mass of buildings. Nine. That's the Lord's breakfast a-cooking, thought Ivy, watching the smoke. I'll try that there little door, and she set off down the hill, Neb racing ahead.

As she drew near, the walls that had seemed a comfortable size from a quarter of a mile away began to loom over her, and she was looking at them so intently that only ears with the keenness of a forest creature's could have caught the light sound of a step on the grass behind her—though it was, in fact, the *sensation* of something approaching that warned her, rather than the very nearly inaudible sound.

"Good morning, Mrs. Gover."

"Good morning. Sir." Ivy half turned. It was that Vicar, drat him. Not looking like a Vicar, this morning. More like a Sunday walking gentleman.

"Beautiful, isn't it," Quentin Henderson said, just moving one hand to show that he meant The Hall, not the morning.

Ivy surveyed the emerald bastion now louring directly above them.

"Glad you think so. Sir."

"You sound very—severe, Mrs. Gover. Don't you approve of The Hall?"

Ivy did not answer directly, but said, "Will you ring or shall I. Sir?"

He set his long thumb on the bell. "It's a good example of Regency Gothic; the original place was burnt down to the ground in 1820." Mrs. Gover on Regency Gothic would be amusing, if one could get her to talk.

Then, alas, Christianity began to intercede. It always had (sometimes he was amused at an impulse to add "Confound it"). Its influence had given to him a depth of feeling which made him, in spite of his wit and his tolerance and his background, unacceptable, in the long run, to those Bloomsberries he so much admired; now, and at Cambridge. He delighted in Cezanne and the French writers of the eighteenth century, but, with a deep, certain, and unshakeable adoration, he adored Jesus Christ, and He had died for Ivy Gover.

There it was; a grace, God knew, but also at times a nuisance.

"Burnt down, was it?" Ivy suddenly repeated with startling ferocity, while the sound of the bell was yet trembling out behind the wall, "Damned good job too. But they built it up again, seeminly. Neb, you sit down and be'ave." Which Neb, having showed Mr. Henderson his teeth, did, and then showed the world a long pink tongue.

"Don't you think the moss adds to the charm?" Mr. Henderson went on, "the first time I saw it, before the war, there wasn't any."

He checked himself. Bloomsbury might find amusement in talking to a Cockney woman as if she were someone of their own class, but prudence told him clearly that it would be unwise to add that Lord Gowerville was hard up. Mrs. Gover might be a gossip, and put it all round the Great and Little Warbys that Parson said as Lord Gowerville couldn't afford to have his walls cleaned.

The Warbys, of course, knew this already, because they knew everything. All the same, better not . . .

Ivy refreshed herself by a downward jerk of her hat.

A click, and the door opened, and there was some sort of a porter, looking at the Vicar.

"Good morning, sir."

"Good morning, Hench. Is the Earl—available?"

"Just at breakfast, sir. If you'll please to come in." He stood aside. "Yes?" to Ivy.

"I want to see Mr. Stone. Sir. Mrs. Gover, of Catts Corner."

"Come in, then." His eye went past her to Neb, who had risen and was standing with an anticipatory pose, ready to bound through the door. "'*E* can jus stay outside, *if* you please. 'E'll do nicely there."

"Why?" demanded Ivy, making no move.

The porter glanced over his shoulder at Mr. Henderson, who was already away on his long legs a quarter of the distance across the vast, quiet, mossed courtyard.

"*Because,*" said Hench, with a change of expression and tone, "Mr. *Stone* don't like dogs. That's the reason. And 'ere the dogs has to stay. It's a rule. That way, please," pointing.

Ivy ignored him, and stepped outside again to whisper to Neb, who instantly assumed an expression of despair and fell, rather than lay down, upon the ground and extended an endless length of mournful nose.

"Does what you tell him, anyways," observed Hench.

"What *I* tells 'im, yes . . . s'pose you was to come with me? This is me first visit," and Ivy smiled.

"No," continued Hench, walking beside her across the great stones, "we got a dog, Mrs. Hench and myself, as nice a little Cairn as you could wish to see, not having any of our own . . ."

"Kids," nodded Ivy, "and this Mr. Stone, he don't like your dog?"

"He's like a child to us, and Mr. Stone can't abide him. Never says a word to him nor snaps his fingers at him nor anything. Mightn't be there, Mac mightn't, for all the notice he gets."

"Some people is silly fools about animals. I've noticed."

"Silly fools!" cried Hench, impressed, "you've about hit it." The observation seemed to him at once so novel and full of good sense that it did just strike him that this Mrs. Gover might be a nice friend for Emmy. Being a Buckingham girl and having grown up in the town, Emmy did find it a bit lonely nowadays. He glanced at Mrs. Gover. No . . . perhaps, on the whole, not. But *he* might run across her again one of these evenings in *The Swan.* He had heard that she frequented it.

The house, lying now to their left, seemed to Ivy to go on for a mile; it was all pointed windows, and in front stretched a long, long terrace, with steps leading up to it and leafless lilac bushes—one long bush, in fact, for its line was unbroken—drooping over the boundary wall.

They were approaching a group of small shabby buildings, solid-seeming but badly in need of a new coat of cream paint. The whole had the air of offices and stables; Ivy could hear hoofs stamping on stone somewhere at the back, and there was a smell of grain and hay, and the muted sound of an unseen boy whistling 'Tea For Two'.

"Mr. Stone's office," said Hench, stopping in front of a small, square place which had been repainted, but not recently, and he knocked on the door.

"Come in," called a harsh, sharp voice, and Hench nodded to Ivy.

"Good day, Mrs. Gover, and I hopes as we'll meet again. Show you Mac, per'aps?"

"Thanks. I'd like to see 'im." Ivy smiled; then turned the smile off like an electric torch as she opened the door and confronted Mr. Richard Stone.

11

"Good morning," said Ivy, "Sir."

Dickie Stone's ambition in life was to marry a rich girl. It would be better, of course, if she were also pretty, but if she were not rich, Richard Stone could never be hers. As Ivy wasn't a girl, and certainly could not be rich (except by the seventy-three-pounds-hidden-under-the-mattress standard) Mr. Stone looked at her without approval. However . . .

"'Morning."

Ever such a nasty voice, put you in mind of a buzz-saw (which was Ivy's name for a mechanical saw). And trying to look through you. Let him try.

"I come about my thatch. Sir."

"Which thatch would that be? I haven't seen you before, have I?"

"The thatch at Catts Cottage. Sir. Them up at *The Swan* advised me to come."

"Oh they did, did they." Mr. Stone was speaking half-turned in his chair while he searched in a small filing cabinet just behind him. "Well," taking out and running his eye down a newly-typed sheet of paper, "according to the notes here, the occupant of Catts Cottage is responsible for all repairs, including the thatch."

He looked full at her, in triumph. She was not a girl, she was not rich, let her hear the bad news at once. Besides, hadn't the old boy himself made it absolutely clear that there wasn't a ha'penny to spare on repairs for anyone, even those who paid their rents on time and had always had their repairs done by their landlord? It was the new rule; the war had been responsible for it; and Dickie Stone had come in with it (following that old dodderer, Pellew) to enforce it.

"Sorry," he added, dismissingly.

"But there's a great 'ole in it. Sir. The birds come in. In and out, in and out, all hours. Not that *I* minds them, but—"

"Of course if you feed them, they will—er—hang round the place," Mr. Stone snapped, recalling various pieces of gossip about the new inhabitant of Catts Cottage that came in helpful here, just at the right moment.

"I *says* I don't mind them," stated Ivy, but she jerked down her hat as if it were a helmet to ward off shrapnel, "only Mr. Gardener the soliciture told me as how the cottage ain't really mine, it's the Lord's. I s'pose the Lord don't want birds in and out, in and out, of a great 'ole in the thatch all hours, does 'e?"

"See for yourself," and Mr. Stone held out the sheet of paper in a thick well-kept young paw.

Ivy, sheltered by her hat, made a pretence of reading; but it was worse than the letter from Mr. Gardener which she had had to take along to Miss Green. Words! Some of them must be the best part of an inch long. It was a take-in, probably. But what could she do? She handed the sheet back to Mr. Stone—in silence.

"Satisfied?"

"*I* ain't got no money," said Ivy, loudly.

"Well, that's a pity . . . What do you live on? You must have some money."

"Two pensions, that's what I lives on. Sir. And a bit o' charing, now and then."

"*Two* pensions?"

"That's right—one from my last husband what was blown up in the Royal Navy, and ten shillins what Maggit and Farrows sends once a week because me second fell off of one of their ladders and never got no better and died eighteen munfs arterwards."

"Well, how much does it come to altogether?" demanded Mr. Stone, who saw no reason for words of condolence on these events.

"Under two pounds," was the cautious answer. If Ivy had been Neb, Mr. Stone would have heard one of his worst growls, and she did not add Sir. What business was it of his?

"Compingsation," was what she did add.

"What?"

"Compingsation. For him falling off of their ladder. Doin' their work."

"I see . . . well, you must save, you know, save. Put a little aside every week. It's your responsibility, that thatch, it says so quite clearly here." He tapped the sheet of paper.

Ivy was silent. Thoughts about the size of The Hall, and being hungry as a nipper, and her father breathing hard in the moonlight, passed through her mind. The Lord couldn't afford the price of a bundle of straw. Just the same as when she was eight years old. Couldn't let you have a bit of pheasant then, nor a bit of straw now, all these years later.

"How much would it cost?" she demanded at last. "Sir. All the time I was saving up, them birds would be—"

"I have no idea. It would depend on the size of the hole. How big is it? His lordship's thatcher would do the job, of course."

She did not reply for a moment, while she calculated. At length she looked up.

"A good size. 'Bout as large as my zinc bath, I'd say. But getting bigger every day with them birds going in and out, in and out, all hours."

Mr. Stone's rather military face, from which youth, in some subtle way, was already beginning to withdraw, assumed a final expression.

"Well, I'm sorry, but it's perfectly clear—Mrs?—I don't think you mentioned your name."

"Gover."

"—Mrs. Gover. You are responsible for repairs of Catts Cottage, and you must pay for the re-thatching. Good morning." He nodded towards her, and looked down at some papers in front of him.

The next minute the room shook to such a violent slam of the door that a fragment of plaster fell from the ceiling. Mr. Stone stared, in indignant amazement.

The small white breakfast room, octagonal in shape, where a few remaining figures of Saxe and Sevres coquetted and pirouetted in the little recesses above the mantel-shelf, looked out over a sweep of lonely green lawn that ended in a barrier of dark shrubs below a hill and its beeches. The air was blue and dim with wood and cigar smoke; the chimney needed sweeping.

"Hullo, Quentin, you're early," said Lord Gowerville, looking up from *The Times*, "have some coffee? It's probably cold, I warn you. Mine was."

"I know I'm early, sir—I'm sorry, but I'm going to London this morning to meet some friends. There's something I want to bother you about. (I won't have any coffee, thank you.)"

"Sit down, then. What's the row?"

Lord Gowerville's father and Mr. Henderson's had been at Cambridge together in the late 70s, and when, in middle-life, Lord Gowerville had come into his inheritance, which included the gift of the living of St. Peter's, he had offered it—subject of course to the Bishop's approval and consent, but that particular Bishop just happened to be an old acquaintance of Lord Gowerville's—to his friend's son, who was then in a North London parish, 'difficult' and slummy. The gruelling routine of the work was rapidly making him into an invalid.

Lord Gowerville had thought it would be agreeable to have a gentleman in the pulpit of St. Peter's; then one would know where one was, as one always had. But since the war . . .

So Quentin had come to the Warbys, leaving the trams and dirt behind him, and also the tube journey to the squares of graceful old houses in Bloomsbury, where he still surprisingly lingered on the fringe of the Set; that Set which he had first encountered at Cambridge and which, since the war, had sparkled and dazzled into such Surprising fame.

"Well . . ."

"Come along, out with it," said Lord Gowerville, puffing out cigar smoke and crossing his short legs, "there, boy, s'sh—" and he bent over the side of his chair to caress, very gently, the hairless head of an old dog lying there, "poor old boy, he's due to be put down this afternoon; Harcourt's coming to fetch him at three, and if I didn't know all that sort of thing was rubbish, I'd say he knew it."

"Poor old Milo," Quentin said absently, "well, the fact is, sir, this is embarrassing. I feel a . . . a puppy. What used to be called a coxcomb . . . but I wouldn't have come if I hadn't—oh dammit! You know Miss Mordaunt, of course?"

"Poor little Angela." The Earl nodded.

"Well, lately . . . really, I can hardly get the words out . . . it's occurred to me more than once that—she . . . er . . . is becoming . . . rather more interested . . . in me . . . than is . . . either desirable or—or wise."

"What on *earth*," demanded Lord Gowerville vigorously, "do you suppose *I* can do about it? I expect she is, poor gairl. Fiancé killed in the war, mother loses her husband the year after, and shuts herself up like Queen Victoria in the same boat, never sees anyone, most of their money gone, hunters sold, can't afford to entertain—I expect she *is* becoming more interested in you than is 'desirable or wise' . . . I suppose you wouldn't think of marrying her?"

"That—is utterly out of the question," Quentin said, and could not keep hauteur from his voice: these old aristocrats, with their passion for killing animals, and sometimes for breeding them, thought it simple to put male and female, any male and female, together, merely because they were male and female. "I hardly know her. Besides . . ." he broke off.

He *actually* could not get out the sentence. If he married, he wanted, not a faded, pretty, nervous creature in her middle thirties, but a young and beautiful girl. A first experience was printed within him like a deep, rusty, hideously-shaped burn. Only perfect loveliness and innocence could erase it.

"Getting a bit long in the tooth, isn't she, poor Angela," Lord Gowerville said meditatively, "Well, it's a great pity, a very great pity. She used to be the prettiest gairl around here. Belle of all the Hunt Balls . . . very sad. What does she do? Make eyes at you?"

His own eyes, ingenuous, small and blue, were not so serious in expression as Quentin would have liked. He kept them fixed attentively on the younger man, putting down his hand occasionally to caress the dog.

"There was . . . she—er—she was *hanging about—*" The words came in a burst, uncontrollably—"outside in the porch last night after Evensong, said there was something wrong with her bicycle . . . I tried to help her, of course . . . then I noticed that she—well, she was in tears. It was *most* embarrassing," he ended resentfully.

Lord Gowerville nodded. (It was all very well for him, Quentin Henderson thought; he had been happily married for thirty years. They had had no children—the heir to The Hall was a cousin-once-removed—but that deprivation had been their only grief—besides, he likes shooting things better than anything else in earth or heaven, probably likes it better than he did his wife, Quentin thought resentfully.)

"There was a . . . a . . . *scene.* She said she was so lonely she didn't know how to bear it, and if she only had *one* friend to talk to . . . really, I didn't know what on earth to do."

"Pat her. Always pat them. Never fails." Lord Gowerville bent over to study Milo, "What's the matter, boy? Lie down—soon be over. Good boy."

"I didn't . . . *dare* to, sir. She . . . she was in such a state . . ."

"Ah well. Very natural. She didn't say she was in love with you, I suppose?"

"Oh no—nothing of that sort—she didn't *say* anything much— just wept, and whispered . . . really, if it happens again I don't know *what* I shall do. I—I told her to pray, of course."

"Yes, I'm—er . . . yes, of course . . ." Lord Gowerville said. "Very proper. But she wants a husband and children.'"

"I said that God understands all our troubles and weaknesses and that prayer brings us closer to Him." Quentin saw no reason why Lord Gowerville should not put up with a little embarrassment.

"No doubt. No doubt," Lord Gowerville's tone was vague, "well, my advice to you is, *don't* give her the least bit of encouragement or before you know where you are, she'll *pounce*."

"She seems so gentle . . . I'm certain she would never do that. She—she did say something about . . . being fond of walking . . . and wanting a friend to walk with . . ."

"Fatal," Lord Gowerville said. "And as for being gentle, the gentler they are the more desperate they get, and the harder they pounce when they do. You be very careful, Quentin . . . hullo! Where's Milo? Good God, the old boy's gone off somewhere . . . never noticed while we were talking. Milo! Milo! Here, where are you, boy?"

The french windows were half-open to the frosty morning and he hurried out through them. The Vicar followed, more slowly, and not thinking about Milo. It was plain as the nose on his face that any 'advice' wrung out of Lord Gowerville was going to be useless.

Ivy purposely walked across the great courtyard at a leisurely pace. Usually, she neither noticed nor cared what people thought. But she was really angry, now, and no one was going to see *her* rushing off in a rage. She surveyed the scene; she gazed up at the low wintry sun; she slapped her hands together against the cold; but her thoughts were so furious, and so absorbing, that she did not notice in which direction she was sauntering.

The next thing she knew, she had just saved herself from tripping over a pinkish-brown mass lying at her feet. She stopped dead, and, coming out of her haze of rage, saw that it was a piteous dog, plainly old, and so weak that it could not lift its head, but lay panting, spread out helplessly, on the stones. The skin showed the crusts of some disease through the thin, matted, lifeless coat.

Ivy dropped on one knee and put a hand lightly on the unsightly body. Burning heat, unwholesome and startling, touched her palm and a faint horrible smell came up to her. The milky eyes, in which there was apparently still some sight, turned slowly towards her, at the touch. She remained perfectly still, and presently saw a faint stirring in his bare stump of a tail. It stirred, then began to move up and down slowly and very feebly, but regularly.

"What are you doing, my good woman?" asked a voice above her head.

She just glanced up, and saw, without really noticing it, an old rosy face, crowned by white hair and finished off by a bushy white moustache, and shabby greenish tweed breeches and coat.

"Should think you could see, couldn't you?" she retorted. "Makin' him better. What's his name?"

"Milo. He used to be a great fighter. He was to be put down this afternoon. It ought to have been done weeks ago but . . . he got out somehow, didn't you, old boy? I was talking to someone and didn't notice. A deuced odd thing . . . do you really believe you can 'make him better'? He's twelve, you know."

"He'll live to fifteen, time I've done with him." Ivy was gently moving her hand down the length of the obese body in a long, sweeping movement.

The Vicar strolled up to them at that moment, exclaiming, "Hullo, here he is," but Ivy was conscious only of slight irritation; all her attention was on the dog. A sweet wind, coming from the beech woods, began to blow gently, smelling of moss and damp leaves; and, as it swelled in power, Milo lifted his head a few inches and uttered a weak bark.

It was answered from outside the gate by an angry, powerful young one. Neb was staring through the delicate tracery of the ironwork, with jealous eyes fixed on Ivy.

"I'll 'ave him walking by the day arter tomorrer, and running by Sunday—you see. I'll see to 'im. Won't I, Milo beauty?" Ivy said; this old gentleman must be Milo's master.

Milo's tail moved feebly against the stones. Quentin Henderson remarked that he must be going or he would miss his train, and was told, in an absent tone, that Hench had a spare bicycle in his yard, which Quentin was welcome to borrow. He could leave it at the station, and someone would pick it up later.

Neither of the other two heard his "Good-bye" or noticed him walk off.

"Are you George Coatley's great-niece?" asked the old gentleman, in a moment or two.

"That's me," said Ivy, not looking up, absorbed in her stroking, "Mrs. Gover. Come up here to see about a great 'ole in my thatch, with the birds in and out, in and out, all hours. Not that *I* objec, mind you, but the place'll get wringing wet. You'd think the Lord 'ud 'ave enough cash to buy a bundle o' straw, and him owning a place this size, wouldn't you?"

Lord Gowerville was not the type of nobleman to tell a tenant playfully that it was just because he did own a place that size that he had to think twice about the price of a bundle of straw.

"So you really do think you can do the poor old chap some good, do you, Mrs. Gover?" he said again.

"Dead sure I can. Done it before—on some worse off than 'im. You bring 'im down to me early artemoon, about two, when the sun's strongest, and we'll soon 'ave 'im about again. There, beauty." She finished her stroking with a long sweep of her small red hand.

"Started you off proper, 'aven't we?" She stood up. "So long." She nodded. "I'll be off, then."

"I'll bring the thatcher down with me," said the old gentleman. "It's all right, Mrs. Gover—I am the Lord—not many people can say that, can they, ha! ha!—About two o'clock. Good morning to you."

12

THE last time that Ivy had seen Lord Gowerville had been thirty-seven years ago, so it was not surprising that she had not recognised him.

She had had her red, ten-year-old arms up to their elbows in the wooden tub full of washing (she and Mum had done the washing out in the back garden that day, it being a fine autumn morning with a strong wind blowing for the drying). She heard a thrilling, confused clamour drawing near, and the next thing she saw was the whole hunt sweeping round the edge of the grassy slope, with hounds in full cry, and the fox ahead of them, streaking across the road making for Belshers Wood.

She stared, hoping with all her passionate heart that it would get away; and there up among the big men on their big horses, as they passed, was a youth on a grey pony, his round red face alight with cheerful excitement.

"That's the young Lord," her mother had said, "enjoying himself, bean't he . . . now you don't stand there a-mooning, Ivy, get on with your work."

Ten minutes later, she had heard the sounds that meant they had killed. She had rubbed at the worn old shirt in the tub as if she would drive her knuckles through it, staring fiercely down into the soapy grey water.

She and Neb now walked home, rather gaily. That had been a bit of luck, that had; but she was thinking more about Milo than the visit from the Lord tomorrow . . . if he was the Lord, if it wasn't a take-in. Lords dressed posh, usually, but if this one couldn't afford a bit of straw, perhaps he couldn't afford posh clothes either. However, now he was going to afford the straw, seemingly.

The next morning, she realised that she had run out of tea.

Even Ivy did not think of having a Lord in her cottage without offering him tea; besides, if he went tealess he might turn nasty and call the thatcher off.

She went up to inspect the hole, before setting off to walk to Nethersham for the tea; it looked bigger and darker than ever with the bright wintry sunlight pouring down through it. She was standing directly underneath, gazing upwards, when something fluttered into the area of brightness and perched there, undulat-

ing its head and cooing while studying her with a bright eye that
yet did not seem to gaze downwards.

Ivy stared back. It was the dead spit of him. Some silly fools,
of course, said that you couldn't tell one pigeon from another,
but she knew better.

"Cooey?" she crooned, holding up her curved hand and arm.
"Come to Ivy, then," and at the low call he came sailing straight
down to her.

"Well I never, all that way," she muttered. "Neb, Neb, come
up 'ere and see 'oo's come to see us. I'm glad 'e found 'is way, I
am that."

Neb came scrabbling up the stairs, and stopped short at the
sight of them. He growled.

"Now we don't want none o' that . . . all beauties together, so
you put that in your pipe and smoke it. 'Ere," in a lower tone to
the pigeon, "want your breakfast?"

She had the remains of a bag of grain, bought from the
corn-merchant in Nethersham in her early days at the cottage
with which to tempt the birds. She now went carefully down the
almost perpendicular stairs, the pigeon rocking in a peculiar way
as it perched on her wrist, and Neb following and keeping up his
protest, of which she took no more notice.

She scattered the grain on her table, and stood for a moment
to watch the bird while it ate, showing more than a pigeon's usual
voraciousness. When it had eaten all she had to give, it fluttered
upwards, with an effort, and after more than one attempt succeeded in alighting on the mantelshelf, in the warm air above the
smouldering fire, and perched there. Ivy saw the wrinkled grey
lids drop over the eyes, and then the tiny head, so suggestive of a
snake's, curved down under its wing and the pigeon slept.

"All that way . . ." muttered Ivy, "now you 'ave a good sleep,
beauty."

Outside in the bright air, with the door locked and the key in
her pocket, she glanced up at the sun. It was still behind the beechwood; the trunks and majestic branches looked black against its
silvery pallor. Only just ten; there was plenty of time.

They did the five miles in just under the hour.

Nethersham High Street was busy; there were as many as a dozen cars standing down its length outside various shops, and three or four customers, sometimes more, in each shop. Jingling the money she carried, man-like, loose in a pocket, Ivy marched towards the grocer's, ignoring the tweed-clad ladies even as Neb, apart from an occasional silent display of teeth, ignored their accompanying dogs.

That shop next to the grocer's, which had been for sale, was sold, she noticed; its bow window was filled with appetizing brown cakes on plated stands, and trays covered by fragile crochet mats with mounds of fancy-cakes and macaroons. Freshly painted above the windows was: 'The Tea Shoppe'.

Too posh for me and who wants all that washy stuff, give me a nice kipper any day, Ivy was thinking, when someone visible through the window waved to her. It was Miss Green.

Ivy stopped, and Neb stopped beside her, and Helen came out.

"I can't stop nor but a minute. Miss," announced Ivy, and added no more. The tea, the thatcher, Milo, and the pigeon remained uncreated, undisplayed to Helen's imagination, behind Ivy's firmly curved, brownish-red lips.

"It's all right—I must fly, too," Helen said soothingly, "I only came to wish my friends luck, they're opening their tea shop today." She nodded at the background. "Do you remember Miss Cartaret—"

"Her as always had a bit o' dead tiger round her neck?" Ivy demanded. Helen should not have smiled, but she did.

"Lynx, not tiger . . . and her sister, the fair one?"

"Lynx, was it. No, I don't remember no fair one."

"How are you getting on? The last time we met was up in the beechwood, wasn't it," said Helen. To say *the beechwood* made for her, once more, the air, the scents, the low light, the two who had walked there.

"We're all right. Neb! say 'ullo to the young lady."

Neb stared pointedly away down the High Street, while Helen silently drew off her glove and held out for his inspection a slender wrist marked by a red scar.

"Your trademark, my boy."

"Well I never. Bit you, did 'e, that night?"

"Yes he did, and I jolly well thought it was going septic."

"Well! And I never noticed."

Helen thought that this was a decided concession, from Ivy; it almost, though not quite, amounted to apology and regret.

"It was all right, thank you, it soon cleared up. I heal very quickly," she said, and indeed, in every part of her except her heart, she did.

They exchanged a few more halting but amiable remarks: it just occurred to Helen to invite Ivy inside and stand her a cake, but she refrained; Coral would not want anyone so poor and common as Ivy in The Tea Shoppe, and, anyway, Helen was not really thinking about Ivy or cakes.

Jocelyn Burke was speeding back to London in the dear little car (the last car, for forty years, of which Helen was to feel fond) and she knew that his eyes were looking darker than usual, as they always did when he was annoyed.

If he had not forgotten his annoyance, *and* the cause of it, already.

They had spent the night in a small hotel in Buckingham and, that morning, Helen had remarked idly that Coral and Pearl were opening their tea shop today, and he had instantly suggested that they should drive over and give moral support.

"Oh." Helen had said.

"Why 'Oh'?"

"They're sure to—at least, Coral's sure to—wonder how on earth we got down so early."

"Tell her we got up early."

Helen gave him a look that was an exclamation point.

"I meant in London, bird-brain."

"It would seem so—so *fishy*. She thinks I hardly know you."

He smiled, and inclined his cheek against hers for an instant, without taking his eyes from the road; they were in the car.

"Do you mind people talking about us?" he asked. "Someone said to me at a party the other night, 'The whole of Hampstead's talking about you and Helen Green'."

"I don't mind particularly—except about Coral. I never really thought about it until this minute."

Mr. Burke sounded the hooter sharply at a chap in a Ford. Really, his love's indifference to public opinion was alarming. A whole-hogger. Yet she never made scenes. Peculiar, really.

"Well, are we going?" he demanded.

"I'd really rather you didn't—I mean, I'd like you to come, of course, but I mind Coral knowing about us. I really do—*mind*."

"I should like to go. She amuses me, and Pearl's very pretty."

Helen received this in silence. In a moment he peered round into her face; the word in those days for his expression was *impish*.

"Make up your mind. The next on the left's the London road. I can drop you there, and Nethersham's only half a mile—if you really don't want me to come."

"Of course I want you to come! It isn't that. I just can't—bear-things-being-chewed-over-by-Coral," Helen ended in a rush.

He shrugged. There was nothing much on in town that afternoon; most of his friends happened to be away that week-end, and it would have been amusing to rag about with Pearl and Coral in their shop.

"As you like, of course."

And in ten minutes she was standing at the corner of the London road, under a hedge of thorn with a grand leafless oak towering behind it, watching the car speed gaily off into the distance.

Helen had begun the half-mile walk. Oh, the unhappiness under the breast of that shabby coat: what must it be like to be sure of a young man?

"Good heavens, whatever hour did *you* get up?" cried Coral, almost at the top of her voice, as Helen came through the shop into the kitchen.

A thin elderly person—Helen decided that most people would call her a *person*, for she was certainly not a lady and did not look like a woman—was standing before a table, running a knife round the bottoms of one or two fairy-cakes that had stuck to the tin. Pearl was also standing at the table, moving a wooden spoon lightly about in a creamy-yellow mass within a creamy-yellow bowl—she glanced up at Helen and slightly smiled.

"Well, I said I'd come. And I got up very early."

"I should just think you did! We stayed at the cottage, last night and Thursday (missed a dance at the Harrison's but it couldn't be helped). Naturally, most week-ends we shan't be here—Daddy put his foot down about that. He wants us at home, of course."

Coral was bustling about, efficiently getting through small tasks while she talked. There was no trace of resentment in her remark about Daddy's decree. She and Pearl were set, like a pair of jewels, in the gold of their parents' devotion; petted, admired, financed, and in return they indulged Daddy's desire for their company.

"Can I help?" Helen asked.

"Oh I don't think so. You might keep an eye on the tea room and just give me a shout if anyone comes in . . . That's right, Mrs. Threader, it can go on the window-sill to set."

Mrs. Threader was the person. She set the walnut cake, which she had just finished icing, in the appointed place.

"Can I have a fairy-cake?" Helen asked. "How are things going?"

"Oh, quite well, it isn't ten yet, and we've sold eight big cakes (Mrs. Threader and Pearl baked yesterday). Then there'll be the teas this afternoon . . . yes, you can have one, but you'll jolly well pay for it!"

"Thanks," Helen was about to slip off her glove when, thank God, she remembered the wedding-ring. Leisurely, keeping her eyes on the bustling Coral, she pulled off glove and ring together and pocketed them. "I'd like a macaroon."

"They're twopence each!"

"I say, you know how to charge, don't you?"

Pearl silently held out a plate with a macaroon on it. She's so *pretty*, Helen thought; I'm glad he didn't come . . . not that anything seems to make much difference really . . . how lucky it had been that the Cartarets had stayed at Sunset Cottage, rather than at that hotel where "Mr. and Mrs. T. Jones, London", adorned the register with yesterday's date. She had addressed Jocelyn as 'Tom' throughout the evening. Very funny, that had been. Oh, *très drôle*.

"This is very good, Pearl. Congrats: who do I pay?"

"I'll take it, thanks." Coral held out a hand belonging to the same type—thick, well-kept, paw-ish—as Mr. Richard Stone's.

"That's one of our ways of keeping the *hoi-polloi* out. They can't afford our prices," she said, on a satisfied note.

Helen wondered what Mrs. Threader thought of these remarks, but decided that Mrs. Threader's manner was intended to keep out everybody except, perhaps, those few who came up to some private standard of truly staggering purity.

"Well, there's someone who isn't *hoi-polloi*, it's a parson," and she nodded towards the shop. A tall man, all height and darkness in the bright morning light except for the white circle of his collar, was standing by the counter looking absently down at the cakes.

"Oh lord—I can't stand churchy people—just go and see if he's up to anything and what he wants."

"He is a clergyman," said Helen mildly.

"I know, but there was that awful old Stewkey."

"I'll go," said Pearl, who had been unobtrusively but rapidly washing and drying her floury hands, and now moved gracefully towards the dividing curtain.

"Oh, let Helen—he only wants a cake—it'll be good practice for her—we might give her a job!" and Coral began to laugh heartily, which disguised from her the fact that she did not like her sister talking to a personable man, even a man who was a parson.

I like his face. (Pearl was going leisurely towards Quentin Henderson.) He looks *good* . . . I forgot about Harry, for the minute! Perhaps I'm Getting Over it.

One young man whom the Cartarets knew had been heard to say that Pearl's new-chicken-colour shingle, and her complexion and eyes, combined with that voice (it was soft, with the ghost of a lisp) were—and here his voice had run up wildly—'damn nearly irresistible'.

But . . . fashions in girls were changing, as they do every fifteen years or so, and Pearl belonged to 1914. That perhaps was why Harry . . .

Quentin Henderson looked up. A girl was standing beside him, wearing blue and white, and as he came out of bitter thoughts with which he was tediously familiar, he was surprised to find them melting into thoughts about lilies of the valley.

"Do you want a cake?" Pearl asked (poor thing, he looked rather miserable).

"Oh—yes, thank you. Er—" he was a little taken aback at finding anyone so pretty and so innocent-looking asking him about cakes in a tea shop. But the lily-of-the-valley was explained; she had on the scent; it became stronger as she moved slightly to pull down the white thing she wore over a blue thing.

"What kind would you like?"

"What kind have you—er—I believe my housekeeper said something about almond."

Of course Mrs. Marzarin had said almond. She had been coaching Miriam, her tiresome daughter of thirteen, for her part in the school play at the time, but she had lifted her dramatic pale face out of her untidy bob of black hair and flung "Almond!" at him as if she were Lady Macbeth.

"I'll just see if there's an almond one left."

Pearl smiled.

Now when she smiled, she showed, amidst the teeth that really were like her name one slightly irregular one. She also had what is called a bee-stung lower lip and a dimple in her left cheek. It really was *not* cricket.

"Thank you." He went up to the nearest table and rather abruptly sat down.

"I'm afwaid," called Pearl softly from the window where she was inspecting cakes, "we don't serve teas until the afternoon. Three o'clock."

"Oh, that's all right . . . I'm only sitting down."

He was sitting down because he felt weak and peculiar, and in order to think over the question, was love at first sight a myth? But coherent and logical thought did not come.

"Just one left." She came towards him; always leisurely, bringing that waft of scent as unbelievably delicious as a theme of Tchaikovsky's, and carrying before her, on a stand, a cake.

"Oh . . . oh thank you. That will do very well. Er . . . This is a new venture, isn't it? It all looks charming."

He managed to take his eyes off her face long enough to glance round the walls of old oak—for the Tea Shoppe had been the parlour of a private house before it came down to being a shop—which were 'stripped' and 'pickled', in the very newest fashion invented by Mrs. Syrie Maugham, who ran a smart interior decorating business in London. Old blue and yellow Chinese plates were ranged along a shelf below the ceiling, and the decorations were three or four hammered copper vases filled with red and white chrysanthemums and sprays of beech.

"I'm glad you like it." Her eyes followed his complacently round the room. "My sister arranged it all. She's very clever at that kind of thing."

"Oh, you're running it together, are you?" He wanted to see if she wore a wedding or an engagement ring.

But, having set down her stand with the cake on the table before him, Pearl had put both hands into the rather mannish pockets of her blue tweed jacket: not that they would have made her look anything but even more delightfully feminine, thought Quentin, if she had worn Rugger boots. But he could not see her hands; only an inch of lily-of-the-valley coloured wrist.

"Yes. Daddy gave it to us. For . . . for a pwesent . . ." (now why did she look sad for just a second?) "We live at Sunset Cottage, near Little Warby; that's Daddy's, of course, but we use it, and Coral, that's my sister, drives us in every morning. She's just got her car; she's *thrilled*."

"Well, I hope the venture will succeed."

"Fank you," said Pearl. She hesitated, then went on smoothly and rather solemnly, "I hope we shall see you in for tea, sometimes."

"Th-thank you; yes, I expect so; I hope so; I live at the vicarage in Tory Lane; my housekeeper isn't particularly satisfactory, poor woman; she can't cook; so I—I expect I shall be."

He paused. I am behaving like a fool and I must look and sound like one, he thought. It doesn't matter. Can I drop the cake on the floor when I take it? Then she'll have to take her hands out of her pockets to help me pick it up and I can see if there's a ring.

No; that might distress her.

I know; I'll give her a note. Hands out of pockets to get change . . .

And then, if two other females did not come bustling out (a libel on Helen Green who, whatever her faults, never bustled) and his girl, turning to the dark fat one, said, "The almond cakes are one and sixpence, aren't they?"

"Yes. Thank you," and, smiling in a manner he thought of as sharply, the dark fat one held out her hand, while Pearl's remained in those pockets.

It was here that Helen saw Ivy through the window, and drifted out to her. Thank God, thought Quentin, the colour of whose thoughts, and their expression, was being notably heightened by his knowledge that something immensely important to him was rapidly going on; that's got rid of one of them.

He never met a girl or a woman who attracted him, that, like some awful transparency, there did not instantly glide over each pretty face, every enticing pair of eyes, the reddened ant-eater profile and the eyes he must always remember. But he summoned his social training, and addressed Coral.

"Your sister tells me that you are living at Sunset Cottage. I expect you know St. Peter's; shall I see you at church tomorrow? I am the Vicar; my name is Henderson."

"Oh my goodness, I'm afraid we don't go to church. Is it dreadfully wicked of us?" sparkled Coral.

"You can hardly expect me to say 'no', can you? On the other hand, I find it difficult to say 'yes'," said Quentin, who had disliked Coral at sight.

She did not quite understand, so she laughed, then suddenly popped on a serious face and a confidential manner.

"No, what it really is, we live in town, and Daddy likes us with him at week-ends."

"Very natural." Quentin did not glance at Pearl, who had strolled away and was wrapping up the cake . . .

"Our name's Cartaret," went on Coral, who had taken to Mr. Henderson no more than he had to her, but knew that a spare man—and he hadn't that married look—was always useful, especially in the country, "I'm Coral, as Pearl may have mentioned and she's Pearl."

Quentin perceived that a special manner should be used with this young woman, but could not quite bring himself to say "Charming."

"Daddy likes jewel and flower names for girls," continued Coral—"hullo, look what's blown in!" to Pearl.

Mr. Richard Stone marched up to the group exclaiming, "Hullo, I just want a couple of iced thingamejigs with cherries on, or are you sold out?"

"Dickie, don't be so *sill-ee*! Mr. Henderson'll think you're bats," with a glance at Quentin, "we're serious business women, you know, it isn't a game."

"Oh, the Padre and I are old pals—you been buying cakes, Vicar? Can't the dashing Marzarin bake cakes?" winking.

"Mrs. Marzarin *is* an indifferent cook, I'm afraid . . . I must go," Quentin turned first to Coral, then to Pearl, who was holding out the cake in a paper bag, "Thank you. I'll certainly come in for tea soon; good-bye." Pearl suddenly, but still silently, fully smiled.

Quentin nodded at that little bounder Stone and strode out, standing aside a moment to let a dreamy-looking young woman in a green coat drift by. What extraordinary relations and friends for an exquisite girl . . . a sister as sharp as a—a *bradawl*, and Stone . . . Stone, who really must be stopped, in some way, from winking when he mentioned Mrs. Marzarin.

And he still did not know if she were engaged. Bound to be: better assume it.

And what an eternity of time ago it seemed that he had been troubled about poor Angela Mordaunt. The knowledge that he was, the feeling that he was, wildly and ridiculously, but also, exquisitely, in love with someone else would give him perfect confidence and tact in disposing of *her*.

"What on earth did you want to jaw to him for, Pearl?" said Coral, after Dicky Stone had been firmly but kindly pushed off and they had sold three more cakes to shopping ladies, and were back, for a moment in the kitchen.

"I wasn't jawing to him. I only said a few words. He was a customer."

"Well, I hope he won't come in for tea. We want a nice, jolly crowd, not clergymen—they're depressing."

"I fink he has a good face," said Pearl, going steadily pink while she slowly drew one long finger round and round inside a bowl Mrs. Threader had not yet washed up.

"We don't want good faces in here. It's a very long face, that's all I've got to say."

"I like him," Pearl sucked creamy mixture off her fingers, looking steadily at her sister out of angry blue eyes.

"I say, you're really wild, aren't you! . . . Fallen in love at first sight?"

"Oh, shut up."

Pearl turned away, and Mrs. Threader, putting a batch of buns into the oven, inwardly shook her head, a gesture with which that organ was familiar. But this was not because of the sisterly squabble.

Mrs. Threader had been disturbed by the appearance in The Tea Shoppe, where everything had promised to be so nice and respectable, by the sudden appearance of that Mr. Stone. Mrs. Threader feared that the stories about Mr. Stone and that girl with the very high heels from Great Abbey were true. It would be *quite easy*, what with him having his own flat up at The Hall; but he was no chicken, *he* would never see twenty-eight again, and he was old enough to know better, and it wasn't nice.

Mrs. Threader closed the oven door with reproving noiselessness.

13

IVY got home in good time to cook two kippers and eat them with a great deal of bread and margarine, followed by a slab of bread-pudding made yesterday for her lunch. She had time to feed Neb, examine Cooey for signs of damage acquired on his long, his almost unbelievably long journey, and then to sit down and peruse (it was more than a mere reading) a postcard which had arrived during her absence.

Win Smithers again. "Hope you are getting on all right. I'll be seeing you again one of these days soon." And love from Win and a photo of Tower Bridge. Ivy did not like the sound of it. She glanced at the fire. No; it would make a bit of an ornament on the mantelpiece; and Cooey might like a peck at it, so that was where she put it.

This Win—she had met her once, at some forgotten gathering of Stan's family, and had never seen her since. But she had heard about Win, oh yes: Win was the one (there was such a lot of them, Stan's folks) that didn't get on with her sister Alice; Alice had pinched half of some house that their mum had left, half to Alice and half to Win—Ivy never listened to family gossip with more than a quarter of her attention, and she neither knew the rights of the drama nor cared about them.

All she cared about was the fact that postcards from Win Smithers had been following her around, from address to address, for years, it must be; and it was nosying-about; and sooner or later Win Smithers herself would be on the doorstep of Catts Cottage, because that was what Win did (said all the aunts and sisters-in-law and cousins); didn't get on with Alice, so she couldn't stay at home, sensible-like, but went round visiting everybody.

If Win Smithers had not so far succeeded in staying with Ivy Gover, it was because Ivy never sent Win a *new* address and it took Win, skilled as she was in the technique of staying with people, much time and detective-work to find that new address out. For six weeks at a time, usually, Win stayed with you; *and* nothing wrong with her appetite neither. Well, Win Smithers wasn't—

Neb sat up suddenly and growled, and there followed a decided knock at the front door.

Ivy opened it to the Lord and Milo, sitting at the Lord's feet and panting, and a thick-set chap with a glummish look who must be Tom Wattis the thatcher.

"Good afternoon. Sir," said Ivy, "'ullo, Milo, beauty." She and Wattis exchanged stares.

"Good afternoon, Mrs. Gover. Wattis will go up and take a look at your thatch, if he may . . . thank you."

She stood aside, and they came in, the Lord taking off his greenish cap and Wattis his old dark one. Milo, who had flopped down on to a mass of withered thorn leaves that had blown against the doorstep, turned his head with a piteous look and a low whine, and Ivy instantly stooped to him, motioning the eager Neb away with a backward movement of her hand.

"What do you think of him today?" Lord Gowerville asked, pausing too.

She had her hand on the dog's back, with the fingers spread out, keeping it completely still.

"Better," she pronounced at last, "'e's only tired because 'e walked most of the way 'ere." She looked up, "Didn't 'e?"

"Quite half the way, I should judge. Remarkable, when one thinks of the state he was in yesterday. He would have been dead by now, Mrs. Gover, if you hadn't come along. Remarkable."

His eyes rested upon her keenly. Not exactly the old type of tenant; picked up that sharpness from living in London—as old Gardener had informed him—no doubt. But knew her place; called one 'Sir' . . . well, he should damned well hope so. We hadn't come to tenants not respecting their landlord yet.

"Can you give me a 'and carrying 'im in. Sir?"

"Yes, yes. Of course."

"The sun's about right, see. Be right for about half an hour."

Together, while Neb looked haughty in a corner and was plainly resisting an impulse to come out and sniff at the recumbent stranger, they lifted Milo's unpleasant body, and carried it inside and laid it gently down on the warm bricks of the hearth.

"You think warmth's the right thing for him, then?"

"'Course it is. Sun's best of all—" (sunlight was streaming into the room through one of the windows that Ivy had weeks ago with difficulty opened) "next to him running in the woods. Now I'll stroke him a bit—and you be off, please," to three mice who were skirmishing down upon Milo's tail. "Your turn'll come later. Sit down, please. Sir."

Here Wattis, having made various thumping and inexplicable sounds overhead, passed through on his way out, touching his cap to the Earl and saying that he would "be over Tuesday".

Lord Gowerville lowered himself (touch of sciatica, must be that walk yesterday) into the Windsor, which he remembered from old Coatley's day. What the dickens was the 'turn' which the mice were to have later? Stroking? They were tame enough to be stroked; he had never seen such a thing in his life; mice running round the room ignoring, and ignored by, a young healthy dog.

"You seem to have a great many cockroaches, Mrs. Gover," he observed at last, arousing himself from a pleasant, lulled, dreamy sensation that had crept upon him as he watched the sweeping motion of the woman's hand, and his eye catching certain slight movements against the grey shadows on the wall behind the hearth, "don't you dislike them? Most women do—that is, I understand that they do."

Lord Gowerville had never known a woman who was, so to speak, on familiar terms with cockroaches.

Ivy shook her head. She did not look up, but at last she announced, rather than said:

"People is silly fools about insecks. They're the same as you and me. Sir."

This statement rather naturally silenced Lord Gowerville. The air smelt of woodsmoke, the grey logs smouldered on the grey stone, the crimson and amber bryony berries thrust into a jam-jar on the table glowed in the sun, and the jar glittered purest crystal. Comfortable here, Lord Gowerville thought, that damned sciatica seems easier. His eyelids drooped.

Then they jerked open, at a short, gruff, joyful sound. Milo was sitting up, and his tail was thumping steadily against the stone; his eyes were fixed upon Mrs. Gover.

She leant back on her folded legs. She did not sigh, but her face seemed to have grown older. Not sadder; that face could no more look sad than could a horse-chestnut, but a horse-chestnut can look old, and so for the moment did Ivy's face.

"We'll 'ave a cup of tea," she announced, "if you could do with one. Sir."

"Thank you. That would be welcome."

He turned to Milo. "Well, old man . . . feeling better?"

Milo got, cautiously and slowly, on to his feet, and flomped down off the hearthstone and walked carefully across to his master, laid his chin on his knee, and deeply sighed, as if with affection and relief. Lord Gowerville gently touched his head. The matted, unsightly pelt along it seemed to have smoothed itself out slightly and even had the faintest sheen, while beneath it on the pinkish skin—Lord Gowerville took out his spectacles because his eyes would not believe what they saw—there was a prickling of tiny, new hairs.

Ivy moved about with a small dark blue enamel kettle and a new packet of Mazawattee tea and the cups and saucers decorated with blue grass. Not a word did she say. The mice were out again, running all round Neb, whose expression was patiently anguished. Occasionally he glanced at her, as if to say "How can you, of all people, bear to see me so humiliated?"

This is the damnedest oddest afternoon I've ever spent anywhere, in the whole of my life, Lord Gowerville mused. He cleared his throat.

"I've never seen a kettle like yours, Mrs. Gover. Er—have you had it long?"

"That's a railwayman's kettle, that is." Ivy splashed milk from a half-pint can into a jug with a broken lip. "My first 'usband was on the railways before he died. *That* wasn't long," she ended sharply, as if a personal injury had been done to her by the death. "Use these kettles for making tea 'side of the tracks, they do. Just 'olds the half-pint. 'Tisn't enough for two but you can always boil it up again."

She snatched the steaming kettle off the fire, scattering drops of boiling water among the mice, who fled. Neb uttered a yelp.

"Now that's 'cos of the mice, and Milo being here, not 'cos you're hurt," Ivy said to him.

She shot the water into a brown earthenware teapot, and sat down at the table.

"We'll let that draw. You like a few blackberries? Sir."

"Thank you . . . tea and blackberries would go well together—I should think."

Tea and strawberries—of course. Tea and blackberries—peculiar. But it was being, as he had admitted, a peculiar afternoon.

Ivy took a saucerful of them from a corner cupboard. Lord Gowerville had been trying to think who she reminded him of, and suddenly realised that it was Aggie. True, Lady Beresford did not call him 'Sir', but her manner and Ivy's had two points in common; perfect confidence, and complete repose. Aggie was 'good' with animals, too, but not like this. Not like this.

H'm. Not quite the thing, perhaps, sitting and saying nothing. Those cockroaches, too . . . very extraordinary indeed. Most cottage women . . .

"I see you have a charming picture," he observed, glancing towards the wall where 'Reunited' hung.

"I bought that picture, see, it was a bargain for 'alf-a-crown, just after my third was blown up in the Royal Navy, and I thought, we'll see, that's what we'll do. I hates church, I really hates it. Sir. But if there's a After Life as they calls it, p'raps it might be a bit like that. The sky's pretty, isn't it? Sir."

"It is indeed." For a moment they studied the two hefty spirits, solidly beautiful in their cloudless empyrean, in silence. It occurred to the Earl, with a most unusual soaring of fancy, that that was how everyone would like to think of Heaven: meeting again the person you loved best, winged and well again, and then he thought of Verena; dear childless wife; dear old girl.

"Sometimes," snapped Mrs. Gover, "I think it's downright soppy . . . 'ow do you say it? Sir."

"What?" Lord Gowerville started, staring, and his thoughts returned to earth. "Oh—the name of the picture."

He got up and strolled over to the wall and took a closer look. The thing had been torn out of some Christmas supplement, and the name appeared underneath.

"Reunited. It—er—means 'meeting again'."

"Thank you. Sir." He noticed her firm lips repeat the word soundlessly: then—

"'E was the one," she said abruptly, "blown up in the Royal Navy. Like I said."

"I am very sorry, Mrs. Gover. Was that on active service?" Lord Gowerville half uncrossed his legs, then resumed his position and bent to caress Milo.

"No, after the war, that was; some fool left a mine in one o' them seas out China way, I don't know, and it blew up. The ship 'it it. A lot went, that way."

"The *Connaught*. I remember it perfectly."

"Liked 'im the best o' the three, I did. Not unlike 'im in that picture," nodding towards 'Reunited', "when we first come across each other. A youngish chap and I wasn't above thirty."

Then her lips pressed together again, as if she had set a full-stop at the end of a paragraph. When she opened them again it was to ask if he would like another cup of tea?

Lord Gowerville and Milo were walking through the woods above The Hall one afternoon, about ten days after his visit to Ivy. Man and dog were enjoying their stroll; Lord Gowerville liked to see Milo waddling ahead, pausing to root into soft patches of earth on the banks at the edge of the wood where primroses would grow in the spring, or to snuff the sharp air of evening, and Milo liked snuffing and rooting and being with Lord Gowerville.

Low rays of lemon light from the setting sun pierced between the massive trunks as they entered the beechwood; Lord Gowerville poked discontentedly with his stick at a trailing bramble, then slashed at an aspen sapling. The place needed thoroughly going over by skilled men. It was a pleasure to walk along the grassy ride running through the forest; no seedlings could grow under that dense canopy of leaves, though ahead he would come on the victorious bracken, edging the slope above the house and yearly creeping down nearer to it, beastly stuff; he trod firmly on the lacy brown leaves of a young plant that had somehow found a footing at the verge, beastly stuff.

Only God knew what the state of the place would be when his time came to go, and young Heriot took over. The price of land was going down as quickly as the value of money. Ah well, no nation could fight as England had fought, for the last four years, and come out unscathed.

Milo waddled quickly past him, uttering the bark that was so much stronger than the weak, hoarse sound of ten days ago.

"What's the matter, boy? Rabbits?"

No—oh lord, if it wasn't poor little Angela Mordaunt, all caught up in one of those confounded brambles. It was all right; he had answered her letter asking permission to walk in the woods with a friendly note inviting her to scramble about and pick all the rubbish she wanted (he had not, of course, put it like that). But he did not care to be reminded just how much rubbish—bracken, brambles, spindly seedlings—grew there.

She was trying to tear her skirt away from the thorns, really pulling at it quite violently, and he was almost certain he could hear muttering.

"Damn . . . damn . . . *blast* . . ." It was such a soft voice, he couldn't be certain. Poor little girl; poor Angela. His wife had had strong views about her mother, that charming woman. But women often had strong views about other women.

"Hullo, Miss Mordaunt, can I be of any help?" Lord Gowerville came towards her, cap in hand. He did not *like* women, particularly unhappy women, picking rubbish in his woods that should not be growing there, but not a sign of what he felt showed on his face.

"Oh Lord Gowerville!" Her mannish hat had got itself tilted sideways and her soft hair, no longer a bright brown and not yet grey, was flying about her face. "How kind of you!"

She tried to turn to him, dragging the tweed skirt unbecomingly sideways, "it's *that* one, right at the other side." She pointed a finger in a worn hogskin glove. "If you can *just* hook your stick round it and *pull*—I think I can reach it—or perhaps I'd better disentangle myself—no, please don't trouble—I've got plenty—if I can just get free of this wretched thing—"

He took the affair into his own hands, seeing that it would take little more to have her in tears, and stooping, quickly and skilfully drew the strong red thorns downwards and out from the thick tweed; Angela had been blindly tearing at them. Then he snapped the bramble with some satisfaction and threw the vicious-seeming thing away.

"There." He drew a little off from her, addressing Milo, while she straightened her hat and ineffectually thrust strands of hair under it.

"Oh thank you—so kind of you—is that dear old Milo? I thought you were having him put down . . . someone told me . . ."

"Oh I was, I was; he was very bad but—er—he made a miraculous recovery."

He really could not go into all that. "Shall we walk on?" he suggested.

Miss Mordaunt had under one arm a great bunch of bracken, beech sprays and silver birch twigs, from which the leaves were fluttering away with her every small movement.

Poor gairl, Lord Gowerville thought. Pity nerved him to heroism—"Let me carry your—er—posy," he suggested.

"Oh, that's very kind of you, but I like to carry it myself, the scent is so delicious." For one unbelievable instant, he thought that she was going to push the thing into his face, "I—I like to carry it, thank you."

They walked on in silence. Angela addressed one or two remarks, of a bluff type which did not suit her low nervous voice, to Milo. Her clothes did not strike Lord Gowerville as being inappropriate; they were thick, they vaguely suggested that she might stand respectfully in his rear while he fired a gun at something; they did not alarm by their emphasis upon her sex; they were not what Lord Gowerville, when he did think of such matters, indulgently classed as 'frilly'.

The yellow light died quickly out of the sky, and the air between the great boles began to grip; soon there would be a rim of frost on every leaf. Shadows, not misty but mysterious and clear, crept up into the distances. Angela pressed a gloved hand against her cheek, Lord Gowerville unobtrusively applied his handkerchief to his nose. They came to a place where the ground sloped steeply away to the left.

"I must hurry," Angela said breathlessly, "I'm rather late and Mummy does so like to have me there for tea . . . good night— thank you so much . . . good-bye, Milo old boy—it—it was so nice to see you both, Lord Gowerville."

"Good night, my dear." He stood, with his cap off, until she had disappeared down the hill between the trees, then replaced it, called cheerfully to Milo, who was scratching amid some writhing roots, and marched briskly homewards.

She must be thirty-five. No chicken. But seemed younger than she was. No hope for her now, of course . . . Poor Angela, hard lines, poor gairl.

The meeting had exacerbated the perpetual excitement of Angela's nerves. It was silly (she knew it) but as she hurried down the hill she began to dream about being proposed to by Lord Gowerville, and gently, of course, refusing him. Her heart was in Peter's grave . . . she wanted to add something really *splendid* to her bunch of leaves! Something to surprise Mummy! She broke into a graceful run; all her movements had grace, not the natural grace of Pearl's, but a controlled athletic one; at nineteen, Angela had been a swift and formidable hockey-player.

As she came to the bottom of the hill, bordered by a hedge beyond which lay the pastures of Binney's Farm, she could see a trail of dim white lying along part of its crest—was it Traveller's Joy? It couldn't be honeysuckle? So late in the year!

She ran forward, humming to herself, smiling, with tears in her eyes . . . honeysuckle . . . "my dear" . . . Peter's grave . . . Peter . . . over the dim grass, under the high cold darkening sky, dropping her largest piece of fern as she ran.

The hedge crowned a highish bank. She pulled off her gloves, stepped across a ditch full of water-plants, scrambled a little way up the slope until she was level with the hedge, then, stretching an arm upwards, groped for the unidentified treasure. It was flowers, she could tell by the texture, cold and soft against her bare hand. It *was* honeysuckle!

Then one foot slid from under her on the slope, softened by yesterday's rain, and she caught at the hedge to save herself, and its small sharp thorns drove into her palms. She gasped with agony, and moved away a little, and her other foot slipped, and her face—her face—

It was dreadful, dreadful, and as she struggled to keep her balance and tried to pull her face away from the wicked dark labyrinth of the hedge, all that she could think of was The Crown of Thorns, pressing into His brow. She had always shuddered away from that thought, and now she knew . . . torture . . . her foot slipped again, a long way this time; she was sprawling, pressed against the agony; she managed to glance down, and there was the ditch, dark and marshy and crowded with plants; she might drown, of course it couldn't be so deep but . . . her skirt was above her knees, her hat had torn free from its pin and fallen off somewhere . . .

"Oh help—help—someone—help—" she called, desperately but still softly—so silly, because there was no one there—and at once a man's voice answered loudly and cheerfully—

"Let 'eeself go, and I'll catch 'ee."

She managed, somehow and with an effort she afterwards wondered that she had been able to make, to turn her head, and saw, standing immediately below her as if he had grown up from the ground that was now scarcely visible, the dark figure of a tall man. His arms were outstretched.

"I can't—I can't—I'm frightened—I'm sorry—I can't."

"Now just 'ee let go, missie, I'll catch 'ee, I say." The voice was coaxing and kind.

Angela stopped thinking. The agony in her hands and the fiery pain in her face were unbearable. She wrenched her head backwards from the terrible hedge, tore her hands away with a moan, and slid down the bank, straight towards the ditch.

But she never reached it. She fell into the arms that grasped her from the back and swung her round so that she was pressed, for a moment, against a rough coat.

It smelt of coarse tobacco and of earth—was it? But she broke free from his arms, and also from a sensation of protection and safety that, after the terror and the agony, seemed to her half-divine.

"There! I said as I'd catch 'ee." The tone was laughing. Angela looked up into a face, a dark face, but pallid in the almost faded after-glow, and saw the shine of his teeth; he was smiling.

"Good thing I were here, weren't ut?"

"Oh—thank you so much—" Angela was now standing three feet away from him and smoothing her hair with shaking hands. "I—my hat—I'm afraid—" She glanced helplessly about her, trembling.

"'Ere we are." He stooped, and held it out. "No, it be sodden—fell into the watter, I reckon." He shook it, and icy drops struck her stinging, burning face, "can't wear that, give 'ee a shocking cold in the 'ead, that wud. 'Ere, put on yer scarf—"

Angela shrank away, but large hands were fumbling with the knot at her neck, capable fingers were arranging it round her head, as if she were a Russian peasant woman, and tying it carefully, as if to spare her scratched face and neck, under her chin.

"Th-thank you." She was recovering her sense of being a lady. "It's Sam Lambert, isn't it? I'm—I really am most grateful to you."

"That's all right." Sam smiled again. "Lucky I heard 'ee hollering out. More of a squeak, t'were."

"Yes—I—I know. It was silly of me, really, but those thorns were—I—I suppose—"

She stopped. One could not tell a farm labourer that Miss Mordaunt of The Beeches had lost her head.

"You'll 'ave to make more noise nor that, missie, if you want folk to hear 'ee."

"I was—I had been out for a ramble and I was on my way home and I—I thought—I was trying to get—I thought that was honey-suckle, on the top of the hedge. Just there." She pointed, then saw her hand, and gasped.

"So tes. Want ut?" With an easy though heavy spring, he was up the bank and down again, dragging with him a rope of leaves and creamy half-withered flowers that since June had sunned themselves into an unusual luxuriance of size and beauty along the top of the hedge. He put it out to her, under her nose, but gently; not thrusting it at her; not risking its touch against her face. She smelt it, and into the throbbing pain, and her shame, and the ache in her throat, there came, like the memory of that moment of half-divine comfort and peace, the ghost of its scent.

"Reckon it don't smell sweet, now."

"There is just a—a—kind of—there's something."

She put out her hand to take the vine, and Sam made a concerned sound.

"T—t! Look at that 'and! You better get along home quick and put boracic on that—and t'other, too."

"Yes, I—I must; I'm afraid my mother will be worrying . . . and when I go in looking like this . . ."

"Mothers," said Sam gloomily, "is always worritting. 'Ness mine knows wheer I be, day *an'* night, she worrits all right. Nags, too."

"Oh . . ." Angela's dignity, that quality which was her armour, and, she supposed, her support, was returning rapidly.

Sam's tone was not exactly familiar, but it was—well—more—*friendly* was the word, she supposed—than it should have been. She was most thankful that he had happened to be passing; she thought that he had been kind (though that was an odd thought, because *kindness* should not really come into encounters between ladies and farm labourers, unless on the lady's side) but she did not want to hear, and she should not have to hear, confidences about old Mrs. Lambert.

"I am very much obliged to you indeed, Sam," she said, standing there with blood dripping over the great loop of honeysuckle and her small face framed by the sporting, masculine, spotted scarf, "th-thank you again. Good night."

She nodded, firmly and pleasantly she hoped, and turned away. Her legs were shaking so that she could hardly walk.

"It were a pleasure," he called after her, not moving, standing there and staring, "mind you use the boracic, me mother swears by boracic."

Angela neither turned nor answered. There had been a note in that last sentence that made her writhe. And her lovely bunch of bracken and beech and laurel and aspen was lying in that ditch. All she had to show Mummy was the honeysuckle, and that (she glanced down) had hardly any scent—well, how silly to expect it to have—and it was covered in her blood.

14

"OH MISS! Your poor—your face! Whatever have you done to it?"

"It looks worse than it is. Don't speak so loudly, please, Mary, I don't want Mrs. Mordaunt to see it until I've bathed it."

"She's in the drawing-room, miss. She waited tea for you. Shall I bring it in now, miss—or—would you like me to come up with you . . ."

"I can manage, thank you . . . take tea in, please, and say that I'll be down in five minutes."

Mary, snubbed but full of not disagreeable excitement, went off.

Angela had never been given a latch-key and had never suggested that she should have one. In the days when she went to perhaps three or four dances a week, ('hops', they were called) at local houses, there was always a maid to sit up for her, or she stayed the night with her hostess. That was a long time ago.

She forced her shaking legs to take her up the wide, well-carpeted stairs and down the passage to the white door of her room.

No time to sit down; Mummy would have asked Mary if it were Angela at the door, and Mary was certain either to look so as to provoke questions, or to say something silly . . . She dragged off the scarf from her head.

And actually started away from her reflection in the glass. White, white, with a horrible scrabble of blood and scratches over her cheeks; her hair wild and flying and scattered over with bits of dead leaf. (Oh *God*, if I could sit down.) She began gently tapping at the streaks of blood with a clean handkerchief dipped in cologne, drawing in her breath with a hiss of pain at the excruciating sting of the spirit. Just as well, perhaps, to disinfect it; she remembered the strictness about cleaning wounds from her months with the V.A.D. (Oh, if I could just *sit down*, and be *quiet*.)

Rub the blood off your palms, and don't be a coward. You were going to marry a soldier, remember, who died a hero's death.

Drag a comb through your hair, put on a cheerful face; get your voice right. Don't get excited. I shan't tell Mummy about Sam; she'll only have a fit—I mean she'll—oh, what a beast I am.

Of course she'll fuss, she loves me, doesn't she? I'm all she's got, aren't I?

She tells me so often enough. (Shut up, you beast.)

She jerked down the cuffs of her silk shirt, straightened her jacket, kicked off her small muddy brogues and slipped on the pretty indoor shoes; yes, that was better. She gently adjusted her skirt so that the pleats were level at her sides, and walked gracefully and steadily out of the room.

"Darling! Are you all right? Mary says you're scratched— Angela! It looks really *bad*, dear—hadn't I better get Doctor Sanderson?"

Mrs. Mordaunt was sitting in a deep chair by a beautiful bright fire where beech-logs burned. Her crêpe-de-chine dress was the same deep blue as her eyes, but its excellent lines were slightly muffled by a matching cardigan on which gleamed a sapphire brooch; blue was 'her colour'.

"I know I must look frightful, Mummy, but honestly it looks worse than it is. And look what I've got!" Gaily, Angela held up the best piece off Sam's wreath of honeysuckle; the bloodstained remainder she had hurled into the wastepaper basket in her room. "Couldn't resist it!"

"Delicious—let me smell." Angela, holding out the relic, carefully put it under her nose. "It must be the very last piece of the year, I should think—but tell me about it, darling, what happened?"

"Oh, nothing much." She managed, with an exertion of her last ounce of control, not to 'sink' or 'collapse' into the facing chair, "I was nearly home—had such a jolly chat with Lord Gowerville, up in the wood, but I'll tell you about that afterwards—and I saw that," nodding at the honeysuckle, which her mother had tenderly pinned to herself with the sapphire brooch, "and of course—I had to have it! It was growing along the top of the hedge."

Inside Angela, a voice shouted suddenly, "Give me my tea, can't you? I'm all in, I'm in awful pain, I hate everybody, *can't you give me my tea? Are you blind*?" Another voice said solemnly, *Don't be a beast*, as she leisurely took the cup held out to her.

"Well, I got over a ditch—" she sipped her tea, "and I slipped, and had to hang on to the hedge—and it was mighty thorny, I can tell you! And then after a bit I managed to scramble down somehow—oh, it *was* killing, Mummy!"

She managed to swallow a mouthful of tea before she began to laugh.

"My hat fell off into the ditch. It's *sopping*. I brought it home in my pocket."

"You surely didn't come home without a hat, Angela?"

"No fear—well, it wasn't exactly a hat, of course, but I—I tied my scarf round my head and under my chin. I must have looked awfully odd, but—"

"Where did all this happen, dear?"

"Oh just—just before you g-get to Binneys." Angela was bolting bread and butter; she could feel strength flowing into her from the old, simple taste, "you know that long hedge—"

"I do hope no one saw you, darling." Mrs. Mordaunt was bending her head, with its knot of black hair that rippled so seductively over her rather large ears, above the cake-stand, in all the seriousness of choosing between Pearl's Sand and her Madeira, "because you know how gossipy cottage people are."

"Oh no, I'm sure no one did. That looks an awfully good cake— I'm going to be a real pig, this afternoon." She cut a thick slice.

"I expect you are hungry, after all that walking . . . darling, you know I understand perfectly about your going for these walks, and how you love to be alone with memories of your beloved— but—now you mustn't be hurt, dearest—I'm only saying it for your own good—don't you sometimes feel, just a little, that perhaps you are getting a little, well, *older*, for these rambles? I do sometimes feel that some of our friends think it's just the least bit eccentric."

Old maids are always half-dotty, screamed the voice inside Angela. The part of her that understood why the voice screamed told it coldly that, for once, it was wrong. She had always loved to walk alone, since she was a child. She did not go for walks alone because she was an old maid.

"Of course I'm not *hurt*, Mummy. But I honestly don't think people *do*, you know . . . Lord Gowerville was simply sweet to me— offered to carry my bunch—oh *lord*—all those heavenly ferns in the ditch, I must go back tomorrow and see if I can find them—"

"Where did you meet him, darling?"

"Up on the Long Ride, in Belshers. I say, this is jolly decent cake. Did Bessie make it?"

"No, dear; it came from that new place in Nethersham, The Tea Shoppe. And what did you talk about? (It's kept by two sisters—ladylike, rather than ladies, I think. But nice girls.) You must drive me in to tea there one day; they've got it arranged so prettily. But go on about Lord Gowerville, darling." Mrs. Mordaunt leant forward to listen.

Angela went on about Lord Gowerville, inventing a pleasant conversation that provoked no questions and no surprise, and omitting the 'my dear', which would have called forth both.

Sam Lambert wheeled his bicycle out from the hedge where he had leant it while he rescued Angela, mounted, and pedalled steadily away.

Whatever Mrs. Mordaunt's friends may have thought about Angela's rambles, Sam did not think the habit eccentric; he accepted it as a symptom of the well-known fact that old maids went queer in the head. Miss Angela was an old maid.

It seemed natural, to Sam, that he should find her half-crying and stuck in a thorn hedge at twilight in December. Other women, at that time, were putting the kids to bed or getting their husband's tea: old maids got stuck in hedges. Sam pedalled on, and his pipe, which was newish and filled with a tobacco with a rich smell named 'Redskin', glowed through the icy dusk.

Poor Miss Angela, mused Sam. It would make a good tale for them up at *The Swan*. Make them laugh all right, that would; her stuck up there with her legs showing, and squeaking like a kitten, and him coming up and her tumbling-like into his arms. He could hear the laughter.

Only—here was a queer thing. Miss Angela up The Beeches, an old maid, lost her young man in the war, going a bit funny because she weren't wed, people laughed when they said anything about her. That was one person. But here was the queer thing. That woman who had fallen into his arms in the twilight, she was all soft, and she smelled sweet, and she was quite different from Miss Angela up The Beeches who would never see thirty-five again and was going a bit funny-like.

He pedalled carefully round the curve that led past Catts Cottage. The windows were glowing, and he could see someone moving about behind the curtains in the red light of the fire. Black hair, yes; but holding *her* would be like holding a wooden plank.

The days drew on towards Christmas, and still Sam had not made them up at *The Swan* laugh over the tale of how he rescued Miss Angela.

The first winter that Ivy spent at Catts Cottage, snow and hard frost came in at the end of December and stayed, unbroken, for a month.

She made few gestures in the direction of Christmas, which she looked on as an interruption of the procession of her ordinary days. On the morning of December 24th, the postman, having clapped his hands together and stamped his feet, handed her three Christmas cards.

As he did so, he peered over her shoulder, where she stood on the doorstep with birds hopping and squabbling about her feet, into the cottage; a delicious breath of warmth came out from the red fire eating the silver logs. Neb lay beside the hearth, his nose on his paws. The postman peered more keenly, and he saw in the dimness a pair of claws, the rosy-purple colour of campion-flowers, gripping the edge of the mantelpiece, and he caught the shine of a cold eye above an arching neck.

"Got a pigeon in there, missus," observed the postman, abandoning, at the sight of that eye, any hopes of refreshment.

"Tell me somethink I don't know," said Ivy caustically, slipping the cards into her apron pocket, "that's Cooey."

"Does he live indoors, then, missus?"

"Since the snow come, 'e does. Any objection?"

"So long as I h'aint got to have him." The postman turned away. The stories about George Coatley's great-niece were true, then. "Messy things, birds."

"Merry Christmas," Ivy called after him, without good nature, as he trudged off through the snow.

Having addressed the birds fittingly, she shut the door and sat down at the table and took out her Christmas cards.

The one from Nobby had a pudding and some candles on it; she liked its gilding and colours, and stood it up where she could look at it from time to time. Next, there was a picture of a fox running off with a goose, from Miss Green.

Helen had gone to some trouble to find a card with secular animals, for she knew that any pleasure Ivy might feel in the Ox and the Ass would be spoilt by their counting as religious: Helen, not a Christian at that time, understood how she felt.

"Cooey," observed Ivy, as she picked up the third card, "you leave that wasp alone; he ain't dead, he's asleep. You like your bit o' shut-eye, don't you? Well, then."

Cooey left it alone, but fluttered down on to the table, where he put his beak confidently into the jam.

"Well I never. Win. Keeps on, don't she?" muttered Ivy, studying a gaudy picture of a coach and horses two-thirds buried in snow, "should think we've got enough snow, outside . . . *now* what's she after?"

She turned the card round, read *Raphael Tuck* on its back with concentration, then repeated slowly under her breath the rhyme printed inside:

> "When Yuletide cheer is on the board
> And snow is deep outside
> Then we recall the days of old
> And friends far off beside!"

"She may. I don't." Ivy balanced the card for a moment, then shied it unerringly across the room into the fire. "Good riddance to bad rubbish . . . afraid o' dawgs, don't like insecks . . . she won't come 'ere. *I'm* safe enough . . . now oo's that, nosying about?"

The impudent, exciting sound made by a motorcycle engine had just ceased outside. It was followed by an ill-tempered knock on the front door.

"Stone," Lord Gowerville had said to his agent, an hour or so earlier that morning, "are you going up to town by train or on that thing of yours?"

Lord Gowerville meant Mr. Stone's new B.S.A., which could do eighty when aroused.

"By the old bus, sir. I have inspected the road and I'm pretty sure she'll make it. Though, of course it's in a shocking state."

When Mr. Stone said *the* road, he meant the ancient track previously mentioned, by which The Hall could be approached in a comparatively civilised manner instead of, as Mr. Stone expressed it to his intimates, sweating through those damned woods.

"I am aware of that, thank you . . . will you be so good as to drop a turkey in on Mrs. Gover for me? It is on your way, and I should like to express a little of my gratitude for what she has done for Milo."

"Of course, sir. Delighted."

"Hench will have it ready for you at the Lodge."

Blasted errand boy, now, was Mr. Stone's thought, as he bumped over the snowy ruts with a goodish-size pale lilac turkey banging on the carrier. He would have a decent Xmas vac. with his people, of course; but Mrs. Threader had been right; he would not see twenty-eight again, and where was the rich girl he was to marry? He'd sooner marry old Coral than anyone, come to that, but her old man, though nicely off, wasn't what Mr. Stone called *rich*; not rolling; not oozing the stuff at every pore, so to speak, and anyway he'd have to die, first, wouldn't he?

About five hundred quid. Say a thou. That's what Coral would get when she married, and probably that would include the blasted wedding, and meanwhile, here he was running about the country with turkeys.

Hence the ill-tempered knocking.

Ivy opened the door with her usual regal swing, and a no-expression face.

"Good morning, Mrs. Gover, His Lordship has very kindly sent you this—" here Mr. Stone dragged the turkey off the carrier by snapping the confining string and thrust it at her—"Oh—and—here—" he fumbled with a leather-gloved hand in his pocket, failed to find what he wanted, swore, and had to tear off his glove to get at an envelope. "Here, take it, my good woman, take it, I can't hang about here freezing."

"Thank you. Sir." Holding the icy mauve object under one arm and the envelope in her other hand, Ivy stood in silence while he kicked at the starter, and the B.S.A.'s angry cough began to splinter the exquisite frozen quiet. "A Merry Christmas. Sir," she added, and then, stepping deliberately over her threshold and taking a few paces into the garden, she stood gazing up at the neatly-mended thatch. With her arms folded: the householder triumphant.

Mr. Stone's glance just followed hers, as he rushed away, and he looked no better-tempered as a result.

"There," remarked Ivy to Neb, as she came indoors, "telling me *I* got to pay for 'aving a bit o' new straw put in me roof, young Mr. Buzz-Saw. Now let's see what this 'ere is."

It was a card from the Lord, with a sort of a shield on it and a dragon, and some foreign words. And some writing inside—"Wishing you a Merry Christmas, with best wishes from Percy Gowerville and Milo." Ivy's face changed, in a grim smile.

She studied the turkey. "Shan't fag with no stuffin'," she decided at last, and began to tie up the legs to the sides with a grubby piece of string before thrusting it into an arctic cupboard. "You and me'll 'ave a feast, Neb, that's what we'll 'ave, and we won't forget the foxes. Nor the badgers nor the rabbits neither, will we?"

15

QUENTIN Henderson strongly disliked the sensation of being a fool. It was the conviction that no one who was attached, even to the fringe, of the Bloomsbury Set could imaginably be thought of as one, that had first drawn him towards the lustrous band which had had its first flickers and sparklings at Cambridge.

In the case of Pearl Cartaret, he knew that he was being a fool. It was actually idiotic, for instance, to have hoped that she might be at church on Christmas morning, because she had told him that she wouldn't.

He had taken to 'dropping in' for tea at the Shoppe (oh, that dreadful 'e') two or three times a week, just to see her, not always to talk to her. The fascinating lispy voice (accent just not quite all it should be), the hair, the eyes, the walk across the shop as if she were a priestess approaching a shrine . . . he learnt that he could bicycle off to Evensong quite content, if he had only been able to look at her. Perhaps a little more content.

It was idiotic to expect a girl's mind and conversation to match her face.

"Tewwibly cold, isn't it?" and the smile. Pearl; pearl-teeth, and that tiny crooked one!

No, they would not be at Nethersham at all, over Christmas, the shop was only a hobby; they could shut it for four days if they wanted to, and Daddy had promised to treat the family to Christmas at a really gorgeous hotel in Brighton. (Servants got bolshier and bolshier and spoiled everything.) So he would not see the black soft hat shaped like a helmet, and the white neck muffled in a collar of black fur, and the face that suggested lilies of the valley and mistletoe and all pale fairy things, in church on Christmas morning.

The vicarage seemed to him to be growing darker and grubbier and more uncomfortable every week, and poor Mrs. Marzarin's cooking more dramatic (Italian, of all things! Part of her liking for opera, no doubt) and less eatable.

In his mind's eye there was a small bright picture, like one seen in the reverse end of opera-glasses, of the interior of Sunset Cottage, where he and that little bounder Stone had once been invited to Sunday tea, the girls staying on over Saturday for the occasion. Chintz with large roses; water-colours of Venice by aunts; novels by Hugh Walpole; mild jokes; wit and passion and learning a million light-years away. But everything so fresh, so cheerful, so unmalicious (was one ever completely free from that faint brassy taint of malice, in the Bloomsbury fringe?) so—Pearl-ish.

Foolish; Pearlish; that *e*; and the voice not quite right but— oh! Pearl. Well, it was going to be the birthday of Christ, and he had better pull himself together.

*

The Mordaunts, he noticed, were at Matins on Christmas morning; Mrs. Mordaunt looking, perhaps, a little too groomed and ripe for eyes that had told themselves, over the years, that they preferred a more intellectual type of beauty; and the poor girl dressed, as usual, like her brother except for a skirt, with her hair all over the place.

Women should be careful about such details. Mrs. Mordaunt's dark furs and her dark beret worn with a splendid diamond clip and the perfect wave of dark hair under it, were a pleasure to look at.

The church was full. The decorations were more than successful; they were a triumph of gleaming dark green and scarlet against the ancient grey stones, and Lady Beresford had sent huge white chrysanthemums from her hothouses. The choir sang its best under the fierce eye of a young organist who hated everything except music. Quentin Henderson should have been filled with the love of God and His glory.

His heart ached because Pearl was not there and because he was making a fool of himself.

He preached a good sermon, he knew, that Christmas morning; touching both on unemployment and the necessity for giving in charity at this season to those less fortunate than ourselves . . . the words came out smoothly, easily, in the light, civilised voice . . . and how is it going to end? the speaker was thinking while he talked; already I want to touch her, just as a child wants to touch something pretty; instinct, mere instinct; I can get along perfectly well with my stipend and Uncle Hubert's legacy, but she would want . . . great heavens, I cannot, I *cannot* be thinking about *marriage*?

And why isn't she engaged? She must be twenty-three or four. One would have thought . . . *why* hadn't she been, as it were, snapped up?

From the moment that he had known that she was, apparently, to be had, he had become . . . *wary* was not a pleasant word.

No, it was not. But was there any good reason why, because of a child's instinct to touch, common-sense and prudence should be put aside completely?

"And now to God the Father . . ."

Angela strode slowly—if such a gait can be pictured—out of church behind her mother, catching the jolly tail-end of Christmas greetings exchanged with that beautiful and perfectly-groomed one. She wanted, yet feared, to catch a glimpse of Sam Lambert.

Was he as tall, and as fine a figure of a man, as she saw him in memory?

She glanced cautiously round Mummy's rich black sealskin towards the back of the church, where the cottagers always sat. There he was, the tallest among those mostly bowed figures, with shoulders well held, clutching a new cap, coming after a dumpy old woman wearing a black and purple bonnet above a cross red face.

The card *must* be from him. It was silly of her to pretend that it could be from anyone else.

"A Merry Christmas from S.L."

It was such a pretty card, thick with glittering frost and crimson berries and green leaves; she had it here, with her, safe in her bag. There had been no trouble at all about its arrival, for she had happened to be in the hall when the postman came, and she had sorted them into two heaps because Mummy did so dislike having her letters mixed up with anyone else's (if Angela had to pretend to be a jolly boy of twenty-four, Mummy showed many of a child's traits without having to pretend at all)—and there, the last of them all, was the envelope addressed to herself—with a penny halfpenny stamp, and sealed.

So that no one should see it except herself. Like a secret between them. The writing was clear and firm; not educated, but what did she expect?

The nice clean-minded boy that Angela had to pretend to be said that it was pretty good cheek of a farm labourer to send her a Christmas card; the boy was a decent chap, of course, and treated everyone decently, but naturally he expected cottagers to know their place. Angela, however, who lived shrinkingly alongside this slangy, cheerful creature, said—and as she said it she could feel her soft voice rising to that other, shocking, screaming voice—Angela said defiantly that it was sweet of Sam.

She cowered behind Mummy, forgetting to stride and to look jolly, because the two Mummys, with their son and daughter behind them, were drawing nearer to one another as the crowd moved slowly towards the door, and in a minute he and she would be face to face.

"Mummy—" she said, and was horrified to hear the word come out in a gasp.

"Yes, darling? (Good-morning, Lady Beresford—thank you for your charming card—and to all of you, of course) what is it?"

"Sorry, but I don't feel awfully well—I think I'll charge on ahead, if you don't mind."

"Of course, darling—sure you'll be all right? It *was* terribly stuffy this morning—I noticed."

Angela nodded dumbly, under her animal-pursuing kind of hat, and began to push her way through the crowd.

It had been a fatal move. Her route brought her out right in face of old Mrs. Lambert and Sam, now nearly at the church door.

What a dreadful, common-looking old woman—but Sam's shoulders were as broad as Angela had imagined, and then the most awful thing happened; he happened to be looking at her at the precise instant she was looking at him, and he *winked*.

It was the tiniest movement of his right eyelid, and it was unmistakable. Disgusting, said the clean-limbed youth stoutly, he knows I'm a lady; Angela, amidst a great shock to which she could give no name—it was plain shock—Angela wanted to giggle and wink back.

Disgraceful, said the young man, asserting himself; it's because I—I fell on him and he *clutched* me . . . the kind of thing he'd do to a *servant* on a *Saturday night* . . . winking. Mummy simply wouldn't believe it. Peter would have knocked him down . . .

She ducked her head on to her chest (the term always used by her dominating companion) and pushed her way onwards through the crowd, muttering excuses and encountering several surprised glances.

Out into the winter sunlight, that seemed to threaten, this morning, with its wild, still, piercing brightness, and across the snowy church-yard.

She opened the door of the car and scrambled into the driver's seat and leant back trembling, with thudding heart.

She did not look towards the churchyard again but kept her eyes fixed on the cold, snow-laden, dark boughs of the great yew that was said to be a thousand years old, yet she saw him come through the door, out of the corner of her eye.

There came her mother's voice, soft yet carrying perfectly over the still air, "Angela! Dear! Can you bring the car over? I *can't* walk through the snow."

Angela put her shaking hands on the steering wheel and set her foot on the accelerator. The car began to move.

The necessity for keeping her mind on what she was doing helped to give her control and to change her mood, but unfortunately it only changed to one of the bitterest self-condemnation. What kind of a woman—what kind of a lady—shook and felt faint because a farm-labourer had winked at her?

Worse—what kind of a lady had felt that impulse to giggle and wink back?

What would Peter, who had *worshipped* her, have said?

Why was she making such a frightful fuss about, really, absolutely nothing?

"Angela?" Her mother, now settled at the back, was leaning forward anxiously, bringing a waft of violets. "You're looking quite extraordinary—are you all right?"

"Don't worry, darling—I'll be all right in a minute. It was only the heat."

They drove away.

It had been unwise, it had been most imprudent, to say "We often come here" to Ivy, when they had met her in the woods that day three weeks ago. But the sentence had come out naturally; she hadn't meant . . . anything.

Helen was alone in her sitting-room on Christmas night, sitting by her fire, thinking.

'We', and 'often', words carrying a ring of permanency in them, a hint of that security for which Helen, without knowing that she did or using the word, longed with her deepest, strongest, suffering self. There was, to a wilful young male, the snapping home of the trap in their sound. So 'we' 'often' come here, do we?

Perhaps, in future, 'we' had better not go there 'often'; not go there at all.

Mr. Burke had not sent her a Christmas card to join the reproductions of paintings by Old Masters, and the one or two painted by artist friends, which stood on her mantelshelf. He had given her four handsome presents—for he was not mean with money, only with love—and kissed her with some enthusiasm while telling her that a family party would prevent his either seeing or telephoning her over the holiday, and then he had driven away cheerfully in his chariot.

Helen was haunted by the suspicion that if he had wanted to telephone her—seeing her, she admitted, would have been more difficult—no number of prosperous inquisitive visiting uncles and aunts would have prevented him.

She glanced at her presents ranged impressively on her table: the book of poems, the scent, the stockings, the gloves. Someone gave you all these handsome things, and you would so much rather have had—all you really dared to want—was something that they had said: to remember.

She sighed; she was good at sighing.

She looked at her small Christmas tree hung with nothing but spun-glass silver balls, where it glittered silently in the firelight.

Oh, what a way to love someone . . . oh, what a dull girl . . . no wonder Jocelyn . . . oh, what a Christmas night.

Five or six kinds of alcohol, perpetual yelling, and unceasing stimulus from lots of jolly, pretty girls, comprised Dickie Stone's idea of a good Christmas. Naturally, when once the B.S.A. had dealt with those damned ruts on that bloody awful road, he gave no further thought to Lord Gowerville, who would dine alone, with the menu that custom expects, with his old butler to hand the old silver. Mr. Stone was only too glad to forget The Hall for a few days, though he was ready to admit that the rooms he occupied there, while being 'out of the Ark', at least saved him a packet.

When he arrived in Golders Green, he had not been at home for more than fifteen minutes when there was old Coral on the phone, to tell him that Daddy had had a bit of luck on the Stock Exchange yesterday and had told her and Pearl they could each bring a friend with them to the Regalia! So would *he* come with *her*!

"*Won't* I?" was Mr. Stone's enthusiastic answer. Who was Pearl bringing? Oh, Pearl was peculiar lately; Coral really thought she had a yen for that parson with a face a yard long down at Nethersham, only she never *uttered*. Actually, she was bringing Betty Simmons. Red hair; probably Dickie didn't remember her.

Mr. Stone, who did remember Betty Simmons, said, no, he didn't, but they'd have a wizard time, and it was frightfully decent of Coral and Coral's governor, and please thank him most awfully.

So on Christmas morning, when most of the older residents of Brighton were just walking or driving home from church, the stuffier among them were provoked to comments about Bright Young People by the sight of Mr. Stone, Coral, Pearl, Betty Simmons and the two young men they had picked up in the Regalia bar snow-balling each other on the Front.

The breaking waves showed yellow foam against the dazzling snow; the sea was a cruel grey, and Coral was not only shouting, but sparkling like anything. Pearl, while defending herself against one of the young men who had resolutely set upon her from the first, was thinking about Mr. Henderson; what kind of a Christmas dinner would that awful woman cook for him?

"Oh, you *wotter*!" A snowball had gone inside her collar.

Seventeen Nelson Street, which was where Mrs. Threader, the person at The Tea Shoppe, lived, was, outside, a gem. No one thought of the little row of cottages, built when the Admiral was at the height of his fame, as eight architectural jewels in a row, because forty years ago their surroundings had not come to the squalid and unbelievable ugliness into which Nelson Street was later on to fall; and their rosy brick, bay windows, two white steps and comely slated roofs were taken for granted in a plain, dignified little street. Not quite cottages, not quite villas, were the eight little gems of Nelson Street. Mrs. Threader never described hers as either, referring to it always as 'my home'.

Mrs. Threader sat alone on Christmas night, sipping ginger wine. Everything demanded by Christmas was there; cards, paper decorations, mistletoe, holly. The two bedrooms upstairs were spotless, icy and, as to their furnishings, hideous; the small fire burned brightly, yet giving an effect of being controlled by some force, unassertive yet irresistible, beyond itself which gently compelled it to give up any attempt to roar or dance.

Mrs. Threader was alone in the sense that no other human being was present. But Monty was present.

Monty was—it was assumed—Mrs. Threader's cat, but in fact, though he may have been, he did almost as he pleased. The death of Mr. Threader, after forty years in the clerical department of the Water Board in Buckingham, had suited Monty to a *t*. No longer did a strongish hand lift him out of one of the two facing armchairs; now, in spite of twittering reproof heard faintly through dozy comfort, he could lie upon whatever bed he chose.

He did not habitually wet in the house, because, as Mrs. Threader explained, a tray had been provided for him from his kitty-wittyhood; but he knew that, should he prefer to do so, he would meet with no rebuke beyond a "Naughty Monty, but missis should have left the window open, shouldn't she?" (a rare action on Mrs. Threader's part, because she always remembered that time the elephant Got Free from the circus procession; also, earth tremors *had* been known in Scotland, and some poor soul had had their china nearly all broke; so it was more prudent to keep windows shut).

Monty was enormously stout, ambitious and comfortable, and Mrs. Threader was fairly comfortable; it was not in her nature to be quite anything. She did yearn towards a majestic, an irreproachable, an almost inconceivable social state which she called *'perfectly respectable'*, but the ambition to attain this state—and she was not completely certain that she had yet attained it—was the only note of the excessive in her nature.

She missed Mr. Threader, of course.

But, on the whole, she preferred being alone with Monty. Occasionally she might say to an acquaintance that she and Mr. Threader would have liked a Little One but it was not to be; and as children, like fires, are natural dancers and roarers, it was perhaps as well that no child had ever lived at 17 Nelson Street.

In dim, satisfied comfort sat Mrs. Threader and stout, Napoleonically-ambitious Monty (he hoped one day to have the house entirely to himself) and neither of them, of course, knew that seventy miles or so away, in Enfield, just outside London, an argument had that very moment taken place—well, words, it was, really, only words aren't a nice thing to have on Christmas Day—between Alice and Win Smithers, which was to affect profoundly the pattern of their days.

16

ONE evening towards the end of January, Ivy was standing beside her door putting out meaty bones, sopped bread and half-boiled potatoes for the creatures living in the woods.

Clouds lowered over the low hills and the beeches looked as if forged from iron against the pewter sky. The only colour in the frozen air was one dim scarlet streak in the west; the snow threw up a clear, eerie light to temper the creeping dusk.

"There." Ivy turned back to the cottage, "That'll keep some of you going fer tonight."

She shut the door. Cooey, Neb, and possibly the cockroaches gave to her entrance that attention given to such events habitual with those who have nothing in the world to do, and sitting down in the Windsor beside the table, having lowered the lamp, she lifted the hot glass chimney with her kettle holder, and blew out the flame.

Then she leant back and fixed her eyes on the window, from which she had drawn aside the curtains.

"Now we don't want no barks from you," she advised Neb in a low tone, "share and share alike's got to be your motter."

Slowly, the twilight came down. The beeches on the hill caught the last of the faint light, then drew into the shadows, faded, disappeared; then the curve of the hill behind their outliers went, and finally the broad climbing sweep of grass, now mantled in snow, lost its nature and became one vast strange glimmer in the freezing dusk. The hedge at the trackside opposite the cottage lost identity too; only the snow-wreaths along its surface gleamed. It was night.

Ivy sat on, still as the snow. Cooey slept; the fire burned in fierce ruby crystals, answering, in ancient obedience, to the law of the frost outside, though its soft yet savage glow and the warm wood and brick and straw of the walls and roof shut the frost safely away.

Ivy's eyelids moved. Something dark was creeping through that hole in the hedge where they always came; now it was crouching in the ditch, as if studying the faint glow coming from the windows.

It was so big! Too big for a badger, even: big and dark, a bent-up black thing against the whiteness frozen to the hedge, crouching.

But not big enough for a man, Ivy decided, measuring it with eyes whose sight was nearer to an animal's than human. She had no ideas about bears escaped from circuses, or about pigs; no circus could get within forty miles without everyone knowing of it; and as for pigs, they liked their comfort. In bed and asleep, pigs would be.

Neb lifted his head with a low growl, staring at the black window, and Ivy made a quelling movement with her hand, below the level of the sill and without taking her eyes from the motionless black croucher. The night was thick.

She saw a white blur, at last, at the top of the blackness—a face. Certain sure! A face—and it was moving towards the house.

She darted up, still in utter silence, motioning to the now fully alert, poised and quivering Neb—and almost leapt to the door.

She flung it open to the freezing darkness, and stood with the welcoming glow of the fire behind her—the very face and voice of Home—and called, not loudly:

"'Ere! Boy! Come in and get warm."

The boy, who had crossed the snow in one rush and was stooping over the pile of bones, stared at her. Eyes! Big as an owl's: that was the first thing she thought about him; she could barely see him, but they were huge dark holes in the white face.

She had called to him as she would to an animal, and though her voice had no country softness, it sounded warm as the glow of the fire behind her.

Now she stepped down over the doorstep and went across to him, crunching through the frozen snow with one hand gripping the snarling Neb's collar.

"There's a pigeon in there. Me and 'im and Neb—" she shook the collar admonishingly, though her tone kept its loving note— "we was just going to 'ave our supper." She came no nearer, but stood looking down at him, and so they remained, in the silent icy darkness, with the glow of the fire coming out from the cottage.

Neb, unable to endure jealousy an instant longer, leaped forward with a murderous growl. Ivy did not stir, but tightened her hold on his collar, and he choked and fell back.

"He's angry, bain't he?" said a hoarse voice suddenly, suggesting the croak of some night-bird. The boy stood up, hesitating, and ready—she could tell—to race off.

"'E'll get over it. You come on in, son." She turned back towards the door.

"I broke a winder," he said, not moving. "You'll tell on me, you wull, missus."

"Not me. You break all the windows you want . . . 'ere, let's get a light, shall we? Can't see a thing."

Her tone was casual now, and domestic. She did not look back as she re-entered the cottage, but she did look down steadily at Neb, who whined, cringed, but turned again to the boy.

"The dog'll 'ave me, missus!"

"No 'e won't. You let 'im smell you—that's their way o' making their minds up."

She occupied herself with re-lighting the lamp, not once glancing up from what she was doing, and as the bluish flame soared and flared, then dwindled to a soft, steady glow, she was enclosed by its light and could see nothing beyond.

"'E's a-smelling me!" came a croak out of the blackness.

"That's all right—you let 'im be, then you come on in."

She went across to the arctic larder previously mentioned, a cupboard with a small window covered in zinc wire which opened direct on to the small garden and the fields at the back.

She felt as she did while luring some suspicious bird or animal to her hand; all her will turned upon calling it, yet she also felt love, so strong that it could override the desire for the creature to come. *Don't come if you don't want to*, was how Ivy would have described this state of mind, in the unlikely event of her being asked to describe it; *don't you come unless it's your very own wish, beauty.*

Another moment, and movements at the door brought from her a casual turning-round, where she was busy at the shelves. They were both in; dog and boy; *he* was about eleven, she judged, corpse-white and them owl's eyes was the bluest blue she had seen in all her life, and his hands were another blue, kind of a purple, more, and he wasn't in rags. His boots were good boots, too; stout and newish.

"Neb, you take 'im to the fire," she said, carrying some tins and a lump of dripping and some sausages over to the table; Neb interpreted this by flopping down on the hearth and putting his long gold and white head along his paws, with a sigh.

"Roo-coo," sleepily, from the mantelpiece; a summer sound.

"You got any more animals, missus?" asked the boy, who was standing by the fire now, rubbing his hands together and staring sleepily into the red crevices, as if mesmerised.

"I got mice. They'll be out presently. And rats, I got. But they mostly keeps outside and shares with the foxes and the badgers. And there's cockroaches, down there at the back and some wasps asleep up there in the warm by Cooey."

He moved nearer to the fire, still rubbing his hands, then suddenly slid to the floor beside Neb and half-lay there, looking intently at the dog. Neb endured this for a little while, then turned his head away uneasily, blinking. The boy too glanced away; towards the pan, where the dripping was beginning to sizzle. A savoury smell floated out into the room, setting the seal on an ancient, rough comfort and safety that was old, old as Man. The cold and darkness outside were only memories, making the moment warmer, when the nostrils breathed in that smell; caves and roasting mammoth flesh were in it. Ivy slapped her one knife and fork on to the table.

"*You'll* 'ave to use fingers," she observed, "I ain't got but one knife and fork. Did 'ave two but—they went. Some'ow."

"At home," said the boy, rolling over a little from where he now lay at full length, "we had knives and forks. My real 'ome, I mean."

Ivy nodded. "Ah. You was a fambly. You want knives and forks where there's a fambly. Me and Cooey and Neb's a kind o' fambly, o'course, but I'm the only one what needs a knife and fork. We'll 'ave tea . . . you fill up the kettle, please." She shook the sausages, browning and spluttering in the tin.

"Where's the water, missus?"

"In that there pail under the sink." She moved her head towards it.

"Ba'int you froze up?" he asked, beginning to pull himself up; he's as tired as he can be, she thought.

"Froze-up! No, we ain't froze up—got a well out at the back, we 'ave, six feet down that water is, all with ferns growing round the top—frost can't get down there."

He dipped the railwayman's kettle, at which he looked with the acute but momentary interest he had given to Neb, into the bucket, and brought it across to her. The huge blue owl's eyes met her own for an instant as she took it from him; they had no expression, just heaviness, as if he were sleepy.

"Best wash your 'ands," said Ivy; in not mentioning that they were smeared with half-frozen fragments of meat and potato, she used tact, of which she had never heard.

He went without protest to the little, pitted dark stone sink and, dipping a cup from the draining board into the bucket, washed his hands thoroughly on Ivy's lump of yellow Sunlight and dried them on her clean old rag of towel.

Been brought up proper, thought Ivy, watching the blue kettle as it sat on the logs and ready to snatch it off the instant before certain hysterical symptoms became imminent—an instant she could judge from years of experience with the blue kettle—but I never seen a boy wash the minute you told 'im before, 'e must be feeling right down, to do that.

"Sit down," she said, "the kettle's boiled."

She poured water into the teapot, and seated herself, and they began to eat.

She gave him her own share of the sausages and six slices of fried bread, making her own meal off two slices and a lump of cheese which she toasted on a skewer. The smell brought out the mice to dart about and sniff, and she noticed how the boy watched them throughout the meal and his three cups of scalding tea.

They finished with two apples apiece from Ivy's store of windfalls in the smaller bedroom; then the boy tossed the second core deftly across the room, still in the silence that had not been broken throughout the meal. He's an old-fashioned article, thought Ivy, not one of your jabbering sort.

At last, he looked full at her, out of the heavy owl's eyes.

"I'll stay 'ere a bit," he said hoarsely, "if you like."

"Suits me," said Ivy, with complete truth, "but won't you 'ave the Inspector after you? Didn't you ought to be getting your schooling? 'Ow old are yer?"

"Twelve on St. Valentine's Day."

"Twelve, are yer. I'd finished with schooling, time I was eleven."

"There won't be no Inspector after me, missus. No one don't know where I got to, see."

"You run away from 'ome, then?"

He hesitated, keeping his eyes fixed on the playing, darting mice.

"I got two 'omes, like," he said at last, "we used to live down the lane, at Bury's. Then they put the rent up, and my dad he couldn't pay it, couldn't get enough work, and—and then me mum, she died, so my dad he took me and my sister off to Portsmouth where me auntie lives. So I—I—"

"All right, all right now," Ivy turned away her eyes from the dirty fair head lowered into the grubby red muffler, "you run away from Portsmouth and come back 'ere to 'ave a look at your old 'ome—and you bin 'iding there. 'Ow long?"

His head came up. "I wasn't 'iding. That's my 'ome, that is. I broke a winder and got in. It's our winder, ba'int it? But—it's all different inside now, with a barfroom and everythink, like it was gentry living there, someone else bought it, I reckon. There was two young ladies—I 'id in the shed most days—but they went 'orf in a little red motor."

"Them two keeps the tea shop in the village," commented Ivy, looking at him thoughtfully, "so that's it. You run away. And 'ow about your dad? 'Ow's he feeling—do you reckon?"

She thought how she would feel, if Neb or Cooey ran away, and she remembered, too, how she had felt that first year, after Stan had been blown up in the Royal Navy.

There was no answer. He stared down at the table.

"Is 'e all right, your dad?" Ivy asked, leaning forward.

"He's all right, my dad." The answer was touched with the indignation she had hoped to hear.

"Don't belt you?"

"Don't use a belt to neither of us. Smacks my ass if I done anything what *he* thinks real bad. Don't never smack my sister's ass."

"'E sounds all right, your dad," said Ivy.

"'E *is* all right." He resumed his study of the mice, but his eyelids were drooping, and when at last he turned to her his voice was slurred with drowsiness.

"You got any paper?" he demanded.

"That's out the back—" Ivy began, but he shook his head impatiently.

"I done that before I came out, proper, at 'ome; paper to draw on, I meant. And you got a pencil?"

"There *was* a clean paper bag, somewhere and I did 'ave a pencil, but—" Ivy was really surprised, now, and staring.

"Don't matter." He got up and went over to the hearth and, stooping, selected a small stick with a charred end, "Where's the bag?"

Ivy found it, rolled into a ball in a corner. It was not large, and as it had contained the sausages it was stained with grease.

He studied it, as if weighing its potentialities; then sat down at the table again, pushing the plates aside. "Got a bit o' something flat? Cardboard'll do."

"There's me pastry board. I don't 'ardly never use it, but I 'ave got one."

"That'll do."

So he knew about pastry-boards; this was no beggar-child. Course, Bury's was a decent place where decent people had lived, otherwise gentry wouldn't have bought it. The Lord owned it, most like. They had been saying down at *The Swan* about him putting up rents all round.

She got up and after some searching found the board propped up against the wall near the outposts of the cockroaches' country, and gave it to him. He settled it on the table and spread out the paper bag, first carefully smoothing its creases. Then his head went down, and in a moment the bit of charred wood began to move in his hand.

The mice were still playing about the hearth. Twice, during ten minutes or so, he looked across at them, pausing, with the stick poised. Then his head went down again.

Ivy sat still. At first she did not watch him, simply because she knew that animals who lived with man became uneasy if persistently watched, and a boy might be the same; but gradually she became charmed by his bent fair head and large lowered eyelids and fore-shortened face, and the movements of the blackened stick in his hand, large for his age, with surprisingly strong-looking fingers.

The soft, brilliant light from the lamp held them all: Ivy, the boy, Neb and Cooey and the drowsy red and grey fire, as if in a golden frame, and Ivy's alarm clock seemed to tick with a sound less emphatic than usual. The warm air was solemn; something was being made.

He put the stick down, and held the paper bag out to her at arm's length.

"There," he said, and continued to hold it until she got up and came over to him.

She looked at it for quite a long time, perhaps three minutes, while he watched her face.

"Well!" she said at last. "Well! It—it *is* the mice!"

He nodded.

"Dancing. Look at them tails! Well—I never saw." She became absorbed in it again.

"Like it?" he asked at last, casually, and as Ivy nodded, "It's for you," he said, and brilliantly smiled.

"Thanks," said Ivy, "very much," she added.

The thought passed across her mind of showing gratitude for his present by taking 'Reunited' out of its frame and replacing it with the mice. Then she glanced at the mice on the hearth.

"Mind you—" she pronounced, "*them's* better," and at once she knew that although she might like to look at the drawing from time to time, even, perhaps, show it to the Lord, she did not want to have it on the wall. It was not that she preferred 'Reunited'; she simply did not want a picture of mice when she could watch the real ones.

He was staring at the mice, serious again now; and it was difficult to remember how his face had looked with the blazing smile.

"'Course the real ones is better," he said at last, "they always is." His voice was lower, and lifeless.

"I'll keep this," Ivy promised, with some vague wish to cheer him up, and she put it away in a drawer containing two skewers and a piece of string, "here, you give me a 'and with these crocks."

She was a darter, rather than a bustler. Now she darted at the table and began to snatch up greasy plates. "Get a move on, son."

Instinct told her to give him something to do. She had never had much to do with boys of his age, but with animals, unless they was asleep, they was always *doing* something, specially the young ones. An idle animal—except for cats—was an ailing one.

They whisked and clattered through the task without a word. The clock said nine.

Ivy swept a ball of newspaper across the table, shining from years of those papery rubbings.

"My mum used to sew or knit, evenings," he said suddenly, looking round at the quiet, tidied room.

Ivy shook her head. "Never had the patience. I'll find you some more bags, and you make your drorins for half an hour, and then we'll go to bed. I'll watch the cockroaches."

"And I'll draw them," he said, eager once more, and they both settled to their work in the warm silence. Presently, Ivy suggested bed, and he lifted his head from his arms with a start.

She made him dash his face with cold water, and clean his teeth with soap and his finger. He was a beautiful boy, and had not yet begun the adolescent's shyness. She wrapped him in half an old blanket and dragged out her mattress from behind the door.

"Good night," he said, standing by the banked-up fire with the brown folds draped over his thin white body, and looked up at her silently.

Ivy stooped quickly and took him in her arms and hugged him, with a great, firm kiss.

"Goo'night, boy. Now you go to sleep."

He got on to one side of the mattress, and stretched, sighed once, and was off. Ivy noiselessly slipped out of her clothes into an immense nightgown made of Locknit, and let Neb out for five minutes into the snow, and stroked his chilled fur when he came back.

She lay listening for a while, with her fox's or badger's ears, to some creature busy with the bones outside. Then she too slept.

17

IN THE morning, at seven o'clock, the boy was still sleeping.

Ivy, awakening, glanced at the black window and saw the ghostly half moon dying down behind the beeches; she could feel, in herself, the frost girding the woods, the cowering hedges, the furrows frozen to iron. Creeping from under the covers, she let Neb out for his run, and stood there for a moment, shivering but not heeding it, while she drew in the pure black crystal air.

Bones is all gone, she thought. Nippy, this morning.

The boy had rolled over towards the glow from the fire, which was almost out, but when she knelt beside it to pack the sunken ash with fresh logs, he sat up, suddenly wide awake, as children often awaken.

"'Ullo."

"'Ullo. You get yerself washed and dressed and give me a 'and."

After their breakfast, eaten in an easy silence, he helped her to wash up and tidy the room, then sat down again by the fire and watched Neb and the cockroaches. His eyes still looked heavy. Ivy climbed the stairs to the larger bedroom and found her thickest muffler and a pair of boots even stouter than those she usually wore.

"I'm goin' out," she announced, "comin'?"

"Me froat hurts," was the answer.

"Best stay in, then. Keep warm. There's wood there—you keep the fire up. Come on, Neb," and Ivy was off.

Let him lie up warm and quiet and he would soon be better.

She took the road to Bury's; this was the only name the large cottage, in its half-acre of ground, was known by, for Burys had lived there for two hundred years and more; they had been there when she was a little girl. My boy's grandad, that was, him as I remember, she mused, marching through the wicked black frost over the frozen snow. May as well 'ave a look at the place.

She already thought of him as her boy; Mike, his name was.

But when she came round the turn in the lane that put Bury's in view, she stopped, and stood still. A little red car and a motorcycle stood in front of the cottage, and she heard voices. She motioned Neb to her side, and walked on.

As she drew nearer, she could hear what the voices were saying, because they were loud with excitement and dismay and the front door stood open. If Helen Green had been there, she would have been reminded of another and more famous conversation.

"Whoever it was *lay on my bed* . . . look at those marks . . . boots!"

"Oh, Dickie, I'm so glad you came past! Isn't it *cweepy*?"

"Don't you worry—I'll soon land him a good one if he does turn up," said young Buzz-Saw's voice, full of manly energy, and Ivy made a face.

"He's opened one of our tins! Baked beans . . . what cheek!" from the back of the cottage, and more faintly, "good thing we hadn't left much."

"Wonder he didn't light a fire."

"Good thing you had the wood locked up, Old Thing."

"Ve cushions are all cwumpled!"

"Oh, I'm always careful about locking up (Pearl's a bit of a scatterbrain, I must say). Daddy bought this place as an *investment*, not to have tramps breaking in and lolling all over our furniture . . . bugs, I shouldn't wonder . . . Oh, I say, this really is the limit, the snow's come in through that window. Look, Pearl. Look, Dickie. All down the wall, and it was only done six months ago. Daddy will be simply livid."

"Has he pinched anything?" Mr. Stone demanded; Helen would have thought that his voice had its fists clenched.

"Well—no—not so far as I can see. But there isn't much to pinch, really. Mummy said we weren't to bring down anything from home that was valuable."

"Jolly good sense." Dickie Stone's tone was respectful; he always remembered to suck up, even if it had to be only verbally, to girls' parents. You never knew when you might need their approval. "You furnished it with stuff from your own place, then?"

"Yes . . . Mummy's been saying for *years* we've got too much, and nowadays of course it's fashionable to have hardly *any* . . . what is it now, Coral?"

Ivy had loitered up the path between the overgrown currant bushes, still listening.

"I *said*, it must be reported at once—oh, would you, Dickie? Thanks."

"Rightee-o!" Mr. Stone cried, and at that moment Neb barked. He was tired of being kept to heel, and scolded for scratching up non-existent flowers, and the arrival of a long man on a bicycle gave him an excuse.

"Good morning, Mrs. Gover," said Quentin Henderson, alighting, "is something wrong? I saw a broken window as I came past at the back." (And was Pearl at home?)

Ivy was for muttering something and marching off, but Mr. Stone, hearing voices outside, looked out of the window, shouting:

"Hullo, there's the Padre! Morning, Padre! Come on in and give us a hand!"

At the same instant Coral caught sight of the retreating Ivy.

"There's that peculiar woman who used to work for a girl we know; she *owns a cottage* round here, if you please . . . I shouldn't wonder if it wasn't some shady pal of hers . . . *stop* her, Dickie!" she ordered rapidly.

"Hey! Mrs. Gover! One minute!" and Mr. Stone charged out of the house, fighting fit.

Ivy did not increase her pace, but paused, and half-turned. She looked at him, without expression.

"Don't run away, Mrs. Gover," Mr. Stone said, and his tone seemed to grasp her by the shoulder, "Miss Cartaret would like to speak to you. Come with me, please." He led the way back to the cottage.

Ivy did not mind any of this pantomime; her one thought was to prevent them nosying along to her cottage and finding out about her boy.

. . . That's it! She stared down steadily at Neb, as they approached the front door. It was now shut, Mr. Stone having been screamed at by Coral not to let in any more beastly draughts as he rushed out in pursuit of Ivy.

A moment, and Neb bounded away.

"Seen a rabbit," remarked Ivy.

"So long as it isn't a pheasant," snapped Mr. Stone, "Lord Gowerville is very severe indeed on poaching."

"I never 'eard of a dog poaching pheasants." Ivy was pleased with her retort, but did not smile.

Quentin opened the door, looking what she had time to dismiss as *soppy*.

"Come along now, hurry up, we mustn't keep the young ladies waiting."

Mr. Stone bustled her inside, carefully shutting the door behind them, and marched her into the low-ceilinged, white-distempered living-room.

"Good morning. Miss," said Ivy, addressing Coral; then directed towards Pearl what may be described as a respectful nod. Then she became markedly silent: not just waiting for the gentry to speak; silent.

Mr. Stone glanced at Quentin. But Quentin was looking at Pearl. So-ho, sits the wind in that quarter? thought Mr. Stone; he really did, although Coral had already told him that she thought it was sitting there. Feeling that it was up to him, as the practical man, to conduct the inquisition, he began:

"Now, Mrs. Gover. A few questions, if you please. And we'd like them answered truthfully."

A telling pause. What a bore the man is, thought Quentin; I wish they'd all go away. Mr. Stone continued:

"Now think carefully, please. Have you seen a tramp round here lately—these last few days, that is. Have you—er—*entertained* a tramp at all, lately?"

Pearl stirred in her chair, re-crossing her long legs, and Quentin controlled a smile. Coral was standing, with her dark eyes moving quickly from face to face.

"Funny you should ask me that. Sir," Ivy began, not too hastily, "I see one about the day fore yesterday. Saturday evening, it was. I was doin' the washin'-up" (as no one but Quentin had seen inside Catts Cottage since she moved in, a picture was presented of lonely womanhood engaged, amidst poor but decent surroundings, upon a humble domestic task. No one so much as dreamt of the cockroaches).

". . . and my dog starts barkin' 'is 'ead off. Thass someone outside, I thinks. Prowlin'," improvised Ivy, who did not mind an audience occasionally. "So I gets the dog by 'is collar and opens the door—and there's this 'ere tramp."

She paused, and plucked at her muffler as if overcome.

"Gwacious, Mrs.—er—Gover! Weren't you scared stiff?"

"I 'ad the dog. Miss. And he's a fighter. So I says, what do *you* want? and 'e pitches me some tale about bein' out o' work and walkin' from London—funny place to come to, the Warbys, for *work*, I thinks to meself—and all 'ow he 'adn't 'ad a bite to eat for two days, so I says 'e could come in and sleep by the fire."

"Very silly of you, Mrs. Gover," said Mr. Stone sternly, "you might have got yourself murdered."

"It was a bitter cold night. Sir. And I 'ad the dog, and the man looked weak-like. Starved, I reckon."

Quentin walked over to the window and looked out at the silent white and pewter landscape. Pearl's eyes followed him. He was feeling sorry for the tramp, and, though Daddy did always say it was people's own fault if they were poor, so was she.

"Well?" demanded Mr. Stone.

"I come down in the mornin'," (picture of a very clean apron and cautious, matronly descent) "and—" Ivy paused—"Gorn. Scarpered. *And* pinched me three spoons what I had left out of the set me Auntie Bessy gave me fer a wedding present," she ended impressively.

That really was a good bit, that was. Sounded so respectable. "Oh, what a shame!" cried Pearl, and Coral's expression became less like that of Nemesis. Spoons given as a wedding present were spoons given as a wedding present, however rubbishy. Wouldn't be silver, of course.

"I miss 'em. Having 'ad 'em about all these years," added Ivy, in a gruff voice more convincing than any whine.

"No doubt. But you brought it on yourself by being so foolish as to let him in at all," said Mr. Stone. He glanced round at the others. "All the same, I think we'll *just* go along to Catts Cottage and do a *leetle* detective work. Eh?" to Coral.

Ivy's mind now worked instinctively, as an animal's does under the press of fear.

"You ain't got no right. Sir," she said, sullenly, but beginning to move towards the door as if realising that it was hopeless to resist the will of the gentry. "I told you I seen 'im, and 'ad 'im in—what's 'e been doing? Broke in 'ere?"

She glanced round with precisely the right blend of curiosity, sympathy, and respect.

"Broke in, smashed a window, and . . ." Mr. Stone was beginning but then he realised that opening a tin of baked beans and eating them, crumpling some cushions, and leaving a dirty mark on a bedspread did not add up to a very imposing total. Fortunately, he remembered the smashed window.

" . . . *broke in*," he ended solemnly, "and Wet Snow has Blown In and Marked the Wall. Look!" he pointed, with drama. "Miss Cartaret's wall, distempered only a few months ago."

"Daddy's wall, really." Pearl got up from her chair, "Coral, I'm frozen. If you're going off detecting, I don't think I'll come."

"Rightee-o. P'raps you can get down to the shop, then; we ought to have been there half an hour ago."

"Oh, Mrs. Threader's there; she'll cope." Pearl turned away, hugging herself and shivering.

Quentin stood with his back to the window, and was silent. He knew that by not moving or speaking, by not adding one conventional remark to the unnecessary things being said, he was behaving with noticeable oddness.

"So-long—" called Coral, from the hall.

"Cheerio, Padre!" Not a sound from Mrs. Gover.

"Oh—er—good-bye. Good luck."

The front door slammed. Pearl stooped slowly, with straight back and the most beautiful movement, and picked up, from its place of concealment half under the sofa, a crumpled ball of paper. She began to smooth it out, keeping her eyes on her work.

"A fox," she breathed at last, "it's *vewy* good. I wonder who did it? Look." She held it out to him, from the place where she stood at the middle of the room. She did not look at him, and he came slowly to her side.

"Cowal's writing pad. Cheek, I suppose . . . but it's *awfully* good, isn't it? An artist-tramp, how killing!" and she gave a nervous little laugh as she glanced up.

"I am very much in love with you," said Quentin Henderson.

Pearl instantly looked down again. She stood very still, but one hand crumpled the sheet of paper and waveringly tossed five hundred and fifty pounds' worth of drawing into the ashes of the hearth.

"Did you hear what I said, Pearl?"

She nodded. She had day-dreamt about this moment. But the words had been different in the day-dream; all the others had said, "I love you."

"Well?"

"Well—what? You—you tell me—that—and then you just say—'well'?"

"I'm sorry—I haven't put it—the fact is, I'm in rather a state, you see. I wasn't—I can't—you see I don't know—"

This was more like it; Pearl began to feel some confidence; she even felt a small rush of happiness, as if she had taken a skip, and a peep over a mysterious solemn wall of some kind.

"It's the usual thing," she said, in a trembling voice, "when you say *that* to someone, to call them—something."

Quentin, too, was feeling more confident. The goddess, the lily of the valley, was rapidly turning before his eyes into an unusually pretty girl who, he suspected, was attracted to him. It was delightful; it was all that it should be; it was only taking him, naturally, a moment or so to get used to a new situation.

"Well, what does one call them?"

She shook her head, still looking down.

"'Darling'? Is that what one calls someone one's very much in love with?"

She looked up, then, and nodded.

"All right . . . darling. *Darling*. It sounds very pretty . . . do you know, I've never called a girl 'darling' before?"

"You *must* have!" cried Pearl, startled out of all feelings but surprise.

"No. It's true. I . . . never have."

"Don't look so sad," she said softly, giving the ordinary small word to the shade of guilty memory and shame that had fallen over his face; and she put out her hand and slid it into his.

And it must be true, she was thinking as she did so, because clergy-men don't tell lies.

By that long, chilly hand, soft and so sweetly scented, he drew her to him until she was resting against his heart. He had a distinct thought that it was a good thing to love a girl as tall as oneself, before he kissed her.

"Oh, I do love you!" she whispered, as she drew away from him at last, "but you—you haven't said it . . ."

"Is that one of the things one has to say, too?"

Strange, strange it was, how love came alive and waxed and strengthened, after a kiss.

"Well, *of course* . . . you weally are extraordinary!"

"Not that, my love—my love. I'm—just not—used to kissing, or being loved. Or—or loving."

"Poor darling," said Pearl, looking up at him rather solemnly, "but—please say it."

"I love you."

"Truly?"

"Truly."

"He hasn't said 'for ever', he hasn't said 'will you marry me' or 'let's be engaged', thought Pearl. (All the others did.)

"I know what we'll do," said Quentin, suddenly and cheerfully, "get your things on, d-darling, and we'll walk round to Catts Cottage and see that they aren't bullying Mrs. Gover."

"Alwight."

While she was arranging her scarf and furs, Quentin recovered the screwed up ball of paper from the grate and occupied himself, quite without being aware of his actions, with smoothing out the creases for the second time. As she said "I'm ready", he began to fold it, but he was looking at her. Then, suddenly, he saw the leaping fox, in his mind's eye and he looked at the paper again "Come on," Pearl said in a minute, "I'm fweezing."

18

I DONE it too quick, that about the tramp, thought Ivy, as she sat in the back of the little red car, into which, to Coral's indignation, she had nipped while Coral and Mr. Stone were absorbed in fussing with their respective chariots.

What's the harm with me having a newy stayin' with me? No reason why they should think anything, is there? So long as he ain't gone out of the place not wrapped up and 'im with a froat;—

now, Gawd, she added fiercely, if you want to show You means well by me, You get my boy 'idden safe somewheres, You make Neb tell 'im *somehow*, and *not* in the W.C., Gawd, because they'll look in there sure as eggs is eggs.

Mr. Stone followed Coral. As he drove, he was feeling such strong envy of her for owning that jolly little bus that he almost disliked his old Coral—and he had had to push the accelerator quite a bit to catch up with her, after a shame-making five minutes with the kick-starter that would not kick-start.

Coral steered the car with admirable judgement over ridges of frozen clay and the streaks of solid black ice lying between them; her sharp dark eyes were fixed upon the track, and she did not notice, as Ivy did, something slip through the hole in the hedge opposite the cottage, wrapped in an old blanket.

There's sense for you, thought Ivy proudly. He ain't like most boys. (This was a fact that became more obvious about Mike Bury as the years passed, and it may or may not have been for his good that, by the middle of the century, being unlike most boys was looked upon as the quality most desirable and exciting in the world.)

Neb was on the doorstep, barking.

"Wants 'is dinner, blessim," observed Ivy, who knew that gentry, especially ladies, expected that sort of thing to be said about dogs.

Mr. Stone now tut-tutted up, looking sulky.

"Hurry up, slow-coach!" rallied Coral merrily as she got out of the car: enjoying the frosty weather, enjoying the tramp-hunt, enjoying teasing Dickie Stone. She slapped her fur gloves together.

"Sorry; she just wouldn't budge. The cold, I suppose." Mr. Stone dismounted, and adjusted the mechanism that balanced the B.S.A. upon its little stand. He stood, sweeping a keen, Peter Wimsey-ish glance over the uncompromising landscape, with particular concentration upon the cottage's windows, until he noticed Ivy, who was fumbling in her jacket-pocket for the key.

"No, Mrs. Gover," cried Mr. Stone, advancing upon her, "you must allow me to go in first." He did not forget to keep up the frightening courtesy.

"Afraid I've got 'im up the chimney, are yer? Sir." Ivy asked, conversationally; she was quite calm, now that she knew her boy was not in the house, "in yer goes, then."

She swung back the door and stood aside, and Mr. Stone strode in, glancing sharply about him and then directing a piercing stare down upon the mattress, as if he expected it to rear up and bear witness.

Coral had followed, picking her way deftly over the ruts, and was now standing at the door peering in distastefully.

"*Don't* come in, Old Thing," cried Mr. Stone, "stay where you are. He may make a dash for it—I'm going upstairs!"

He marched to the door that concealed the staircase, wrenched it open, and began to stump purposefully upwards as fast as the almost perpendicular stairs would allow. Ivy put a log on the fire and told Neb that it wasn't dinner time yet so it was no use looking like that. A few large flakes of snow drifted past the door in the lowering light.

"Found 'im?" Ivy asked, when Mr. Stone had finished stamping about overhead and reappeared at the foot of the stairs.

"This is not funny, Mrs. Gover," said Mr. Stone, "you may be getting a visit from the police this afternoon."

He looked across at Coral, rosy-faced in her red coat and high black fox collar; a magazine-cover girl against the whiteness of the now rapidly falling snow. "Come in and get warm, Coral, while I start up the old machine . . . there doesn't seem to be anything here. I'll just have a dekko—er—round at the back."

"I could have told you that, and saved you and the young lady all that trouble. Sir," said Ivy, as he disappeared. A few moments passed.

Coral, who had been tempted by the fire, and was standing by it warming her feet, shrieked loudly.

"What—where—what is it—where is he?" Mr. Stone thundered as he reappeared, looking rapidly round in several directions.

"Not the tramp—*cockroaches*!" cried Coral, pointing in horror, "hundreds of them—behind the fire! I can't bear them! Oh, oh—let me get *out* of here!" She rushed out of the room into what was now a snowstorm.

"Cockroaches are a sign of dirt, Mrs. Gover," Mr. Stone almost shouted, turning to Ivy as he hastily followed. "I shall report this, of course, to Lord Gowerville . . . the tramp *and* these beastly insects."

"Very well. Sir," said Ivy. "Neb, you be 'ave yourself," as, aroused by Mr. Stone's loud tone, Neb uttered a terrible growl, "but don't trouble yourself about the insecks—he seen 'em. We was all in 'ere together, a few weeks ago."

The door slammed. Ivy went to the window and idly leant there, with Neb standing on his hind legs beside her, watching while the two figures, almost hidden by whirling snow, hastily started up their machines. Mr. Stone was telling Coral that he really must be getting back to The Hall, though, of course, the old boy didn't keep a check on his movements, as if he were in the bally Army, and could she 'manage', in this blizzard? He would phone the police. Coral replied smartly that she would be a fool if she couldn't, but also thanked him warmly for his help.

"Get a move on, damn yer," murmured Ivy, "my boy'll be freezing."

It seemed a long time until the car and the B.S.A. had got into movement and the ugly and irritating noise of their engines died away.

Gradually, the silence of winter came back to the scene, the whirling snow seeming, by its silent sweep, to add to the quiet. Ivy waited a few moments, then hung wide the door and gave a shrill boy's whistle.

Out of the white confusion stumbled a small snowman, blanketed in wool and whiteness, with a wicked red face laughing up at her out of the folds.

"Come on in with yer—come on in." She put an arm round his shoulders. "Neb tell you all right, then?"

"He come a-barking and a-barking, and then he fair pulled me outside." Mike dropped the snow-laden blanket from his shoulders on to the floor. "I don't know. I 'ad a sort of a feeling, like I had to hide. I reckoned the Inspector might be coming. So I run out and I got down in them bushes behind the hedge, under the leaves. There's dry leaves there. But I got dancing about to warm meself, and I'm as warm as warm. Feel!"

He gripped her hands in his, and, as she felt the blood running through them under his smooth child's skin, there came a loud knock on the door. They stared at each other almost in horror, so strong had their happiness and triumph been, and now—

"Mrs. Gover! Mrs. Gover! Are you there?" It was a shout, in a man's voice.

"It's all right, it's that Vicar. 'E ain't much, but he ain't so bad as some . . . best let 'im in." Ivy hurried to the door, while Mike sat down On the edge of the hearth, as if calmly deciding that he had hidden enough for one morning.

"May we come in?" Mr. Henderson did not wait for assent but stepped over the threshold, "It's too bad for Miss Cartaret to walk . . . Thank you." The fair one, as Ivy now thought of her, followed, looking around with calm interest.

"Perhaps," Mr. Henderson said quietly, "you could supply us with chairs," and Ivy, who was not looking pleased, dragged forward the Windsor and carelessly swirled it over with her apron. "Get a chair for the gentleman, Mike," she ordered, and Mike brought out the one with the sound seat from its corner. The unwelcome visitors sat down.

"And who are you?" Quentin asked him, so struck by the size and colour of his eyes, and a quality in their expression, that he omitted from his tone the patronage, even the kindness, he would have used to most cottage children.

Ivy opened her mouth, then shut it. So far, there had been no putting forward of Mike as 'my newy': and perhaps it was best to let the lie remain untold.

"Mike Bury." And he turned away and sat down on the hearth again and stared into the fire.

"Are you warmer now?" Quentin asked in an undertone of Pearl, who was looking grave.

"Oh, heaps warmer, thanks," and she smiled.

"Got caught in it, did yer?" observed Ivy, not from the motives inspiring a hostess, but because the Vicar might be wondering why Mike was not at school, "come on very sudden, didn't it?"

"It did indeed . . . have you a holiday from school, Mike?" said Quentin, turning to him.

"'E's got a bad froat," said Ivy loudly, at the same instant that Mike turned round, with a marked effect of facing his questioner, and answered deliberately:

"No, I ba'int on holiday. I—come away from my other 'ome. Come away after school one evening." He paused. "See?" he ended loudly.

"Ran away, you mean."

Mike nodded. "That's it."

"So 'e's stayin' with me," put in Ivy, "ain't you, Mike?"

"S'pose so." Mike turned away to the fire once more.

"Do you mind if I smoke, Mrs. Gover?" Quentin took out his case and paused, looking at her. Ivy said briefly, "Smoke away. Sir," and he smiled and offered the case to Pearl, who shook her head. The snow was coming down ever faster and thicker, and Ivy, seeing that there was little chance of the visitors leaving yet, and feeling the need for action, began one of her routine rubbings of the table with a ball of newspaper. "Gets a nice shine on it. Miss," she observed to Pearl, and Pearl smiled and nodded.

It was not about himself and Pearl that Quentin wanted to think while he smoked his cigarette. He could not do that here; he needed solitude. He really was resting, now, on the thought of Pearl, and he wanted and meant to continue resting: let the 'road wind uphill all the way' if it was going to, dammit; he was going to think about this child with the eyes, who had drawn a fox with the assurance and skill of a genius of forty. In a moment, he inhaled the last lungful of smoke, and stubbed out the cigarette into a saucer hastily shoved at him by Ivy.

"Thank you, Mrs. Gover. Mike—you drew this, didn't you?" He held out the crumpled sheet of paper.

Round came Mike's head. "Me fox!"

"I thought so . . . why did you throw it away?"

Mike was smoothing out the wrinkled sheet.

"Dunno. It weren't—when I done it, I weren't—the real 'un, he's better than this one be—so I throwed 'im away . . . but . . ."

his voice faded off, as he realised where the drawing must have been found.

"That's my sister's paper—out of her box—a fwiend gave it her for Christmas," Pearl said reprovingly, "it was you broke into our cottage, and stole our baked beans and made marks on my sister's bed with your dirty boots, wasn't it? It was vewy naughty of you."

"It ba'int *your cottage*, it be *my home*," he shouted at her, turning on her, twisting his lithe body round to face her.

"That's enough, Mike," Quentin said severely, "it belongs to the lady's father now. You're in the wrong, you know."

"No, 'e ain't," snapped Ivy, rubbing at the table furiously, "and whose business is it, that's what I'd like to know?" She looked at no one as she spoke.

"Well, mine, Mrs. Gover. It's my business because I've chosen to make it mine, and because I want to help Mike. He draws—that's a beautiful drawing, that fox. He mustn't get into trouble with the police because he broke a window and got into someone else's house—"

"I tell you it *ba'int* theirs—it's *ours*." Mike beat with clenched fists on the stone of the hearth.

"Sh—sh—it ain't no use doing that," said Ivy. "You listen."

"—they'd probably take a lenient view—I mean, nothing very bad would happen to him, because he's a child, and because of the circumstances, but I'm afraid—"

He paused.

"*She'll* 'ave 'er knife into 'im," supplied Ivy, "and so'll young Buzz—Mr. Stone. Won't they? Sir."

"Er—naturally, Miss Cartaret is annoyed."

Quentin paused again. He wanted to say that Coral was a spiteful girl making a fuss about very little, and the bounding Stone an officious ass, and that nothing in the affair mattered but getting Mike safely out of it so that he could go on making drawings as beautiful as the leaping fox.

But it would be exceedingly imprudent to say so. Coral was Pearl's sister; Stone would, Quentin was certain, make a tediously persistent enemy if once offended; the Vicar could not really side with cottage people against gentry, no matter where his true sympathies might be. And Mike was undeniably a runaway from home and school; that would count heavily against him. Any defence of him could rely only on a plea of natural affection for his old home, and the startling power he possessed of drawing a fox . . . Quentin could not imagine Coral and Mr. Stone and the local policeman being wooed into lenience by either fact.

"It's always bad to get into any trouble with the police, however slight," he said, "we just don't want it . . . Mike, how do you get on with your father?—has he got a father?" to Ivy.

"'E gets on with 'im all right. Tell the gentleman, Mike. He said as he wants to help you, and we don't want no police nosying round 'ere, now do we? Tell 'im, go on."

"I get on with 'im all right," Mike said, slowly and sulkily at last.

"Then why did you run away?"

"Dunno." He turned to the fire.

Ivy was making an extraordinary face, the result of forcing features that were not by nature expressive to convey information.

"'Is mum. She *died*," she mouthed, and Quentin instantly nodded. Guilt endured over the years sometimes—not always—bestows on those who suffer it a quickness of understanding denied to happier people. Much seemed plain to Quentin now.

"Mike."

"What?" He did not turn round.

"I shan't tell the police—I shan't tell anyone, that you broke into the cottage where you used to live."

"All right," said the boy, in a moment, keeping to his stare at the fire.

"But I think you ought to let your fa—your dad know where you are. If I don't tell the police, you'll write to your dad and let him know you're here, won't you?"

"And you won't go telling *her*—Miss Carter—neither, will you? Sir," demanded Ivy, leaning forward, in her eagerness, across the scraped and gleaming table, "nor that Mr. Stone?"

Pearl sat upright.

"I do *fink* Coral ought to know."

"That would stop the whole plan dead," Quentin said, very decisively, "we won't tell anyone . . . but you and I can talk about that later . . . well, Mike?"

"I *like* it here," Mike burst out, twisting round again, "Neb and Cooey and the 'roaches and *her*," nodding at Ivy, "I don't want to go home, not to my other home I don't. I like it *here*."

"Your dad must be very worried, missing you, and wondering where you are." Quentin tried to use simple words.

Mike muttered something; it might have been "*I* been miserable," but Quentin could not be certain. A glance at the window showed him that the snow, with its lovely and infuriating capriciousness, had ceased. Pearl was clutching her coat about herself.

"Now that's enough," announced Ivy suddenly and loudly, hurling the ball of newspaper into a corner, "no more jawing, Mike; you write to your dad or out you go. See? I'm not 'aving you here with yer dad worrying, and the police nosying about . . . we'll say you've 'ad a bad froat and you're staying a month with me to get set up again, and then 'e can come and fetch you away. 'Ow's that?"

"A month's four weeks," Mike said, with his eyes fixed on her face, and a light beginning to shine far down in their blue depths. "That's a long time, a month is."

"'Course it is . . . now you show the gentleman the drawing of the mice what you done for me. In the drawer, it is. Go on, show un.

Pearl stood by the door, ready to go. She felt strongly that the naughty little boy ought to be punished; only not, perhaps, by the police; that would be too severe . . . how peculiar men were! getting so interested in a drawing and a child he had never seen before, when *she* was there, and only an hour ago he had told her that he was very much in love with her! Well, I shall *speak my mind* on the way home, thought Pearl; I still think Coral *ought* to know; but not Dickie, perhaps.

"Remarkable," said Quentin, at last, "almost more remarkable than the other; such a strong sense of design . . . have you shown anyone at school your drawings, Mike?"

Mike looked up and laughed. "Says I can't draw for nuts, they do, 'cause I won't bother with their old jugs and boxes."

Quentin laughed; if he had not felt that a little adult serious-ness might do no harm, he would have liked to pull the artist's ear. He could, however, give him five shillings, telling him that it was to be spent on pencils and paper.

When they were out of sight of the cottage, leaving Ivy and Mike almost as cheerful as they had been before the visit, Quen-tin drew Pearl's arm gently within his own.

"Where do you want to go, dearest? Back to the cottage, or to the shop?"

"Oh, the shop, please. Mrs. Threader gets rather fussed if neither of us are there, and I don't know where Coral's gone off to—wushing wound to the policeman, I expect."

"Probably. Well, you and I can't help that . . . the policeman won't know the boy's there, if Mrs. Gover keeps him out of the way, and we're the only people who know he's the villain." His long legs twinkled over the snow like those of some great black bird, and he almost pulled her along, but Pearl liked it.

She wanted to punish him just a little, however, for being so interested in that boy and his drawings, so she said in her smooth-est voice, with the lisp very marked:

"You weally don't fink we ought to tell Cowal?"

She did not dare to say, "I think I ought to tell Coral."

"Certainly not, darling. You aren't serious?" He stooped his tall head to look into the face under the black helmet. "Your sis-ter's—er—sense of property is unusually strong. If she's told, it could lead to all kinds of trouble for that boy."

"But it *was* naughty. It might be for his *own good* to tell the police."

"He broke into *his home*, Pearl, not into *your* cottage. Can't you understand? He came back here to find the life they used to live here with his mother."

"How extwaordinawy . . . I didn't know that . . . I'm sorry . . . poor little boy."

"You can see that it makes all the difference, can't you? And how important it is that nothing's done to make the boy . . . go from bad to worse?" Quentin insisted.

The thought *would* obtrude itself that any one of his Bloomsbury friends would have understood, and agreed with him,
without a word of explanation being necessary. The road undoubtedly was on a slight rise at the moment. But her face was like a
rose, fresh and pink in the icy wind, and, after entertaining and
then dismissing a notion of addressing her as 'rose-face', he suddenly swooped and literally snatched a kiss.

"Oh!"

"Are you going to marry me—I mean, will you marry me,
darling?"

"I—oh, it's all so—you *are* a hustler, aren't you?—yes, I suppose—but do you—?"

"Do I what?"

"Well, love me?"

"Of course," was his stout and emphatic answer, "of course
I love you."

"Ven I will," and Pearl smiled deliciously, enjoying, even as
her sister had enjoyed the frost and teasing Dickie Stone, the look
on Quentin's face and the warm clasp of his arm about her own.

"Darling!"

They were almost at the bus stop by now, a place, usually, of
a final loneliness, with a road and hedges curving away on either
hand towards the hills, and very rarely a horse and cart, and
almost never any of the dozen or so cars in the neighbourhood,
to be seen on it.

Need it be said that on this occasion, when Quentin had just
become engaged to Pearl and had her arm drawn within his
own, that a cousin of Mrs. Wattle's, solid, and in full possession
of unimpaired eyesight and ears, was planted squarely under
the stop?

"Good morning, Mrs. Terry."

"Good morning, sir. Good morning, miss."

"Good mom . . ."

One of those young ladies from The Tea Shoppe. Holding her
arm. Bold as you like. Oh well, they're engaged, that must be it.
There's a bit of news. Must tell Mary.

Quentin wished that the warning mournful lines would stop saying themselves in his head:

"Does the road wind uphill all the way?"
Yes, to the very end."
Will the day's journey take the whole long day?"
From morn to night, my friend."

He then recalled the line "beds for all who come", and, finding himself dwelling with satisfaction upon at least one aspect of the situation, he smiled at himself; and Pearl, seeing the smile, thought affectionately that it was nice to see him looking so happy.

And, of course, she was happy too, if twenty-three had not been rather young to settle down. But they could have a nice long engagement.

19

"BECAUSE I ba'int going to write it."

"You know what I says, Mike."

"Go on—you won't turn me out—not you."

A week had passed of the month that Ivy had promised to her boy, and the letter to his father had not been written.

Every evening—that is, on those evenings when they had not been out roaming the budding woods with Neb until darkness came down—she had put out the penny bottle of ink, and the black wooden penholder with the J nib, and a sheet of writing-paper and an envelope from a shilling box bought for this important occasion at the post office in Nethersham; and every evening Mike had settled down to draw, only shaking his head absently when his attention was called to the preparations.

For once in her life, Ivy was helpless. Usually, she was silent; or lied or found some way of dodging, or told some exciting yet convincing tale when facing a situation in which she wanted her own way; and this was how she had dealt with her three husbands, until Stan had taught her to live with him in a partnership of silent, loving give-and-take. But she knew that she could not use her tricks with Mike, because she loved him more than he loved her.

She did not make the mistake of threatening. He would see straight through that: he knew that she would no more turn him out than she would turn out Neb or Cooey.

"Then *I'll* write it. I will, straight," she said, one day when the writing materials had been laid out as usual, and, as usual, ignored.

"Go on and write it, then."

Ivy was rubbing the table, with long, slow, round sweeps; she was not so small-minded as to jog against the pastry board on which he had his drawing-paper, and the table was based so solidly and straightly on its stout legs that it did not shake. It was raining, with the long lances of silver that fall in early spring shining in the light filling the cloud-filled sky; birds were singing in the fresh wetness.

Ivy did not want to write it, because she wanted Mike to stay with her and it was hard—that was how she put it to herself—to have to write a letter sending him away; also, as Helen Green had guessed, she could neither read nor write properly. Yet, when it was written and posted, she would feel easier.

Thoughts, angry and disturbed, of bursting out, "You aren't half mean," were crowding in her mind, when there came the noise of a car's engine outside. A van, thought Ivy, willing to turn her attention to something else; that's a van, all right. Stopping too. Hope it ain't—

There was a pause; Ivy disdained to go to the window like some old nosyer, and Mike was absorbed.

A heavy knock on the door.

"If that's your dad, it'll serve you right," said Ivy, as she went to open it, and at that Mike did look up, startled.

"He 'asn't got no motor, you're barmy, 'sides, he don't know where's I be."

"We'll see," Ivy said darkly, but when she opened the door there stood Nobby Clark.

"'Ullo, Ive."

"'Ullo—well, fancy seeing you. What you come all this way for?"

"I see *you're* just the same," Nobby said, with emphasis. "Some people might arst a chap in out of the wet."

"Oo's stoppin' yer?" At which, Nobby resignedly stepped over the threshold.

His eyes at once fastened upon Mike, who, seeing that it was not his dad, had gone back to his work. Nobby glanced inquiringly at the hostess.

"That 'ere's my nephew, Mike," she said instantly, "stayin' with me but only for three week. Mike, this 'ere's Mr. Clark, an old friend o' your Uncle Stan's."

Mike grinned. It was at the lie, not in greeting to Nobby, but the lighting up of his remarkable eyes and the alluring change that took place in his usual disinterested expression caused Nobby to grin back. Ivy was beginning to clash her tins about.

"You stayin' long?" she enquired. "You may as well sit down, go on, sit down by the fire, for Gawd's sake."

"Thanks, I'm sure." Nobby heavily seated himself, and glanced around. "You got it looking better, Ive," he pronounced. "More—'ome-like."

"Want to stay to dinner, I meant?" Ivy ignored the tribute.

"If you can put up with me. I wouldn't wish to put you out in any way, I'm sure."

"There's enough for three. Mike'll go short if anyone does, 'e's the youngest."

Silence now descended. Ivy darted about, slapping a shilling's worth of New Zealand scrag into a biscuit tin, stooping agilely under the dank sink to scoop water from an old bread-crock which left a moist ring on the bricks, wrenching three or four skins off some onions and tossing them straight across the room into the heart of the fire.

"*Ive!*" Nobby almost groaned. "Them'll smell your place out."

"Well, if you come in unexpected you must put up with it, mustn't you?" But her tone was friendlier. She had had a good idea; Nobby wrote a clear hand, and he could write the letter. It would mean letting on to him about Mike, but she could think up something . . . once get that letter off, and she *would* feel easier; yes, she would. She would not let herself think about the

time when her boy had gone; she only knew that she would feel
easier. He ought to be at home. It wasn't as if his dad was a bad
lot, or beat him.

Nobby sat, in indignant silence, amid the reek of burning
onion skins. This spring which was budding outside was Nobby's
forty-seventh, and he was feeling that it was time he got married
again; poor Polly had been gone seven years, and he had collected
around him a nice circle of widows and desertees and cheerful
plump women with little businesses, any one of whom, he knew,
wouldn't say no.

There was also Eileen.

And finally there was Ive, who had continued to stay in his
memory, irritating as a hangnail, haunting as some tune you
couldn't get out of your mind. He had acted upon a sudden idea,
and driven down to see if she was still just the same, and his first
glimpse of her, standing there framed in the doorway, in her dark
dress with a navy and white spotted apron and her hair screwed
up very tight, and her first words, had showed him without any
doubt at all that she *was* just the same; like a tidy gipsy; ignorant
and slap-dash, and unlike any other woman he had ever known,
and unforgettable. The only sign of improvement was in the cottage; that did look a bit more comfortable, and Neb seemed less
like a mad dog.

"'E's come on a lot," Nobby observed, indicating Neb where
he lay by the hearth.

"Suits him, livin' 'ere," said Ivy. "I'll 'ave a bit of a sit down
while it's cooking," and she pulled up a chair opposite to him.

Nobby glanced at Mike. Then he looked into the fire for some
moments; his thoughts were unable to keep as clear as he would
have liked, because of the reek from the onion-skins, now in their
final convulsions. Frying onions was one thing; Nobby liked the
promising smell of frying onions; but onion skins—and chucking them on to the fire like that—straight as a bowler, never see
a woman who could throw as straight as that—but it was all part
of Ivy's annoying fascination.

"Been keepin' well?" she asked suddenly, with her smile, and
in her warmest voice.

"Ive!" Nobby leant towards her, speaking low, "you thought any more about—you know—what I arst you?"

Ivy hadn't, and she had to think for a moment before she remembered his proposal. But she answered, "Well, I 'ave, Nobby, but the answer's still 'no'. Thanks all the same."

That ought to do it; now 'e'll be all soppy, and 'e'll write that letter, she thought.

Nobby's eye, embarrassed, had strayed from the shrivelled onion-skins, caught by slight movements at the back of the fire.

"Ive! You know you got cockroaches?" he exclaimed, in something like horror, sentiment forgotten.

"'Course I know. What of it?"

"They ain't 'ealthy, that's what."

Ivy shrugged. "They don't do no 'arm."

Nobby was silent—from sheer thankfulness. For the second time he had been shown, as if some appalling and fathomless chasm had opened before his feet, what being married to Ivy Gover would mean.

It had been a narrow escape, and no error. Now he could eat his dinner, and go off back to London, and forget his old mate's widow except for a card at Christmas.

But some soreness lingered, and quite a lot of wounded male vanity.

"I don't remember no nephew of Stan's or yours . . ." he began, seizing on a small puzzle that was teasing his memory.

It took Ivy an hour, while dinner was cooking, to get her story told, because Nobby was one of the kind who says—"But I don't see as 'ow—" while having something told to him; and how long it would have taken had she brought in that recent brief and amiable visit from the local policeman, whose father had known her father, she could not think. The lie about the nephew was explained by the necessity of keeping Mike hidden because of the Inspector. Nobby understood and sympathised about Inspectors.

When all—or so Nobby thought—was explained he experienced one of those changes of feeling towards Ivy which had made their acquaintanceship, since her widowhood, so uncomfortable.

Here she was, doing the right thing. Not encouraging the boy to stay with her, but set on getting him back to his dad. Where he ought to be, thought Nobby, severely.

But acting, as usual, just as you'd never think she would. He could have bet on her hanging on to the boy; he was company, and women always liked kids. No, a man could never be sure *what* Ive Gover would be up to, and the vaguest of thoughts about thanking the vaguest of Gods for his escape drifted through Nobby's mind.

"So we thought as how we'd arst you to write the letter for us," Ivy concluded.

"Me? Wot letter?" Nobby stared.

"The letter to his dad." Ivy could not control a touch of impatience. "You write a good 'and, and I never was one for writing, and 'e," nodding towards Mike, "won't do it."

"You ought to make 'im, Ive," Nobby said, and a gleam came into his eye, "*I'd* make 'im." He glanced without indulgence towards the fair, freshly-washed head bent over the table.

"Now we don't want no trouble," said Ivy rapidly (blast the men, they was more bother than any animal). "'E'd only run off into them woods, runs like a hare, 'e does; we'll 'ave our dinner and a cup o' tea and then I'll get out the paper and him and me'll tell you what to write."

Nobby reflected. The dinner smelt good. "Mark you, Ive," he said earnestly at last, "I think you're doin' right. You're doin' what's *right*. Otherways, I wouldn't 'elp you."

"Thass settled then." She got up lightly from her seat and began to slap things on to the table, "out of the way, please," to Mike. "You can 'ave the knife and fork," to Nobby, "seeing you're company."

It had taken Ivy an hour to explain to Nobby about Mike; and it took all of them two hours, until the sun had almost fallen into the black net of the beech boughs and the light was low and thin and crystal-yellow, to get the letter written, addressed, and stamped, with the crumpled penny-halfpenny one that Ivy had carried for a week in her purse.

Mike refused to dictate it, so Ivy and Nobby did it between them, with more hesitation and consultation than she liked; it was a fine afternoon and if Nobby would have pushed off, she and Mike and Neb could have been up in the woods. Many a long pause, many a hovering of the black wooden pen in Nobby's big hand above the sheet of paper—*Gawd!* and Ivy's eyes gleamed, and Nobby more than once asked what was the matter with Neb? it was like his old temper, growling like that; and slowly, very slowly, the words got on to the paper. Then, of course, they had to be copied out.

Dear Sir,

Your boy Mike is safe and well, staying here at the above address with me. He run away to see his old home. But as he has had a bad throat he wants to stay with me for three weeks more.

Can you come along and fetch him about 4th April.

Yours sincerely,

Mrs. Ivy Gover.

Mike sends best wishes to you and Elsie.

"That'll 'ave to do, Ive," said Nobby, when the pink blotting-paper had been thumped, and he sighed; writing letters, especially writing them with Ive, was work. "Was you thinking about a cup of tea?"

"That's just what I was thinking about—and thenks." Ivy gave him her smile, and darted towards the blue kettle, "drippin-toast we'll 'ave."

In those days, cold dripping was always savoury with rich meaty gravy that had worked into it, especially at the bottom of the bowl. Nobby's spirits rose—then he glanced towards the cockroaches, and remembered the candles in those bottles, and his spirits steadied themselves. Yes, a card at Christmas would do nicely between him and Ive Gover for the rest of their lives.

The fire was strengthened, the hot dripping toast eaten and the tea drunk; it was all comfortable enough, but Nobby did have a feeling that Ive and the boy and that dog—and the pigeon, for all he knew—were sitting on the edge of their chairs wanting him to be off. Well, he was not all that anxious to spend the evening there, himself.

"Well—so-long, Ive. I expect I'll be seeing you again some time," said Nobby, at the door, "so long, sonny," to Mike. "Don't you go running away again."

"So-long." Mike did not look up from an old copy of *Comic Cuts*.

Ive actually put out her hand: perhaps it was gratitude for his help in writing the letter, perhaps what might be the last sight of his large worn face for ever brought back memories of Stan and the old days; but there it was, a small red hand, looking strong and alive. Nobby took it and gave it a good clasp. Ivy said nothing; was he going to hang about until the last light had gone?

"Don't ferget to post it, now!" she screeched, as he sat for a moment in the van, with the engine running, looking back at her.

His reply was to take the letter out of his pocket and silently hold it up. It looked very white in the growing dusk. Then he drove away.

Mike and Neb were already at the door, capering silently. Ivy whirled indoors, snatched her hat, jacket and muffler off a nail, and whirled out again, slamming the door after her and the three were off; across the lane, through the gap in the hedge, past the hollow where Mike had hidden, along the side of the freshly-ploughed field, and on up the white hill; white now, not with snow, but with one vast sheet of glimmering snowdrops, and towards the darkening woods.

Nobby paused in Nethersham, not without some deeper feelings, to post the letter. It would catch the seven o'clock. Doing an old mate's wife a turn, doing the kid's dad a turn, fulfilling a promise. That was a good job done.

On the way home, he thought, not of Ive who had fascinated and shocked and annoyed him for close on seven years, but of the others: plump widowed Mary who had kept on the small sweets-and-tobacco-and-newspaper business at the corner of Gillet Street near The Nag's Head; Kathy, the cheerful support of an old mother who was no misery and who contributed her share to the household by Board school cleaning (so *she* would not be a burden on a new son-in-law); Cis, a bit house-proud but keeping her two rooms and the son now thirteen, whom her husband had deserted, tidy and clean. And there were one or two others whom he did not know quite so well, but who were all suitable for a man who was looking about him.

And there was the one with red hair, the one who was a bit slap-dash but liked a laugh (Ive's laugh could put you in mind of the witch in panto) and a bit of fun; the one who never nagged or grumbled; the one who seemed to make the lights go up and shine brighter when she came into a room; the one that Nobby finally did marry; even Eileen.

For the next weeks, Ivy and her boy revelled in the turn of the year, just as they had enjoyed the frost and snow. They rambled through the softening woods, neither calling each other's attention to the sunsets nor pausing to pick primroses; Ivy expected flowers to give good service, if she did stuff a handful into a jam-jar, and she considered anything less than a week spent in water, and still fresh, a waste of time spent in the picking.

The three would wander home at nine or ten at night, soaked in cool air and the delicate nameless scents of earliest spring. Any remarks they exchanged during these ramblings were barks, or hollow, mindless shouts. All three were very happy; they put the short, colourless letter from Mike's father away in the drawer with the piece of string and the drawing of the dancing mice and the one of the fox; and neither thought of it nor spoke of it. He would come round about April 4th; time enough to think then.

Every night, and only then, there was a hug and a kiss before they went to sleep. What Ivy used to notice, as his great blue eye approached her own, was its expression; *you never see a dog look at you like that*, she would think, and that was the nearest she came to recognising the look of love. But sometimes she wondered, for the first time in her life, if her childlessness had been such a lucky escape after all.

Deep blue light began to die down behind the giant branches of the beech trees, lasting a fraction of time, a mere minute or so, longer every evening. Millions of primroses came thrusting crinkled leaves up through the warming earth. Helen Green walked in the budding woods on Sundays, alone.

So did Lord Gowerville, except for Milo, who was now apparently rejuvenated, and had grown a new coat; not so silken and thick, naturally, as his youthful one, but thick enough, and fitting his portly later years.

"What's the matter, old man?" his master called to him, one beautiful evening when they were on their way home through Belshers; it was the first week in April, and Mike and Ivy had just a few more days to be together.

Milo had been investigating a thicket of birch a little way ahead, and now came waddling importantly back at the call. Lord Gowerville approached the thicket; he could see that the bright young grass beside it was crushed, and he frowned; this part of his woods was closed to walkers.

As he came level with it, someone reared up out of the autumn bracken, scrambling to her feet, and stood staring at him, with parted lips. A young woman in a green coat; not a cottager, he judged. An unusual face; thoughtful, and very pale.

"Am I trespassing?" she asked faintly. "If I am, I—I'm sorry."

Lord Gowerville lifted his cap. Voice all right; manner lacked confidence. But then she *was* trespassing.

"I thought I might be, but it was so beautiful—I just walked on, and then I lay down and—and I went to sleep," she continued.

"This is my land. But don't worry about it," Lord Gowerville said.

She did not seem to be worrying about it, but stood looking vaguely off into the distance. It was about six o'clock; the air was marvellously clear and still, but so full of life that, to Helen, there was an actual, invisible welling and throbbing in it, partly expressed in the loud singing of the birds and in the myriad faint scents that gathered into one ruling, penetrating sweetness, but expressed too in something beyond them: a tingling? *Tingling* would be a difficult word to work into a poem . . .

"It must be marvellous to own a beech wood," she said dreamily, bringing her light green eyes back to his face.

This remark displeased Lord Gowerville, causing him to dismiss her with poor Angela Mordaunt, as *another arty, cranky gairl*. He also disliked *marvellous*, as applied to his ownership of Belshers, which he was at the moment faced with the choice of selling, in order to get the money to prevent the roof of The Hall from literally collapsing in upon it within the next ten years. *The beeches or the house.* The words, when he would let them, rang in his head over and over again, like some rhyme of doom. Usually, of course, he would not let them. But anyone who said something that brought them into his mind became temporarily unpopular with Lord Gowerville.

"May I suggest that you walk on?" he said abruptly, "it will be almost dark in an hour."

"Yes, I will . . . thank you."

She stopped, and picked up a floppy beret and an old rucksack from among the bracken stems.

"Nethersham is about six miles on. Take the ride on the left when you come to the crossed paths. It is a longish walk," he added, slightly relenting.

"Yes, I know. Thank you. I like walking. Good-bye."

She smiled down at Milo, who had seated himself almost on her feet, glanced once at his master, and turned away into the woods and the evening light.

Lord Gowerville replaced his cap and also walked on, watching her as she went swiftly out of sight. She walked well, with a springy stride that was full of energy, and, Lord Gowerville thought, did not match the graveness of her young face.

20

"GOOD afternoon, Miss Mordaunt," said Coral, as Angela came into The Tea Shoppe; she thought with satisfaction that you had to be really young to stand up to a wind like today's, "chilly, isn't it? Your usual?"

"Tea and toast, please, yes. It is cold. But I'm warm—I've walked from Great Abbey."

"You ought to get yourself a little car," said Coral contemptuously; if there was one kind of person, she told herself, that she despised more than another it was people who had come down in the world and were stuck-up.

Angela smiled, and said that she used her mother's. Young women like Miss Cartaret did not make her nervous; she had the resources of birth. Unfortunately, her smile was a gracious one, and Coral walked off with much determined movement of the hips.

She had been in a temper since Pearl and that long-faced parson had walked in at home unexpectedly and as cool as you please one evening last week and announced their engagement.

This made Pearl's *third*, and Coral had always taken it for granted that *she*, Coral, would be *married* first. And Daddy had been heard to express the opinion that the parson's Head Wasn't Screwed On the Right Way; which meant, Coral knew, that Daddy thought Quentin (what a name! I ask you) would never be a bishop, which was apparently the only job in the Church that was decently paid. Mummy actually seemed to like him, and to be pleased.

And having to tell people your sister was engaged to a *clergyman*! Where would Coral be able to look?

Angela sat in her corner, waiting for her tea and toast, with a new novel by John Galsworthy which she had taken out from the twopenny library at Great Abbey.

"Any room for a little one?"

It was a moment before she realised that the man was speaking to her, and that he was Sam Lambert.

His cheap, badly cut overcoat, cloth cap, and gaudy muffler could not hide the fact that he was a fine big man; the fact that he was nervous, however, was well hidden.

"Good afternoon, Sam," said Angela quietly, giving him the cold, gentle smile she would have given to a family servant.

"I expect you're wonderin' why I ba'int at work," he said, sitting down on one of the place's small chairs and eclipsing it, so that he seemed to be sitting on air. "Well, I'm here on business for Mr. Binney. His new Ford, she's taken to makin' a noise inside her, so I brung her down to be looked at in Webster's. Says it'll

take an hour. So I—I come in for a cup o' tea. What you reading?"
He craned his head sideways to see.

"Oh, nothing—that is, it's a novel—a story—by a writer I like
very much."

"Ah . . . you read a lot, I reckon? Must be quiet up at The
Beeches, I've often thought as it must."

"Yes . . . I . . . I never thanked you for the pretty Christmas
card. It was," said Angela slowly, "sweet of you."

"It weren't nothing. I reckoned you was glad I come by, that time
you was in a fix, and I though it were a pretty card, so I sent ut."

"I—I was very pleased to have it." Angela could not help, here,
from turning a swift glance on Mrs. Threader, who now crept up
with the tea and toast—did *she* know him? But Mrs. Threader's
face retained its usual suggestion of an unawakened bun.

"What's for you?" she droned, turning to Sam when Angela's
order had been set before her. This was because Mrs. Threader
did not like Sam being a big man, and sitting down opposite
poor Miss Mordaunt 'like that'. Enough to upset her. Usually,
Mrs. Threader's formula with customers was, "what may I get
for you?" which sounded nice, she thought.

"Pot o' tea, missus, and see it's good and strong, and some o'
your cakes."

"Our tea his always excellent," said Mrs. Threader expres-
sionlessly, and, confirmed in her low opinion of Sam, crept away.

"You'll hev a cake—me standing treat—won't you?" he asked,
when his own order had come and Mrs. Threader had made a
second slow departure, with warning and disapproval in every
line of her sparse figure.

Angela knew that it would not matter if she accepted. Kindness must always be shown to inferiors. But what would matter
would be the tone in which she did accept.

"I'd love one," she answered, exactly as she would have spoken
to young Evelyn or to any of her women friends, and she let the
kind-to-servants smile warm into her natural one.

Sam smiled too. He said nothing, but allowed himself to lean
back in the exiguous chair, which creaked in protest. There weren't
nothin' in coming into a place like this and speakin' to a lady, he

thought; nothin' to it at all, if you just kept cool. It weren't like bayonet-fighting, where you had to go mad-like. (Not that he'd fought with the bayonet, having been in R.E.M.E.)

His plan had been laid some weeks ago, when he had learned from local gossip that Miss Angela regularly walked into Great Abbey on Wednesday afternoons, then on to Nethersham, and had tea at The Tea Shoppe.

"Know what I did?" he asked suddenly, bringing his clear eyes so suddenly round on her that she actually started. She shook her head; she was eating toast, and could not speak.

"Worked out all this here."

"H-how do you mean? I'm sorry—I don't—"

"Seein' you. I kept my best coat hid up at the farm, see, and this muffler, and this morning, it *being* Wednesday, see, I hears a foony noise inside the old Ford. *Didn't hear it until this mornin', comprenney?* So I tells the Guv'nor, and we decides I'd better bring it down here to be looked at. Most of the afternoon that'll take, I reckon." He grinned widely, and snatching his teapot, poured out a stream of darkest brown liquid, then silently held out the plate of cakes to Angela.

"You . . . it was . . . a kind of . . . plot," she said faintly, staring at him.

The decent boy who was supposed to share her emotions here spoke up; his voice was lowered in disgust and warning, but Angela's feelings were not of his imitation-deep kind; they were truly deep, and truly powerful and they were frightening. I can't think properly, she thought dreamily; the smell of tobacco and fresh air from his coat is so strong.

I ought to get up and go.

Yes, and at once, said the boy sharply.

"Know why I planned it all out?" Sam asked suddenly, leaning towards her.

She shook her head.

"What I was hopin' was—s'pose you was to come to the pictures with me one evenin'?"

"It's very kind of you," Angela almost whispered, at last; the voice of the boy had stopped; all her self-command and her social training seemed to have vanished.

She only felt, in one awful storm of feeling, that for years, since about two years after Peter had been killed, she had been growing desperate.

Desperate for a husband and a home and children of her own. The endless years, perhaps thirty years, with Mummy stretched before her, and she saw them in imagination with horror.

And his eyes were good. So clear; clear as the water running in any ordinary ditch beside any hedge where forget-me-nots and ragged robin grew; ordinary, and kind and good.

"No, it bean't kind . . . I'd like you to come. Reckon you don't get much of a life, up in that big place, alone with your mother!"

"It is—I'm—I do get very lonely," Angela blurted.

"Ah. And I reckon your mother just about sits on you the way mine sits on me. (Or tries to—she doan't get away with much, not with me, she doesn't.) Now, doan't she?"

Angela tried to pull herself together, that exercise which used to be all too well known to young Englishwomen.

"You . . . oughtn't to say . . . things . . . like that, to me . . . Sam."

"True, though, bean't it?"

"Yes," she answered simply, "yes, she does sit on me. She loves me of course but she—she still manages me. As if I were a little girl."

"Likes their own way, old women does—old ladies, too, I suppose." Sam leant back comfortably, ignoring the squeaks from the chair, "but I lets mine get on wi' it. Rant away, I say, and I hopes the weather holds. How do you manage wi' youm?"

"Oh, I—I just . . . give way, I'm afraid. (I ought *not* to be talking like this, you know, it's *disloyal*!) After all, she is my mother—and I'm all she's got, now."

"Now that's nonsense-talk (pity you'd ordered your tea, you could ha' shared mine)." Sam emptied his cup at a draught, and refilled it. "Got a gurt house full o' furniture, and a car, and money comin' in, hevn't she? Nice-lookin', too. Though not," and here Sam fixed his eyes upon Angela's face and spoke slowly, "so pretty as what *you* be, when you smile . . . she might marry again, one o' these days."

"Oh, that's out of the question, Sam! She's absolutely devoted to my father's memory."

There was terror and guilt and shame in talking to Sam Lambert, but Angela was also enjoying the novel sensation of chatting about her situation with a man under sixty; her uncles, and the family solicitor, and various friends of her mother's might regret that she had never married, but they accepted, without question, her fate: she would live with Mummy, and the memory of Peter Stevenson, until she died.

"Oh well. Widders," said Sam tolerantly, looking at her over his tea-cup, "only needs some decent kind o' chap to come along, and they soon come round, I reckon."

Angela considered for a moment, while she bit into one of the cakes ordered by Sam. "Soon come round"—how vulgar, what a low view of the solemn devotion to their ideals in which she and her mother shared. And how sensible, and how much more cheerful! It occurred to her that all her life she had been taught to be truthful, but never to be truthful to herself about what she felt and wanted.

She thought in sudden terror, *I don't love Peter any more*, and fixed her eyes wildly on Sam.

"Didn't mean to upset 'ee," he said at once, and across the table came a great hand in a coarse brown woollen glove, and grasped her own, "eat up your cake, little burd."

His tone was commanding but quiet; it sounded beautiful to Angela. She ate the cake, not tasting it, and only half-listening to the voice of the boy babbling inside her. It kept reminding her that she was a lady. Its tone was growing steadily more frantic, but fainter, and when it used the word *disgusting*, Angela told it furiously to shut up. This is probably my last chance, she thought calmly, in the inner silence which followed, and I'm desperate, and his eyes are kind. (And don't—and don't . . . *count* . . . on it.)

"Now how about the pictures?" Sam was saying, "there's a change o' programme Thursdays."

"I—I'll come, Sam. I will, and—and thank you—very much—but of course I shall have to ask—my mother—" she broke off. She had not meant to say *ask*.

"Woman grown, aren't you?" he said impatiently, "you *tell* her you're comin' wi' me."

"All right. I—I—will. That's what I'll do." Angela gave a nervous laugh, and got up.

"That's my brave girl." She looked like a girl, too, with that colour in her face, and her hair slipping about.

Had he said 'my brave girl'? Angela did not know what to do; whether to pay her bill or leave him to pay—he must earn terribly little—or how to get out of the shop, or what would happen when they got outside . . . and there was her book! She had nearly forgotten it.

As Sam got up from the chair it gave a last hopeless sound, and fell away from him, broken. Several ladies glanced round, and he looked casually backwards on the ruins; you do not become agitated over a broken chair in a tea shop when you have had thirty-six hours under German bombardment.

"Go on out, and wait. I'll drive 'ee back in the car," he ordered, without fluster, and Angela, dazed by now, wandered out of the shop, only half aware that Mrs. Threader had crept towards the scene of disaster while Coral was bearing down upon it rapidly.

She waited, under the splendour of the evening sky. A half-moon hung in the clear orange west; the willow trees were in bud above the stream and she could hear it rippling in the dusk.

I *must* keep my head, she thought, and felt a hand on her arm. Sam was grinning; about the chair, she supposed.

"Cold, are yer?" She shook her head, smiling faintly; she had just discovered that she liked to look at him.

They walked down the High Street together, and for the first time in her life Angela was on the outside of the pavement when walking with a man; they also passed Mrs. Rawnsley of The White House, an old friend of her mother's, who stared, smiled and said "Good afternoon, my dear," and stared again. Angela held her head high and straight. If you had a big, kind man to walk with down the High Street, that was what you did. But her heart was beating so heavily that it was painful.

They stared at the garage, too. But Mr. Binney's van was ready, and Sam made everything easier for her by acting in silence; opening the door for her, paying the bill, backing the Ford out of the garage yard, all with competence, and with none of the grins, or excuses, or mumblings, that she had had time to imagine, and to dread.

It was dark when he pulled up the car outside the gate of The Beeches. The moon shone, white and hard, in the hard black sky.

"Won't Mr. Binney want to know where you've been? Aren't you rather late?" said Angela; the drive had passed in silence, except for a few remarks about weather, the car, that sort of thing, and she felt the need to talk because she was frightened.

"If 'e does, I'll think of summat to say. Mr. Binney he weren't at the war, see, and us chaps as *was* in the war, we learned a thing or two," and Sam's left eyelid came down.

That was the first time, that evening, under the sky still keeping the cruel look of winter, that Angela laughed with Sam Lambert. She came out with a silly sounding hysterical sound, but it was a laugh, and not the smile she kept for servants.

He stood, looking down at her kindly.

"Now what are 'ee going to say?"

"Please don't talk to me as if I were a little girl!" Her starved womanliness spoke in sudden anger.

"Ah. But that's how she treats you, bean't it? Like a little gurrl. You show her you mean to hev *your* way, for onc't."

"I—I—all right." She stood, looking up at him, with fear in her eyes even as there was kindness in his; it was not fear of him, because he seemed to her, as he stood big and dark against the sky, not Sam Lambert, not the tractor-driver on Binney's farm, but Man, strong and dependable, who had wonderfully taken command of her; it was fear of facing Mummy.

"Good night," she muttered; she was hoping, passionately, that he would not try to kiss her.

"Good night, little burd . . . now you remember. Say your word and stand by it. I'll be outside the Palace in Great Abbey next Thursday, quarter to sivin."

He turned away; Nature sometimes dowers the simplest men with the right instincts to meet the moment, and he felt strongly that it would not do to touch her. He was starting up the Ford, and in it, and away, almost before Angela had come out of her daze.

The lights in the house glowed at her with steady reproach as she ran up the drive but she was thinking, *I do like it when he calls me little bird.*

What a silly thing to call a spinster of thirty-five, said the decent boy disgustedly.

I'll wear my blue frock and coat, thought Angela blithely, through her fear.

Mary, who opened the door to her, went back to the servants' sitting-room and Cook with sober thoughts about being an old maid; walking about in the cold and dark, and coming in all flushed up and barmy-looking; better have anyone that asks you—except Charley Wattle, of course, cheek—than get like poor Miss Angela.

Angela went straight into the drawing-room.

"Hullo, Mummy," she burst out, on a high steady note, and threw her hat, which she had been carrying, on to a chair. "Sorry I'm late, I hope you haven't been worrying."

Mrs. Mordaunt put down the *Daily Telegraph.*

"I was beginning to get a little anxious, it's after six. But I supposed you'd run into someone you knew at The Tea Shoppe, and stayed chatting . . . was anyone there, dear?"

"Sam Lambert." Angela lowered her shaking legs into a chair and clasped her hands over her knees. Her engagement ring flashed modestly in the light.

"Sam Lambert? Oh, that man who drives the tractor at Binneys . . . I've seen him out lately in Binney's wonderful *new van.* I don't know what things are coming to . . . he was actually in The Tea Shoppe? Not *having tea?*"

"Oh yes." Angela looked straight across at her mother, and had the odd thought that this was the last time they would see each other. Mrs. Mordaunt wore soft black chiffon, this evening, with diamond brooches glinting here and there. The classical-ly-knotted hair, still so dark, the unlined skin and the sad and placid beauty of her face . . . She's had everything, thought Angela fiercely, *but she won't let me.*

"Oh yes. He sat at my table. He's asked me to go to the pic-tures." Mrs. Mordaunt laughed. "Darling, don't rag. It makes me feel quite . . . I don't like it, Angela, and if any of our friends heard you—"

"But it's true. He did ask me. And—I'm going."

Now her mother looked alarmed. She leant forward and said, softly but urgently, "Angela, are you all right? You haven't caught a chill, have you? You're very flushed."

"I'm perfectly all right, thank you . . . I thought it was sweet of him to ask me, so I . . . I . . . said yes."

"Angela! You didn't—you can't have!"

"Oh yes I did. What's so shocking about it, Mummy?"

"But the man's a farm-labourer . . . of course, you're joking, darling, but I don't think it's a very *nice* joke. If I must be truth-ful, Angela, I think it's in bad taste."

"I daresay. A lot of . . . things that are true . . . are."

She swung herself up out of the chair and stood looking at her mother, with her hair spraying about her face and her tweed jacket, which she had unbuttoned, hanging bulkily about her. "Anyway, I'm going. Next Thursday evening."

"I don't believe you," Mrs. Mordaunt pronounced, sitting upright now and staring. "I know you behaved perfectly when he asked you—one doesn't return insolence with insolence—but I *never*, in *all my life*—I never . . . I do *not* know *how* it's all going to end. If these creatures can walk into tea-rooms and sit down with ladies and—and—ask them . . . the *pictures*! Like Mary, or Cook . . . but you aren't well, dear, are you? That's it, of course . . ."

The tall piece of elegance rose, and drew near to her, and cold, ringed white hands groped for her own.

"Darling, Mummy understands. It's the shock—a low, coarse man like that. Any nice girl would feel the same. Wouldn't you like to go and lie down, and I'll have some dinner sent up to you?"

Eat up your cake, little bird.

"No thank you. I'm perfectly all right, I'm not shocked or disgusted or—or anything like that. I was . . . only . . . surprised that he should ask someone . . . like me."

"Well, really, Angela, what a strange way to look at it! Of course, he would think it the most tremendous feather in his cap if you ever did such an unimaginable thing as to go out with him. I never *dreamt* of such impertinence—oh, if only your father were alive! If only you'd had a brother—he would very soon have put the man in his place . . . oh, if only Peter . . . that dreadful, dreadful war . . ."

"Peter's dead," said Angela. "I'll just change, Mummy, and be down soon . . . don't mind too much, darling."

She gulped as she rushed out of the room, and then the clean-limbed boy struggled in vain as he was swept away in a torrent of tears; frightening, scalding, that stopped her at the foot of the stairs, sent her crawling and shaking up to her room, and kept her lying helpless on her bed almost until the gong sounded, an hour later.

She came down, calm and red-eyed, wearing a calm dark evening dress; and Mary, unable to prevent herself from an occasional scared glance from one white, silent face to the other, served dinner.

"Angela," Mrs. Mordaunt said in a new voice, when the girl had gone out of the room, "you're wearing lipstick, aren't you?"

"Yes."

"I thought we had agreed, some time ago, that ladies don't paint themselves."

"Yes, we did. But I've changed my mind."

Mrs. Mordaunt carefully laid down the silver knife with which she was peeling an apple, and now it was her turn to put her hands up to her face and cry.

21

MIKE drew. The pencil, which was part of some materials bought with five shillings given him by Ivy, in order to match Mr. Henderson, flew over the paper; dashed; poised; swirled heavily on a thick line; crept; and the flames on the hearth danced; they, and his moving hand, were the only objects moving in a dreaming silence charged with energy and magic.

Ivy sat by the hearth in the Windsor, reading over a letter which had arrived that morning. It was certainly the most ominous communication she had yet received from Win Smithers, with its references to not having seen her for ever so long, and it being a nice idea if Win could come and stay with her for a bit, though, Win added, she was not really one for the country, finding it v. dull.

Don't say nothing about *when*, Ivy mused.

She was, if she had known, only being treated as Win's prospective hostesses always were. Win never did state a month, or a season, much less a day, on which they might expect her; she had done so at first, in the early days of Alice's turning nasty, but had learned that a clear statement of plans gave people the chance to write and tell her not to think of coming on the fourteenth, as that was Alec's birthday and they were putting up Mum and Uncle Ted, while after that, in the spring, they were having the kitchen done. Some of them added that they did want her visit to be comfortable, hence these excuses. But the result was always the same: a put-off; and Win had learned.

Ivy suddenly put the letter on the fire, thinking, that never got 'ere, that didn't. Posts is funny in the country. She glanced at the window. Sunlight was pouring in, and the greening hedge across the lane was shaking in the wind.

"I got to go to Great Warby. Comin'?"

In answer, he silently held up what he had been drawing; underneath it was written 'The Grinning Dogs'. It showed Milo and Neb fighting furiously, with bodies twisted in two circles so that they made a black, writhing pattern, with exaggeratedly, but beautifully exaggerated, teeth exposed in angry smiles.

"Like it?"

"'Course I like it, might *be* them, only you've made 'em look different, somehow, but don't you go and let Neb see it, might start 'im thinkin'. He'd do for Milo in one go, he would."

"Here, Neb—what's this?" Mike held out the drawing in front of the dozing Neb; his voice was low and exciting and mocking. Neb slowly opened his eyes and stared. "You and Milo. Fightin'. Goin' for each other. See?"

"Dawgs don't see the way we does ... don't be silly," said Ivy, looking at him as he bent over the dog and thinking what a lovely boy he was, with his cheeks that were red and hard now, after the weeks spent in cold country air, and his eyes—never see such eyes, thought Ivy, (and indeed, the eyes of genius are marvellous, and awe-inspiring). In a week he'll be gone—and such pain seized her that she was astounded.

Couldn't believe I'd a' felt like that about him, she thought fleetingly, while they were walking quickly and gaily along the Great Warby Road. Good thing I got old Neb. She had put 'The Grinning Dogs' away in the drawer, with the leaping fox, and the mice dancing their eternal, airy round; so funny, so non-human and endearing, that the eye seemed to exclaim aloud in joy at its first sight of them.

Win Smithers sat upright in her corner of the bus, nursing her two baskets of pale, smooth, shining woven straw, which fitted one over another into a neat strapped case. All of Win was neat; her navy coat and skirt and hat, her jumper of wine-coloured wool, and her carefully tended fox fur, hanging its wretched and horrifying little pinched mask round her meagre shoulders. Her face was long and meek and pale.

"Catts Corner," announced the conductor, looking without pleasure at Win Smithers.

"Gracious! What a desolate, isolated spot!" said Win, slowly proceeding down the bus and addressing, not the passengers, who looked at her in surprise, but herself, "if it was *me*, I should 'ave chosen some pretty village. Is it far from the shops?"

"Nethersham five miles, Great Warby two. Careful miss," and the conductor helped Win and her case down into the mud and wind-rippled pools of the track that here led off the road.

"Is it far to Catts Cottage, Mrs. Gover's home, do you know?"

"Sorry, I can't say," lied the conductor, and rang the bell. As the bus jolted off he exchanged glances with the nearest passenger.

For nearly an hour, Win picked her way down the track, between what she thought of as 'great ponds' and the mud. "Quite remote," she observed, "but do I see smoke over that hedge? Yes, from a chimney. I do believe Winny is going to be lucky. In spite of it being so muddy and remote, I really believe Winny is going to be lucky."

But when, turning the corner, she confronted the low, white-washed little place, standing in a piece of ground with bones and unidentifiable mash trodden into its surface, and when a flock of big black-winged birds that were pecking at the mess whirled up wildly at her approach, she paused in dismay.

"Perhaps Winny should have stayed at Auntie Bella's . . ."

Half an hour later, when Ivy and Mike came splashing down the lane, each holding one handle of a shopping basket, she was sitting on her case on the doorstep with her skirt well gathered around her legs from the birds, who had returned to their meal.

"Gawd, it's 'er," Ivy muttered, but not pausing in her march.

"Who?" Mike's eyes flared coldly on the stranger.

"Win Smithers. Now don't you say one word to 'er, or take me up on a word I says, and we'll 'ave her out o' here after dinner."

"Well, good morning, Ivy. Here's Winny—all ready for her lunch. I s'pose you got my letter yesterday—or it might have been the day before, I *believe* it caught the quarter past ten from Southend—I been staying with Stan's Auntie Bella—but the plate was a bit worn, it might have been the quarter past three, Winny must look quite strange, sitting on your doorstep, but really, dear, why don't you have a nice little porch and a seat for visitors? I would, if it was me."

Win always advanced upon her hostesses, whom she by now sadly presumed to be reluctant, with a flow of words, in order that they could not 'start on the excuses'; and the only occasion on which this method had failed had been that awful time when Cousin Joe had used the period during which she was talking to marshal his forces, draw in his breath, and come out at the conclusion of her remarks with a roar of "Sorry-can't-'ave-you-here-on-no-account-full-up."

"Never got no letter. Excuse me." Ivy reached past Win, who was now standing up, to unlock the door.

"Oh, but you must have, dear."

"Well, I didn't never saw a sign of it. The posts is funny round 'ere."

"And who is the little lad?" asked Win, with her head on one side, as she followed, uninvited, into the cottage.

"That's Mike. Stayin' with me . . . for . . . for a few days. Mike," called Ivy fiercely, "this here is Win Smithers, on my 'usband Stan's side."

Mike did not look round; he was throwing sticks for Neb just outside the door.

Leaving it open, Ivy bustled about, ignoring Win; splashing water into biscuit tins, throwing a handful of dried sticks on to the fire, tearing apart the skin-links holding six sausages, and dropping a craggy lump of dripping into a tin lid. She ignored her guest.

Win had seated herself meekly in the Windsor, nursing the case on her knees.

"You know, dear," she said presently, having had a close lock round and taken in everything, including, with an incredulous start, the cockroaches, "you h'ave *not* made the best of this little place. If it was me, now, I should h'ave it very different."

"But it ain't you, is it?" snapped Ivy.

This was the first time, in all her years of visiting, that anyone had replied to Win's stock, meek criticism with this obvious retort; even Cousin Joe had never said it.

Win came of a kindish, timid clan, inarticulate and shy, living in tidy little houses on the outskirts of small towns, with a bit of well-worked garden; owning a pet bird or a dog; relishing something tasty for tea at six, and liking a pink lampshade in the lounge. She had about as much chance with Ivy as a shrimp with a shark.

Nevertheless, feeling it was time that she got herself established—really awful though Ive's home was—she tried again.

"I cannot understand, dear h'ow it was you say you never received my letter."

Ivy was pouring a basinful of haricot beans and the water they had soaked in all night into the prehistoric saucepan.

"P'raps you never posted it?" she said.

"I'm as sure as I am this h'ere is my right h'and," and Win held up a gaunt member gloved in black. As the sun went in at that minute, a kind of solemnity was imparted to the avowal, a here-I-am-and-here-I-stayishness, which Ivy did not like at all.

"I just said, as I h'adn't seen you for some time, I thought I might pay you a visit," said Win, after a pause.

I know, Ivy thought, advancing, for now was the moment, on to Stage Two; show 'er upstairs.

"You better see where you'll 'ave to sleep, then," she remarked, and then made Win jump by one of her effortless shrieks, "Mike, you and Neb come in and keep a eye on the dinner!"

"Nice dog—nice dog," said Win, retreating, as Mike and Neb bounded in, flashing blue and shining gold. "I h'ope he doesn't bite."

"'E bites them as 'e don't know." Ivy was now leading the way up the stairs, which, even without the biscuit tins and the cockroaches, were enough to discourage anyone older than fifteen.

"I must say," Win observed, "that you live in a more isolated part than what I expected, dear. H'ow far would you be from the shops, now?"

"Five mile. I hates shops," and Ivy flung open the smaller bedroom door.

This remark, so unbelievable to the natural female ear, was still ringing ominously in Win's *(hate the shops?)* as she stared in upon bare boards and walls, a mattressless bed piled with holey blankets and—Win's eyes seemed to bulge—*bird's mess on the floor.*

"It was not getting my letter, I suppose," she said at last; she was making a rapid re-arrangement of her plans, and wondering whether she could arrive at Auntie Bella's niece's sister-in-law's at Catford late that afternoon without one of her preliminary letters. "Though it seems funny . . ."

"Mike," screeched Ivy down the stairs, "see to them sausages, boy."

"Can't. I'm drawing," came up an absent-sounding shout.

"Blast 'em," Ivy said, very loudly, and darted downwards. She never swore aloud, as a rule, though her silent oaths were blasphemous and strong, but she wanted to shock Win.

And the bird's mess, see her face when she saw that! She won't be 'ere not a minute after she's stuffed her lunch down herself, Ivy thought gleefully; her plans were going well.

"You ought to make that boy mind you, dear. I would, if it was me." Win was gingerly following down the stairs. (Really, enough to break your neck.)

"Well, it ain't you," Ivy said for the second time; no snap, now; just a batting back of the ball, and Win felt that every time she ventured to say what *she* would have done, she would get the same answer. Weeks and weeks of it . . .

It wasn't nice, talking to anyone like that.

"I'll air the blankets. Muss be damp," Ivy said over her shoulder.

Win's reply was a plaintive request to be told the whereabouts of the Houses of Parliament?

Some confusion followed. Win had to explain, which embarrassed her dreadfully; Ivy didn't seem to have heard of any of the nice names for the W.C.; but really what could you expect? Only a Christian traveller among a tribe of cannibals with unusually repulsive habits could understand what Win was feeling, as she came back from that deplorable black sentry box standing up dour and shameless among the primroses: picking her way through wet, tangled green and white grass, shrinking from the boisterous cold wind.

After lunch, she decided, she would ask the time of the next bus to the station; yes, she must have her lunch first, and then Winny would be on her way.

"Come on," called Ivy, slapping down a plate overflowing with gravy, sausages, boiled potatoes, and haricot beans, "you can 'ave the knife and fork."

Even the dreadful little kitchen stub, sharp as any razor, and the bent, yellowing fork, could not prevent Win from feeling better after eating the savoury hot plateful. And Ivy was so pleased over the success of her campaign that she suggested a cup of tea by the fire. Mike and Neb had silently rushed out into the afternoon gaiety of wind and sun.

"Where d'you live, when you're at 'ome, then?" Ivy asked suddenly; the fire was glorious and orange-red, the tea scalding and sweet and strong; in a few minutes she was going to tell Win Smithers that the next bus went at four o'clock, and all these facts made her feel less vicious towards her. "Seems a funny idea, comin' stayin' in the depths of the country in winter—see what I mean. Not your style."

"My h'ome is in Enfield," Win did not precisely drop her aitches but she sketched, rather than sounded, them. "Mother was an invalid. Passed over three years ago and left me and Alice—Alice is the elder, by seventeen years, Alice is—the h'ouse between us. But I told you, Ivy. I distinkly remember telling you at your wedding that we lived at Enfield, though of course, Mother hadn't passed on then."

"I'd forgot." But Ivy did not speak sharply, because she was seeing Stan at their wedding, big and smiling in his blue suit, and herself in a navy costume with a white hat, and a bunch of flowers that he had given her. Oceans of beer, there'd been.

"But . . . I'm not often at h'ome," Win was saying, with a kind of desolate dignity.

"Whyever not?" Ivy demanded. "Should think you're the home-sticking sort, aren't you?" and she laughed, a witchy, ringing sound, and drank scalding tea, with her eyes—as near black a pair as I ever saw, thought Win—fixed on her.

"Me and Alice don't get on," murmured Win, hypnotised with the warmth and hot food and tea and by her relation-by-marriage's eyes. "Ever so nasty, Alice can be. It's not a nice thing to say, but she was jealous. About me h'aving h'alf the h'ouse and the furniture. What she said about the willow-pattern! Shall I ever forget it! Never again, Winny, I said to myself, never again. So I . . . stay with people . . . relations, of course, not taking advantage . . . and of course I always go h'ome at Christmas, so I should hope, but Alice isn't always very nice, she has Christmas with the lodgers."

"'As lodgers, does she?" Ivy's eyes seemed to snap and sparkle in the firelight, "in your part of the 'ouse?"

"I s'pose it is, really," said Win feebly, "only I can't do nothing . . . that hard, Alice can be."

"You stand up to 'er," Ivy commanded, sitting upright and keeping her eyes fixed on Win's long, meek face. She reached up her hand to fondle Cooey, who flew down off the mantelpiece into the firelight, and pointed a finger imperiously at Win.

"Go on. You stand up to her. Tell her you'll go to the Law. I knows a lawyer what my uncle went to. In the village, name of Gardener. You tell Alice you want the money she gets from them lodgers in your part of the 'ouse. 'Ow much is it?"

"A good thirty-seven and sixpence a week, it must come to. That I do know," Win murmured.

"Then you see you gets it. People'll kick yer teeth in if you let 'em. You go straight 'ome, and tell Alice you're 'aving that bleeding thirty-seven and sixpence or you'll know the reason why. Frighten her."

"She's nearly seventy, Alice is . . ."

"All the better. Old 'uns frightens easier." Ivy drained her cup and stood up; Cooey fluttered back to his place in the warm shadows.

"Now I spec you'll be thinking about being off . . . if you're going to 'ave it out with *Alice*, the sooner the better; you won't want to be stayin' 'ere."

"Well, I think Winny *will* be on her way, dear—seeing you never got my letter, and it's so remote h'ere."

"The bus is at four. Just time," Ivy glanced at the clock, "if we steps out."

She was whirling herself into the mauve muffler, and now flung open the door on the glittering day. She hoped Mike would not be out with Neb until after dusk; hours had been wasted with this here Win, and she wanted every minute with her boy.

"There's no *reason* why I should h'ave it out with Alice, is there, Ive?" Win murmured, half-way down the lane.

"'Course not. It's your rights. You remember. You got the Law on your side. You tell her that and keep on telling."

Win felt full of unfamiliar energy and courage as she followed behind Ivy, forgetting to be careful about the 'ponds'.

Not one of the numerous relations with whom she had stayed had ever said the things that Ivy Gover had said straight out; they had said it was a Shame, they had said it Wasn't Right, they had said Alice Ought to Know Better, they had said Your Own Sister, but not one of them had said, *You stand up to her*. That had been left to the gipsy, the one who lived worse than a beggar, with cockroaches on the hearth and bird's mess on the floor.

"Oh, I dunno—bound to be one some time," Ivy cried, in reply to Win's hasty question about trains, as she mounted the bus step with the help of the same conductor. "There's a tea place in the 'Igh Street—you can sit in there till there's a train. Posh, it is—just suit you! Toodle-oo!"

She waved, standing between the hedges covered in emerald buds, with the brown trees rocking in the wind that swirled her muffler out in the air; she waved with fierce satisfaction, as the bus carried Win Smithers far and far away.

22

SUCH a nice respectable place, thought Win, as she settled herself in the corner of the Tea Shoppe farthest from the door, and here was a nice, respectable person coming towards her to take her order.

"I must warn you," began Mrs. Threader, pausing at Win's table, "that we are Quite Out of macaroons. I should have been baking all this afternoon, but our waitress is away Off. Never let us know until half-past two, if you please, and then phoned—*phoned*—to say as she'd gone into Great Abbey *to buy an engagement ring*—and her not eighteen and hasn't told her mum yet. Well, Reeny, I said, it's your own business, but did you give a thought, just one thought, Reeny, I said, to those as you was Putting Out? Yes, miss?"

"Oh, I don't want no macaroons, thanks all the same. Just a pot of tea and a slice of cake—some people h'ave no thought for others, do they?"

Win felt she must have that slice of cake, to carry her through the journey back to London, and then across London to Catford, though it was a piece of extravagance, she knew, and she was still packed up with lunch.

"I'm so sorry to trouble you," she said, when Mrs. Threader crept back again, "but do you h'ave any idea h'ow the trains run back to London?"

"Five-ten; fast," put in Coral briefly, who happened to be passing at that moment. "Marylebone Station."

"Oh thank you—how kind of you" (this must be the proprietress, and Win gazed admiringly at the smart young business lady). "Would it be troubling you if I was to sit here for an hour, and wait?"

"Rightee-o." Coral smiled; she did not encourage poor old things of this kind in The Tea Shoppe but she could see, and relish, the artless admiration. "The station's about ten minutes' walk."

"Thank you very much—what a very nice place you h'ave h'ere, if I may say so—do you and your husband manage it together, like?"

"Heavens! I'm not married—plenty of time!" Coral sparkled and moved her waist and hips, "no—my sister and I run it together," and she went off.

Mrs. Threader, in spite of being fully occupied during this, the busiest hour of The Tea Shoppe's day, contrived to pause at Win's table for a word more than once. The fact was, Win's appearance and manner appealed strongly to Mrs. Threader's thirst for perfect respectability. Never taken such a fency to anyone in my life before, Mrs. Threader used to say afterwards to anyone kind enough to listen; well, it just showed. It was to be.

"Have you all you require?" she asked, half an hour later, when two or three retired Colonels and some tweedy ladies, full of tea and cake, had gone out and The Shoppe was emptier.

"Oh yes, thank you. It was all ever so nice, and such nice, respectable people you h'ave h'ere."

"Miss Cartaret is particular as to who comes in," Mrs. Threader droned, "very particular *indeed*, she is. She does not want Ladies Being Annoyed—that kind of thing, you know."

Mrs. Threader's face darkened, recalling the great brute of a man who had sat down opposite poor Miss Mordaunt some weeks ago. The dreadful thing that had come of it—*her at the pictures with him*—seen going in by Mrs. Threader's own eyes; and everybody soon knowing that they were 'going about together', and those who did not know being told about it by Mrs. Threader. And her a *real* lady.

"And seems all the nicer to me," the nice respectable person was saying, "because I've just come out of *an awful place.*"

Mrs. Threader drew back in spirit. A recent, whispered criticism of the Ladies at Nethersham Station recalled itself . . . but no, here was not one who would mention a Ladies, at, so to speak, the drop of a hat.

"Oh, whay was that?" Mrs. Threader could not, despite her confidence in Win's respectability, bring herself to say where.

"My cousin by marriage's h'ouse—well, h'ovel, I'm afraid I must say. You never see. Bird's mess on the floor and beetles all round the chimney."

"Some people," said Mrs. Threader remotely, "don't Seem To Know, do they?"

"They don't indeed."

Mrs. Threader here glided away in response to an imperious beckon from Coral at the entrance to the kitchen, leaving Win to pick up the crumbs of her slice of cake with a moistened finger, and watch what was going on, until it was time to walk to the station.

The air in The Shoppe was warm, and the sun shining; just for now, she would put the thought of standing up to Alice out of her mind.

Coral was really irritated, this afternoon. Pearl was no more use in The Shoppe than a sick headache since she had become engaged; today, for instance, she had hurried through the baking and left an hour early in order to lunch with that man at Great Abbey; and as for Reeny, Unemployment might not have existed, so chancy, impudent and unreliable was she. Coral was feeling upon her middle-class back the first faint stinging from that whip which, forty years on, was to lash without mercy the broad back of the whole of England, and she did not like it at all. Pearl ought to pull her weight.

. . . Really, it was enough to make you get engaged to Dickie!

So, when he put his head round the curtain separating the kitchen from the tea room about four, with the greeting, "Hullo, Face!" she was pleased to see him because there was always something doing when he was around, but she vented some of her crossness upon him.

"Hullo—what do you want?"

"Well, that's a nice thing to say to a chap who's playing hookey to see you—I ought to be looking at old Saunders's fence." Mr. Stone appeared hurt.

"Sorry, but I'm fed up. Do either come in or go out."

"You come out, then. Got something to tell you and we don't want Theda Bara drifting around." This was Mr. Stone's name for Mrs. Threader.

"Oh, all right." Coral came lounging out, with much useful hip-work, and sat down at an empty table. There were only three customers left in the shop now, including Win.

"Well," Coral said, in a bored voice, "what is it?"

"Bit of gossip—regular bombshell. Keep it under your hat, though it'll be all over the Warbys and Great Abbey by tonight."

"Oh, Dickie, don't be so—I'm fed up. What is it? Has the old boy put your screw up?"

"No such luck—or *you* know what I'd say, don't you?" with a look.

"Don't be *sill-ee!*" But Coral showed the beginning of a sparkle. "Come on, tell me."

"Guess who's bolted—cleared out, run off, skedaddled?"

"How should I know? Go *on*, you are maddening."

"Angela Mordaunt, that old spin, up at The Beeches, with Sam Lambert who drives the tractor at Binney's."

"I don't *believe* it!" Coral cried, but believing it instantly, and delighted at the appalling, the unbelievable height of that stuck-up creature's fall. "Who told you, for heaven's sake?"

"It's absolutely true. The old boy himself. She wrote to him—yards of it—saying he'd been so kind and she looked on him as a father or an uncle, you never heard such stuff, and would he take care of her mother, and she and Sam were going to be married in London and she was all right for money because she had three hundred a year of her own and—"

"Sam's all right for money, too, I should think," said Coral significantly.

"Exactly what I thought. It can't be anything else, she must be forty if she's a day, and nothing to look at."

"Yes, she's so *utterly* washed out. But what on earth made him show you the letter?"

"Oh, he was worked up. Shocked, you know. 'Dreadful thing, one of our class going off with a farm labourer,' and so on. Wanted someone to blow off steam to, I honestly do believe. Made me promise to keep it dark, of course."

"Well, so it is a dreadful thing," Coral said. "She must be bats."

Dickie shrugged. "Any port in a storm . . . can't you come out for a run?" His eyes were shining with triumph.

Coral stared.

"What in? I'm not making a fool of myself on the back of that machine of yours."

"Not suggesting the poor old B.S.A. Come outside . . . got something to show you."

Win had overheard this conversation with the strongest interest, gathering as much from their glances and expressions as from their words; though it did seem as if someone, or two people, had been behaving in a way that was not at all nice. She watched them go out of the shop, and pause before a small, smart, plainly brand-new car; saw Dickie Stone's smile, and Coral's stare, and then her little jump and her clapping of hands, right out there on the pavement in front of everybody.

Bought a car, thought Win. Wish them luck—nice respectable young people.

And presently the young lady came back into the shop calling, "Mrs. Threader! Mrs. Threader!"

"Yes, Miss Cartaret?" Speaking almost inaudibly, in order to reprove the loudness, Mrs. Threader materialised beside the kitchen curtain.

"Look here, will you close up, please? I'm off—my friend's just bought a car—we're going for a run."

"Yes, Miss Cartaret; that'll be nice for you, it's a nice evening." Mrs. Threader smiled dimly; perhaps some youthful essence from Coral's gaiety and her pleasure had crept through to that respectable heart.

"Oh—I *must* tell you—what *do* you think? You know that Miss Mordaunt, who used to come in regularly every Wednesday?"

"Yes, Miss Cartaret. Tea and toast. Miss Mordaunt from The Beeches."

"Well, she's *run away*. With a chap who works at a place called Binney's Farm."

"Well, I never," Mrs. Threader droned, "and there was me feeling sorry for her, thinking about that time that awful man come and sat down at her table when she was just having a nice read. Perhaps," and Mrs. Threader's voice sank, *"that was him."*

"I'm pretty sure she must have encouraged him," Coral said, pulling down a straw helmet over her head, in front of a looking-glass on the wall, "stands to reason."

"Well, as to that, of course I couldn't say, Miss Cartaret. I only know as Miss Mordaunt's family has lived at The Beeches these fifty years. I used to see her about as a little kiddie."

It occurred dimly to Mrs. Threader, as she looked at Miss Cartaret's ripe and lively face, that there were different kinds of ladies.

"Well, she's got off at last!" Coral cried, and almost ran out of the shop to Dickie and the waiting car.

If he was going to pull his socks up, and get a move on with cars and things, she might really think about saying yes when he said—as she knew he shortly would—"Well, Old Thing, how about a spot of double-harness?"

Mrs. Threader crept about, drawing veils over unsold cakes, snapping off lights, giving the kitchen and the shop over to shadows that were less gloomy than the shadows of winter; putting dead snow-drops from the table-pots into the rubbish bin. The orange sunset was fading. Venus looked in with her brilliant eye through The Shoppe's window, and Win Smithers sat on in her corner feeling increasingly sad.

Before her lay the journey to London, through the pretty fields and woods she was leaving behind, then the journey past smoky old houses at Catford and her surprised reception by Auntie Bella's niece's sister-in-law; she had never stayed there before, but she had always heard that Auntie Bella's niece's sister-in-law had a temper: no one had ever said it was a nasty temper, but, to Win in her present state, a temper was bad enough.

And then tomorrow, but not too early because they might as well give her a bit of lunch, the journey back to London and across it to Enfield, and having it out with Alice.

My mind's made up, thought Win. No one *likes* words with their own, but when I do make up my mind, I stand by it.

Win believed this, though in fact she had never made up her mind deliberately about anything since the age of six.

"There," observed Mrs. Threader, approaching, "now we're all ready for tomorrow, and I'm sure I hope Reeny thinks better of it and comes in; my feet are quite exhausted."

"H'ave you mice?" Win asked with interest, glad to come out of her thoughts. "If it was me, I should be afraid; try as you may, crumbs will fall, and it would Tempt them."

"Oh, Miss Cartaret wouldn't have them," said Mrs. Threader, on a note approaching decisiveness, "she's very particular about pests." She glanced at the clock. "Now it's half past four. I am going to my home. Shall we walk down together? It is on my way."

Win was pleased to be asked, though she did not like the idea of half an hour's wait on a station. Together they crept out into the marvellous beauty of the afternoon; not much was going on in Nethersham High Street; the children were out of school and at home, by now; shopping was done; no motor-cars about; a trap stood outside The Ploughboy, with the horse contentedly mumbling in its nosebag; the cream weatherboarding houses and their thatch or silky grey slate roofs seemed dozing in the brilliance; every tree and shrub and hedge was clothed in that first unbelievable green of earliest spring.

Down the road they went; Nethersham was having its tea, and they met no one. They agreed that the evenings were drawing out; they stopped to admire, in a restrained way, the spring millinery on show in one window of Cutter's the draper's. Gradually, the stir in the cool air began to invade their spirits.

"I will tell you what," said Mrs. Threader, "what do you say to you catching the *seven-twenty* and coming along with me to see my little home? And I *might*," she said, with caution yet playfully too, "find us a boiled egg. My name," she added, "is Mrs. Amy Threader."

"Well, that *is* kind of you. But are you certain it won't be putting you out?"

Mrs. Threader considered. "No," she said at last, "it won't be putting me out. Being a widow, you see, I am free to make my own plans."

"Ah, it comes to some," said Win. She tried to sound mournful, but she was feeling much better now that those journeys were postponed by two hours . . . "My name is Miss Winifred Smithers."

"Not but what it wasn't nicer when Mr. Threader was with me," Mrs. Threader went on dutifully, "but I *have* been left a bit. Not millions, of course," a thin, squeaking laugh, "but enough to live respectable. He left me the house, too."

"Ah." Win sighed. "There I *could* speak of trouble; being left houses and h'alfs of h'ouses."

"Houses is a mixed blessing," and Mrs. Threader turned aside into the delightful short length of Nelson Street, with its little rose and white half-villas, half-cottages basking in the evening glow, and Lord Gowerville's great hill crowned by his noble beeches, now in their early green splendour, in the background.

Beauty vanished abruptly when Mrs. Threader opened her front door; slowly, cautiously, as if expecting to find a lion in the hall. But there was nothing but a faded fawn wallpaper decorated with green blobs, a hatstand suggesting the antlers of a very old and plain stag, and a clothes-brush, new and shiny, hanging on the wall.

"Just h'ow I would h'ave h'ad it if it had been me," breathed Win, after she had seen the yellow wallpaper, mauve silk eiderdown, and pink linoleum of the spare bedroom; she was allowed only the fleetest, most modest glimpse of Mrs. Threader's own bedroom, all in shades of cold blue shrieking one against the other; the outlook from both windows was over small gardens suggesting neglect and chickens.

"I always say I have a nice home," said Mrs. Threader in a tone of the deepest melancholy, opening another door, "and this is my little lounge."

"You h'ave a *beautiful* h'ome, Mrs. Threader," Win said solemnly, surveying the 'little lounge', "and the loud speaker and all. Pussy, Pussy," to Monty, who had been asleep in Mr. Threader's chair, and now opened his eyes and gave her a glare of hatred.

"Well, I will Just See about those eggs—if you will make yourself at home, Miss Smithers," and Mrs. Threader crept away to the back premises.

When she came back again, there had been a change of some kind in the room—she was not sure—something—yes! Monty was on the hearthrug and in his chair, sitting very upright and holding out her blue hands to the fire that neither roared nor danced, with a faint, grateful smile on her long face, sat Win Smithers.

"That's right," said Mrs. Threader. "If I've told him once not to sit in that chair I've told him a thousand times, but does he take any notice?"

"Oh, you shouldn't have," said Win, charmed by the table spread with a cloth that had a crochet border, and bone china, a knitted patchwork-cosy over the fat teapot, and a plate of wafery bread and butter beside two eggcups wearing caps matching the cosy.

"I believe in having things comfortable, you owe it to yourself, in this world," Mrs. Threader said. "Sugar? Yes—you do. I noticed."

Monty lay on the hearthrug, hearing the unaccustomed rise and fall of two voices. If he had not been too lazy, he would have sprung up and scratched the pair of them, but it was many a year since Monty had sprung.

Presently, Win had finished telling Mrs. Threader all about Alice. Then she asked her advice; should she have it out with her, like her relation-by-marriage, her that had the bird's mess on the floor, had advised?

"No," said Mrs. Threader slowly, at last, "I wouldn't have it out with her, not if I was you. Not to say have it out with her. That sort, not meaning to say anything about your sister, mind you—they can always talk you round. I wouldn't say one word," Mrs. Threader's voice droned on, and the fire ventured on the ghost of a dance, and Monty lay seething, in the comfortable quiet, "about the tea set, nor her having Christmas with the lodgers. Just you go in—mind you, this is only what *I* should do, if it was *me*—quite pleasant-like, and tell her straight out that from now on *you're* having that thirty-seven and sixpence a week. And no more nonsense."

Mrs. Threader paused. There had been no large moments in her life, because she not only did not want large moments but had decided that they were not all that other people said they were. But she felt one upon her now. It came over me, she was to say later, like it was to be.

". . . and you tell her," concluded Mrs. Threader, "as you're going to live in the country with a friend. That's me, the friend." She nodded and, leaning forward, just gingerly patted Win's knee.

"Well, that *is* kind of you," said Win, dazed, "but of course you would have to let me give you something."

"Not one penny more than ten and sixpence a week will I take for that room upstairs!" Mrs. Threader almost cried.

"I could give you a h'and in the h'ouse, too," said Win, an instant's vision of seven and sixpence a week dying down like a Verey light.

"Of course you could."

"It 'ud be ever so peaceful, with Pussy and all." Win put down a respectful hand to stroke Pussy, who thought it best to feign sleep, or he might lose control.

"Well, you bear it in mind. Tonight you sleep here, and tomorrow we'll talk it all over. How about a listen-in? Mr. Threader was very fond of a listen-in. And shall we make it Winny and Amy?"

Win nodded. No one but her mother, and she herself, had ever called her Winny.

*

The having it out with Alice went off ever so well: Alice seeming to have gone old all of a sudden with having bronchitis all the winter; went on something surprising, begging Win not to desert her own sister, and crying; enough to upset anyone, unless they had made up their mind, with all the fierce coldness of a newly-aroused instinct, to get something out of life at last, to have that thirty-seven and sixpence a week. Alice, coughing and shaking and sobbing, swore on her mother's grave that she would send it regular.

It cannot be said that Mrs. Threader and Win flourished. But they did not want to: all they wanted was to wither comfortably, and this they did.

Alice soon died, and left her share of the house to her sister, and Mr. Gardener of the High Street arranged the sale of it, for the staggering sum of seven hundred and fifty pounds.

"Winny is a woman of wealth now, you know," Mrs. Threader would say mysteriously to those of whose respectability she was certain, "but it has made No Difference. None at all."

It had made some difference to Mrs. Threader, who was jealous. But, to be fair to Mrs. Threader, she told herself that jealousy wasn't nice; and as, at the time of the sale, Monty astounded Nelson Street by running away, and going to live off rabbits and such in the woods, there was something else to talk about.

They agreed that though of course Winny would always be polite to that Ivy Gover because she was a relation by marriage;, there was no need to Ask her Over. She was not respectable, and the fact settled it.

They lived on. They lived on, withering in their desired, dim, druggingly comfortable respectability: but both were spared the bewildered pain of living on into an era when respectability had become, with chastity and honesty, one of the crimes.

23

"PROB'LY the last time," Ivy said suddenly.

The three had been out all that afternoon, wandering through the woods, and now dusk was falling; the sky was a solemn blue, and they were passing through a clearing where bluebells seemed to be drawing down the deep colour into themselves; piercing scents hovered up from the ground, cold breaths from petals and moss.

"Go on," Mike hurled a stick for Neb, who raced after it.

"It ain't 'go on', Mike. Your dad said he'd be here round about the fourth, I looked on Wattle's calendar this mornin', it's April 4th this very day."

"*You* won't send me off."

"I got to," Ivy said earnestly, "I got to. We said a munf, and the munf's up today."

"Well, I ain't going."

Ivy felt what she thought of as 'too bad' to start a struggle with him, and what would be the use? The beauty of the beech wood at this hour hushed angry voices, and 'going on' at anybody, especially her boy, her own boy. Just for a moment, she wondered how she would ever manage without him; then she told herself not to be a silly fool.

Mike seemed to think that the question had been settled: he wasn't going. He tore down the hill after Neb, through the sheets of fading snowdrops and over the turf that answered to the flying foot, and vanished through the hole in the long line of green hedge before the cottage door.

Only hope *he* ain't sitting there, waitin', Ivy thought, following at a swift, but slower, pace. Had enough with Win Smithers.

S'pose she went off 'ome to *Alice*. Last of 'er, anyways.

She dismissed Win, who was at that moment peacefully seated at supper in 17 Nelson Street with Mrs. Threader.

Mr. Bury was not sitting on the doorstep that evening, but the next afternoon, while they were preparing to rush out into the air after a hasty dinner, there came a knock at the front door.

"That'll be your dad, prob'ly," Ivy said casually, "you can open it."

She did not look round, but went on scraping the prehistoric saucepan, which she had intended to leave unscraped while they went out . . .

"'Ullo, Mike."

"'Ullo, dad."

Ivy turned round. A smallish man in the late forties, decently and roughly dressed; grey skin, thin but broad-framed, with Mike's eyes but lacking their thrilling brilliance and their depth of colour.

"Good afternoon," Ivy said, wiping her hands on her skirt, "I'm Mrs. Gover. You're Mike's dad I—I expec'. Come in. We'll have a cup o' tea."

"Thank you, missus, I could do with one," and he came into the room saying "'ullo, boy," to Neb as he did so. Neb actually moved his tail.

Now they wouldn't be able to go out—never go out again.

Silly fool.

"Sit down, Mr. Bury," she said firmly, "Mike, get your dad a chair."

Mike drew up the Windsor to the fire, keeping his face turned away.

Mr. Bury observed, as if to himself, "He can sulk, when he likes."

"Could you eat a kipper? We 'ad ours for dinner but there's a couple lef'," Ivy asked, and she smiled at him. Mike's dad.

"Ah, I could, and thanking you, missus. I caught the workman's from Portsmouth this mornin'. 'Aven't had me dinner, not today."

"*He* looks all right," he said, in a moment, studying Mike, who had sat down at the table with paper and pencil, "drawin' as usual, I sees. Always drawin'. But they don't think much of it at his school. Says—what was it now—got too many ideas of his own."

Silence fell. Ivy was furiously rushing water into—Mr. Bury stared—a biscuit tin, setting out the knife and fork on a rough-dried white cloth she snatched from the drawer where the sketches of the fighting dogs and the fox and mice were kept. He stared slowly round. He knew the inside of old George Coatley's cottage, of course; but it used to look better than this, when Maria Coatley had been alive.

But one of Mrs. Gover's grandads, Elkanah Lee—Mr. Bury remembered him—had been a gyppo. That accounted for *her* eyes, as near black as he ever saw, and her slummocky ways.

The kipper was slapped on to a plate, Ivy having drained off the colourless water in which it had been steeped. Its plump, coppery, delicately-oiled body smelt faintly of the sea and of the oak-chips in which it had been smoked.

"Help yourself. Tea's just ready." She pushed the loaf and margarine towards him, and darted at the little blue kettle, which was showing those symptoms of boiling which she alone could recognise.

"Elsie's all right," Mr. Bury observed to the head bent over the paper opposite. "Had her fourteenth birthday last week."

Mike did not answer, and Ivy, having poured tea for Mr. Bury and offered a cup to Mike and received a shake of the head in answer, sat down by the fire and sipped her own, with no expression on her brown face. White sunlight streamed into the warm room; Neb stretched himself to his full length and whined.

"Come on out, boy!" cried Mike, springing up, and made for the door.

Instantly, the glances of Ivy and Mr. Bury locked. Ivy just moved her head.

"You can't go out, Mike," his father said at once, "we're off, when I finished me dinner, and got me pipe going. Off home."

"This here's home." Mike stood by the door, staring under the big, lowered curve of his brow.

"No it ain't," said Ivy, after some silent movements of her lips. "You been staying with me, that's all. You 'ad a nice 'oliday, and now you go off home with your dad. Right place for you," she ended, choking over a mouthful of tea. "Went down the wrong way," she muttered.

"You'll see the boats. You like them," his father said; the kipper was eaten, and he was packing his pipe, with broad hands that were, he knew, capable of wrenching the boy along beside him with no trouble except the bother of it; Mr. Bury worked in Portsmouth Docks now, which form of labour develops the muscles.

"I likes it here better."

"Well, you can't stay here, Mike. Mrs. Gover won't 'ave you and I say you got to come with me, and that's all about it . . . got your things?"

Ivy nodded. "Upstairs. I'll get 'em." She darted away.

When she returned, carrying a canvas bag filled with underclothing and socks she had bought for Mike, Mr. Bury was saying, with a patience and kindness that hurt her strangely, both because she knew that he was a good father, and because she wanted no one but herself to be good to her boy—

"Don't forget your pencils and stuff, son. That's a nice pencil that is," picking up a dark green Venus BB from the table, "you'll want that, you don't want to leave that behind."

Mike sullenly began to cram pencils, chalks and paper into the top of the carrier.

"I've had to tell the police, 'course," his father confided to Ivy almost in a whisper, "had to. But the sergeant's all right—got three of his own—I'll go round and tell him tomorrow. I s'pose he come back to see our old place, was that it, d'you think, missus?"

He looked into her face earnestly, but all Ivy answered was, "Must a bin," and turned away to the drawer where the sketches were kept.

"'Ere, Mike," she said, holding the three out to him, "you'll want yer fighting dogs, and the mice, and yer fox."

He took them in silence; the sight of the broad, strong, yet childish hand held out for them nearly broke Ivy's control: there would never be any more evenings with her sitting stroking Neb's head against her knee while she watched that hand moving the pencil over the paper; and magic had been made there in the wooden hut at the edge of the forest, as it is made in the witch's hut in the fairytale.

Then, suddenly, everything was done: the last pencil stuffed into the carrier, the muffler wound round Mike's neck ("lost yer cap, I s'pose," his father said resignedly) and Mr. Bury's pipe set comfortably between his teeth. They moved towards the door, and Ivy swung it open wide.

"Well . . ." said Mr. Bury, and held out his hand to her, "so-long, missus, and thanks for keeping a eye on him."

"That's all right." The two hands, the small red one and the big one with skin thickened from the hardest of work, met in the loose, brief clasp used by people who feel, but neither want to speak, nor can speak, their feelings.

"Goo'bye, Mike," Ivy said loudly, "'ere's Neb wants to go with you." She gripped his collar firmly. "You—work 'ard at your schooling, and p'raps you'll send me a card, some time. One with—them ships on your dad was saying . . ."

His lids lifted slowly and the glowing blue eyes, dark with fury and suffering, met her own.

"I won't never send *you* a card. Not never. You're making me go, you are. I don't never want to see you again."

"All right," Ivy said, with a smile that was all love, "please yourself."

"You shut up and come on, now," his father said roughly. "Thank you, missus. So-long again."

He turned away, dropping one heavy hand on Mike's shoulder and pushing him forward, so that he stumbled, on his first step away from her.

Ivy stood, watching, while Neb fretted and jerked under her grip, whining. Down the dry ruts of the lane, past the celandines glittering under the hedge, towards the curve that would take them out of sight. She drew in her breath, her hand was on the door, to pull it inwards and shut it on her loneliness.

They had stopped, they were saying something to each other. Ivy paused, staring. How those little flowers shone in the sun. Mike was feeling about in the carrier bag while his father waited; he did not look impatient.

Then Mike broke away, and came racing back along the lane, with something white fluttering in his hand. She saw that his face was ugly in the grimaces of crying, and when he flung himself against her and her face came down to his, she felt the hot tears.

"They're for you," he gulped, thrusting the sketches at her, "The mice, and my fox, and them two fighting—*you* have 'em."

She clutched at them and him; one fell on to the threshold, and then he was flying back to his father; he was beside him; Mr. Bury nodded, and they set off once more. Neither looked back.

The turn in the lane hid them from Ivy as she stood staring after them.

She picked up the drawing.

She shut the door. She screwed up a piece of newspaper, and began to polish the table; in long, round, vigorous sweeps. From time to time she glanced over at the three sketches, which she had propped up on the window-sill, but, quite soon, she could not see them except as one white blur.

24

ON A glaring summer evening in the early seventies, the procession of home-going traffic was jerking its way through Nethersham High Street; past the Chinese restaurant and the betting shop, past the young, hot, harassed policeman on point duty at the corner of Nelson Street. The curved concrete lamps would not shed their mauve glow for two hours yet, and the television aerials stood up against the clearest of blue skies crossed by dissolving white vapours; lines suggesting to an over-developed imagination the tracks of gargantuan, celestial snails.

"I'm sorry about this, Aunt Helen," said Clovis Standish, leaning back resignedly in his white Corydon and addressing the elderly lady beside him, "it's always peculiarly awful just here, but there isn't any other route unless we go round by Great Abbey, which would mean . . ."

"It's all right, dear. It is awful, but in a minute, and *if* you can get out of this, I'd like to go up to look at a place I remember."

"I'll try," doubtfully, "where's the map?"

Consultation; the dark, beautifully-cut head of hair and the greying one bent together.

"Here." Clovis's long finger pointed. "That's a lane. We can turn off there, it's a few miles out of Little Warby—if everyone else hasn't got the same idea."

"I expect they will have—oh!"

"What?"

"They've covered in the stream and cut down the willows."

"Where those new houses are?"

"Yes . . . never mind." Helen leant back, and fixed her eyes with determination on the sky; those ancient *Huns*, she thought, *who worshipped the blue sky*: and well they might. A swelling roar began, miles at the back of the crawling, mile-long queue; it grew swiftly to one vast, shattering, unbelievable and unbearable noise which dominated, for some seconds, the grinding and roaring and gasping of all the engines round about.

"Good heavens," Clovis said mildly.

"Yes, it's that beastly thing."

"Well, we can't see it, anyway."

"We shall in a minute . . . yes, if you want to see it, there it is." She pointed, with a finger in an elegant grey glove.

"It really does look exactly like an insect, doesn't it," observed Clovis, with his amusing nose turned to the sky.

"Yes, one that's gone mad . . . thank God," as the roar began gradually to abate. At the same moment, the traffic loosened, and started to move forward; a huge van labelled *Filley's Frozen Foods* had turned off down the lane for which Clovis was making, and the white Corydon proceeded on its way, past pretty villas whose gardens were adorned by a great deal of aubretia, with an occasional field of pale gold stubble peering between them. There were no animals in the fields of sun-bleached grass; they were hidden in air-conditioned, clean buildings, accurately fed and comfortably sheltered. Some of them were kept in darkness.

"Here we are." Clovis turned off down an uninviting lane, its grass borders littered by papers and rubbish left by picnicking motorists, and drew into the hedge.

"What will you do with yourself while I'm gone?" Helen asked. "I shan't be more than half an hour. It *is* nice of you, dear." She knew that her nephew preferred a few things to the country.

"I've got *The Financial Times*." He smiled, pulling it out of his pocket, and Helen smiled too. "Where are you going? Up to those beeches?"

"Yes."

"All right, then . . . don't get murdered."

"I'll try not to."

She set off down the lane. Gradually, the dismal drone of engines, that sound so seldom out of the ears of late twentieth-century people, began, blessedly, to lessen, and soon she was slowly climbing the great hill down which she had so often swung with Jocelyn Burke. About halfway to its summit, she paused.

Pure air, and stillness; she was more aware of them than of the distant noise, and there, ahead of her, soared the Nether-sham beeches.

And not changed—not changed, she was saying in her heart as she climbed towards them; it's forty years since I saw them and almost everything else has changed, but they haven't. Now she was entering their shade; not cool, warmed by the long sun-light of the day and by the long shafts of light driving under their thick layers of dark, late summer leaves. The noble trunks and the giant branches above her head were transformed in that light to an eerie blend of silver and gold. There was silence, and the last calling of hidden birds.

She stood, looking about her and murmuring aloud, "It's so beautiful—it's so beautiful." Then she walked on. The trance of delight began to lessen; she looked about more critically, and saw that someone—who?—was taking care of the realm of the Nether-sham beeches; there was no defamation of litter, and raw, slim stumps among the moss showed that a trained and firm hand was being taken with the newest generation of the intruding saplings which had pained and irritated Lord Gowerville. The grass of the ride between the giants was short and green. 'Footpath to The Hall: Walkers only', said a notice among the trees, amateurishly painted on a board whose green exactly matched the bronze-green of the leaves.

Who? Because it didn't look like a public park; the stultifying civic neatness was absent. Who?

Suddenly, and with strong irritation, she saw a woman tramping (Helen felt that this was the word) towards her along the ride; wearing smart country clothes and accompanied by four dogs. One of them, a young Jack Russell, ran at Helen and leapt up, in an effusion of friendliness, against her skirt.

"Down, Jacko, heel," said the woman sharply.

She was sweeping past Helen, barely glancing at her, when Helen said:

"Don't we know each other? Aren't you Coral Cartaret?"

The tramper paused, and stared.

"I'm Coral *Stone*—have been for nearly forty years—God! doesn't it sound awful—and surely you're Helen Green."

Her voice made Helen think of gin, and bars, and hearty uproar; it was strong and fruity.

"Helen Standish," Helen said gently; she did not think it sounded awful to be married to someone for forty years, and she perceived that they had not changed her old acquaintance in the least.

"Well, I shouldn't have known *you*," Coral said; by the stoniness of her face, Helen gathered that she would have known her, if she had bothered to look, and that she disapproved of her, and of her appearance, as strongly as ever. But now the reasons were different.

"Do you live round here?" Helen asked.

"All among the hippies—no thank you. We've got four acres and a bungalow at Warby New Town. And this is the family," indicating the dogs, who were occupying themselves as dogs do when their owner stops during a walk to gossip.

"What on earth are you doing down here?" Coral went on, "Thinking of buying a cottage or something? Because I can tell you, *at* once, that you won't get a thing for less than seven thousand; we had to give ten for our place . . . remember the old Tea Shoppe?"

"Of course." Helen was warmed by a sudden lively memory of young faces and light hearts and sorrows once deemed heavy.

"Well, Dickie—I don't think you ever met him—"

"Once; at one of your parties, I seem to remember."

" . . . Dickie took it over when Pearl gave up when she got married. Turned it into a restaurant. Of course, he couldn't carry on during the war—he got a desk-job in Whitehall—and I was Citizens Advising—but we put in our old Mrs. Threader and a pal of hers to run it for us, and it went like a bomb . . . after the war we opened another in Great Abbey, and the year before last, when they joined the Warbies up into Warby New Town, we opened two there. So now we've got four . . . didn't you notice The Tea Shoppe? Did you come through Nethersham?"

"No—I—I—didn't, I'm afraid." Helen did not want to tell Coral that she had been too shocked by seeing the little stone bridges gone, and the willows cut down, and the Nether covered in, to notice anything else.

"It's called La Traviata now."

"Oh . . . yes . . . then I did."

She vaguely remembered an impression, gained through large windows, of near-Egyptian darkness, plain board walls, and strings of things; bottles, onions, grapes.

"I'm glad you're . . . doing well," she said, feebly, she feared. But she had always, she remembered, had to go on tip-toe with Coral.

Coral's plump ruddy face darkened, and her mouth, coated with raspberry paint, drooped.

"*Staff's* the problem, my dear," she said bitterly, "absolute bastards they are, nowadays, and then this blasted S.E.T. on the top of it—you have to pay them the earth, and they've *no pride in their work*, haven't a *clue*. (Of course, the hoi-polloi are on top now, that's the trouble.) We could be simply *coining* the stuff—well, we are, come to that—but we could be making three, *four* times as much if we could only get staff."

"I hear it's difficult everywhere," Helen murmured. ". . . I suppose you don't know what happened to that cleaner of mine, Mrs. Gover? She had a cottage somewhere round here, an old uncle left it to her."

Coral laughed. "Oh, our Ivy. She was quite a character—got into the local rag eight years ago, just about the time Luke inherited The Hall (and wait till you hear about *him*). She . . ."

"Do you mind if we go on?" Helen asked. "I've got a nephew waiting for me at the foot of the hill."

"Suits me. I've got to look in somewhere."

They turned, and began to walk back along the ride, the rejoicing dogs scampering ahead.

"You surely aren't trying to *walk* along that road? We call it the Warby racing-track," Coral said.

"Even I am not so fond of walking as that," Helen assured her, "he's in a car."

"What sort? Do you drive?"

"A Corydon. No, I don't." Helen thought of adding that she detested cars, because of what they are doing to England, but decided against it.

Coral's face became stony again, as always when she heard of any-one owning something desirable that she had not got, and she said nothing: someone who had not known her long ago would have thought that she was condemning the Corydon as not the thing at all.

"Do go on about Ivy," said Helen.

"She must have been ninety when she finally passed on, I should think. Still living in that awful old hovel—a perfect disgrace to the neighbourhood—and Luke's father had sold most of the land round there and there were some really nice houses going up and naturally people didn't like it—you don't pay ten thousand for a house to have a dotty gipsy and hordes of birds on your doorstep—no one could grow any soft fruit—and the local Health people wanted her to go into an Old People's Home at Great Abbey—and, trust her, of course she *wouldn't*."

"Good for Ivy." It was a murmur.

"What?"

"Nothing . . . do go on."

"Our Luke inherited, just at that time, and for once he did the Lord of the Manor stuff, and went down to see her (he's mad about birds and animals, too. Well, I like dogs, myself, if they're properly trained). It seems he went poking about, and found three sketches, stuffed away in a drawer, by *Mike Bury*."

"Good heavens. The man who did the frescoes for the Council Chamber in Ibona, last year."

"That's the one. Well, I'm no highbrow, as you may remember," and Coral laughed, "but even *I've* heard of him."

"He's known all over the world, I should think. There never has been such a painter of animals."

Helen broke off, remembered the reproductions, in a Sunday supplement, of the mighty and solemn creatures seeming to float like clouds, yet to march with the rolling sound of thunder, across the vast bare walls of the Council Chamber in the newly-built African city; elephant, rhinoceros, hippopotamus—archetypes from a dying world.

"How on earth did *Ivy* get hold of them?" she demanded.

"Oh, he stayed with her once when he was a kid—or so she *said*—and Luke took the drawings in exchange for the cottage. So there she stayed, defying everyone, taking in the fox one morning just as hounds were on it—you can imagine the fuss with the local hunt!—Not that there's much room to hunt round here, nowadays—and one morning the milkman found her, dead. Lying on the doorstep with birds hopping all over her. Rather gruesome, really."

Coral paused, to charge ahead and speak sharply to a dog. She's like a raspberry that's got too fat, Helen thought dreamily. The sun was setting, steeping the beeches in fire, and the still air rang with the languorous calling of wood-doves.

"Luke makes *the* most awful fuss about his blasted wild-flowers; won't let dogs have a scratch or anything . . ." puffed Coral, returning.

"Do tell me about him, Coral." Helen's voice was lulling, her small ears listening, with all the naughty enthralment of forty years ago, to Coral being Coral.

"Luke? Oh, he's dotty . . . he inherited very young, and he's the real student-protest type—you know—he won't use the title, such nonsense—Dickie and I both think it's a *pose*."

"I think I met the old Lord once. I was trespassing."

"Of course, we keep in touch with The Hall, Dickie having been agent . . . well, you couldn't trespass now, he's opened the woods to the public . . ."

"How on earth—? There's not one scrap of litter." Helen's eyes swept in a glance of love over the brown slopes of the forest, the turf over which they were walking, the dark green brambles and their red berries on the verges.

"Oh, that's his awful friends—about twenty of them—all living at The Hall and growing vegetables and sleeping with each other— I'm broad-minded, but when it's a big local land-owner . . . they call themselves The Tribe of The Beeches. They act as gamekeepers, sort of. Tidying up. And he keeps a regular zoo in the grounds . . . and paintings all over the walls in the house . . . The weirdest goings-on—drugs, for all I know."

Helen said nothing.

"But he's been offered *nearly a million* for the land, Helen." Coral's voice was fruitier than ever, deep as ruby port with real feeling. "Think! You could build *luxury flats* and *treble* the value of every house in the district. And he *will not* sell."

Helen did think. Thank God for Luke, Lord Gowerville. My Home Counties seem to belong to Coral and Dickie Stone now-adays.

They had left the warm shadows of the wood and were beginning the descent of the hill.

"I've got to look in at The Beeches. Sally, Angela's eldest grand-daughter, has just had her first, and wants me to be god-mother," said Coral.

Helen shook her head. "Never knew an Angela."

"Oh—so you didn't, I forgot. She used to come in to The Tea Shoppe . . . ran away with a farm-labourer, *the* most awful scandal. They came back here from Belgium just after the war broke out. They'd bought a farm there, on *her* money, and were doing well. *Four* kids, she had—and everybody thought she was a regular old maid! Just shows you never know, doesn't it."

You do sometimes; I knew you would be like this in forty years, Helen thought.

"Dickie and I got quite thick with old Sam, the labourer. He got rather fond of the bottle after Angela died, a year or so ago, and used to spend most of his time either with us, or at *The Swan*. Bit of a nuisance sometimes . . . but he wasn't a bad old boy . . . They pulled *The Swan* down last year. High time too, it was a dreary little hole and losing money all the time. There's a big new place there now, hotel-and-restaurant type. Coining the stuff, I hear."

"And how is Pearl?"

Helen had not quite yet come to that age when one hesitates to ask after a contemporary not seen for years. But she was on the edge of it.

Coral turned aside to swear at a dog.

"Oh, she passed on. About five years ago, it was. Married the parson at Little Warby. They moved up North, quite early on. They seemed to get on all right, I must say, though I never could stand him."

That, from you, means that they were happy. I'm glad; I liked Pearl . . . how pretty she was! Helen mused, remembering.

Coral had paused; they were at the foot of the hill.

"Well, I turn off here," she said, "cheerio, it's been nice, seeing you again." Her hard dark eyes stared into Helen's. "Give me a ring some time, it's a Great Abbey number."

"Perhaps I will. Goodbye, Coral," Helen said.

Coral turned away, swinging her hips and shouting instructions at the dogs, and Helen walked on towards the lane made unappetising by the picnickers.

She was just sufficiently on rising ground to have a panorama of the scene below; neat white houses in trim gardens, crumbling cottages of a shape already beginning to look like drawings in an old book, the flat, beetle-like tops of the cars jerking, stopping, jerking, stopping, behind the hedges whose lower branches were clotted with litter and grey with dust.

She turned, for one backward glance at the beeches.

There they stood, high above her and far away, solemn and still in the waning fire of sunset; towers and castles of rustling green; benign father-gods of the woods; filled with their gently-stirring life in the blue air of summer or roaring slowly in winter's gales.

And *they* don't belong in any sense of the word, to Coral and Dickie Stone, thought Helen.

She went on, down the hill where the snowdrops used to grow.

THE END

FURROWED MIDDLEBROW